THE
DAWN
OF A
DESPERATE WAR

THE GODLANDERS WAR
BOOK THREE

By Aaron Pogue

The Godlanders Trilogy
The Dreams of a Dying God
The Wrath of a Shipless Pirate
The Dawn of a Desperate War

The Dragonprince's Legacy
Taming Fire
The Dragonswarm
The Dragonprince's Heir
Remnant (short story)
From Embers (short story)

The Dragonprince's Arrows
A Darkness in the East

Ghost Targets
Surveillance
Expectation
Restraint
Camouflage

THE
DAWN
OF A
DESPERATE WAR

THE GODLANDERS WAR
BOOK THREE

AARON POGUE

47NORTH

Text copyright © 2014 Aaron Pogue

Published by 47North, Seattle

www.apub.com

Amazon, the Amazon logo, and 47North are trademarks of Amazon.com, Inc., or its affiliates.

ISBN-13: 9781477824269
ISBN-10: 147782426X

Cover design by: Kerrie Robertson
Illustrated by: Chris McGrath

Library of Congress Control Number: 2014932944

Printed in the United States of America

THE
DAWN
OF A
DESPERATE WAR

THE GODLANDERS WAR
BOOK THREE

(1)

In southwest Raentz on the Dividing Line, at the farthest end of the civilized Godlands, the woodsmen dressed in shades of green and brown, the better to hide among the gnarled trees. Though they went with axes to their tasks, not a man among them went without a dagger at his side and a bow upon his back. These woods rested on a dangerous frontier, in easy reach of the Wildland savages and the fearsome creatures that roamed there.

These days, a stranger walked among the woodsmen. He wore the same clothes, though he was clearly uncomfortable in them. He wore the dagger on his belt, but something in his gait suggested he was more accustomed to the weight of a heavy sword. He swung an axe with strength and stamina, but with scant weeks of experience in his form. No matter how he pretended, he was unquestionably an outlander.

Still he put in a hard day's work, and the locals saw it in him. Day after day, he'd found a place among them and earned their respect, until they might overlook the implications of his sudden arrival. He was hiding from something. Something grave. It took some effort for a man to overcome those suspicions, but he was on his way—well on his way.

It was hours yet until sunset when the woodsmen headed home. They were hard workers, but no lord would risk his men on that frontier at dusk. They leaned their axes on their shoulders, hauled the day's last logs toward the nearest flume, then trudged toward their homesteads—modest houses made of stone, with solid bars behind the doors and lamps already burning bright against the coming night.

The stranger found his way among the other woodsmen, and though he showed no clear intention, he soon ended up in step beside a man named Endan Wade. Wade nodded to the stranger as he arrived, but still they walked awhile in silence, eyes watching the woods around them. The stranger had more to fear than raiding savages. Three months in this disguise had not been enough to dull his edge. More than any other here, the stranger walked as though ready to do battle.

Endan Wade gave him a sigh. "No one would mistake you for a common woodsman."

"I am not anything common these days, no matter how I try."

"Try harder. You must keep hidden."

The stranger growled. "What more can I do, druid?"

Endan Wade looked around at that, but no one could have overheard the stranger's words. The druid lowered his voice nonetheless. "Watch your tongue, Corin. That's precisely the sort of slip—"

"No!" Corin Hugh snapped. "I grow tired of this charade. When will we begin to move?"

"It will take time to plan a war against the gods."

"I have given you weeks."

"And it may take years! If you persist in defying us—"

"I have done nothing to defy you," Corin interrupted, frowning. He thought for a moment and then shrugged. "Not for several days."

The druid snorted. "Did you think today's meeting would go unnoticed?"

The ever-present thread of Corin's fear twisted tighter in his breast. What meeting? What had the druids noticed, and why hadn't Wade said something sooner? Corin forced a calming breath and asked the question: "What meeting do you mean?"

"You can drop the act," Wade said. "We know how you hope to use the Nimble Fingers."

Corin shook his head. "I have not yet set that plan in motion."

"Give over. The other men were discussing it this afternoon. A dozen outlanders arrived in the village near midday, asking for directions to your cottage. They were joined by a lord all dressed in black."

The fear pulled taut, squeezing the air from Corin's lungs.

The druid cocked his head. "Good lord, Corin! You've gone pale."

"Aemilia," he whispered. "Wade, you have to help me. I did not bring anyone to the cottage today."

"But the man in black—"

"It wasn't me. I've been hard at work, maintaining my disguise." A bitterness twisted his voice, and he didn't try to fight it down. He dropped the axe from his shoulder. "Go to the Council. Bring everyone you can find." Corin was running before the words were out.

Wade called after him. "Why? *Why*, Corin? What's happening?"

Corin didn't even try to answer. He ran. That fear clamored inside him now, wrenching at his heart.

He didn't know. He didn't *know* what had really happened, but weeks of constant fear seemed realized now, the trap snapped closed. Wade had been right, after all—Corin made a lousy woodsman. He was a pirate, a scoundrel, a city rat. He did not belong here, but that very fact had made it an ideal hiding place.

Until he was discovered. How? How had they found him so quickly? And who had come for him? His terror told him that the figure dressed in black must have been Ephitel himself— king of all the tyrant gods—but surely it was not. Surely he would have sent a soldier in his place—a watchman or a justicar. Even a wizard would have been better than Ephitel. But it was he. Corin knew it was he, with a certainty that drove him to near frenzy.

He didn't have his sword. It had been too great a risk, too valuable a resource, so *Godslayer* rested in its clever little vault, hidden. Without that sword, he couldn't face Ephitel. *Please, Fortune,* he prayed, *Let it be someone else. Let Aemilia be away. Just . . . let her be safe.*

But she wouldn't be. She would be home. She was part of his disguise, and she played the part well. That pretense had been the only brightness in this whole charade. He'd shared three months with Aemilia while the druids pumped him for every fragment of his memory.

He'd pretended to be a country lad. He'd pretended to be a cooperative asset to the aggravating druids. And he would have gone on doing all of it for an endless age if he could have kept pretending to be part of a happy family with Aemilia. She'd made him a very happy home.

Tears burned in his eyes, but he refused to shed them. It had all been for naught if Ephitel had found him. Corin slowed in his mad dash. He bore the hope of the world within his memory, and all the angry fires of justice stoked to render final judgment on the tyrant Ephitel. But as Wade had said, it would take time to accomplish such a thing. It was no easy task to strike down a god, and all their plans would come to nothing if Corin fell into the monster's hands.

He strained his eyes in a vain attempt to catch some glimpse of the distant cottage through the woods. He wasn't close enough yet. He could still run away. He *should*, to save himself. Or at least find some hiding place and wait for Wade to bring the Council. He could not afford to charge right in. His quest was far more important than the life of one man. Or one woman.

It didn't matter. He couldn't leave her—not without knowing. For all of three paces, he had slowed, but now he ran harder yet.

"In the village near midday," Wade had said. These men had come hours ago. What could Corin hope to find? It didn't matter. He ran harder.

He didn't *know* it was an enemy. It could even have been the Nimble Fingers. Perhaps they were looking for him—to beg his aid or warn him of some dark rumor. Or it could be some plot of Aemilia's. She was almost as sharp a schemer as Corin himself.

It was probably something harmless. Almost certainly.

Still, Corin never slowed.

The cottage sat alone in a little clearing, far from town, far from any roads. It had been a druid sanctuary through long ages, and for a short while it had become a home. Corin darted from the tree line, heedless of the risk involved. He leaped the low, neat hedge that bounded a modest garden.

He sprinted for the warped oak door, noting as he passed the sharp-edged boot prints in the turf, the trampled lawn. He tamped down the quiet fury in his heart, clenched his jaw, and flung a hand up toward the door.

But the door opened ahead of him. And standing just inside, clearly surprised at Corin's sudden arrival, was Ephitel himself.

The tyrant god had come a-calling.

❦

Corin flung himself at Ephitel. Surprise flashed in the eyes of the cruel elf, but not a spark of anger, not a glow of hate. No real emotion showed at all. He leaned almost casually aside, twisting at his narrow waist, and Corin's desperate momentum flung him past.

Corin crashed against a wall, and pain exploded in his shoulder. He stumbled, and Ephitel caught him with one hand, steadying him. Corin jerked free of that grasp, shrank backward half a step, then stood his ground and raised his chin.

"What have you done with her?"

Ephitel frowned. "She was a druid, you know? In the ancient days, when they still held some power. Filthy creatures, really. Scarcely better than the witches."

Corin stomped forward. "Where is she? What have you done with her?"

Ephitel drew himself up proudly, but still no emotion touched his voice. "They are outlawed, outcast, exiled from the lands of righteous men. And yet they linger on. They skulk in shadows, meddling in the affairs of holy nations. This one tried to end the Vestossis' reign."

Corin snarled. "*I* did that. Aemilia—"

Before Corin could say more—before he even saw the flash of motion—Ephitel's hand clamped hard around Corin's jaw and lifted him from the floor. Casually, unstrained, the tyrant god drew Corin up to meet him face to face, and for a long moment Ephitel considered him.

Corin couldn't move his jaw. His whole weight rested against that rock-hard grip, and bright bursts of agony bloomed in his neck and shoulders. He slung a vicious jab at Ephitel's unarmored belly, but he only bruised his knuckles in the process. Ephitel had bathed in the Waters of Aubrocia, and Corin knew of only one weapon that could do him true damage.

For his part, Ephitel showed no indication that Corin had made the attempt. He licked his lips, thoughtful, then spoke in a quiet voice near Corin's ear.

"You did me a favor, manling, in killing Giuliano. He was a spoiled child and something of a bother. For that, I'll let you live. And you did me another favor too, by leading me to one of the druids. For that, I will forget your name. I will forget everything about you, and you can spend the rest of your miserable life in some shade of peace. Let it not be said that I am unmerciful."

Through all the speech, Corin did not stop struggling. He caught the elf's forearm in both his hands and tried to heave himself up against the strangling grip. He gasped for air and forced words past his bruised throat. "Where is she? What have you done with her?"

Ephitel shook his head. He dropped Corin to the floor and turned away. "Even manling farmers know what to do with vermin, child. I exterminated her."

Those words stabbed at him like lightning bolts. Aemilia was dead. Ephitel had killed her. The words cut all the sharper for the monster's dull tone. Corin found his feet and flung himself upon Ephitel's back. He pounded uselessly on the elf's shoulders, wrenching at his head, but Ephitel tossed Corin aside with a vigorous shake.

He sighed. "Leave off this show of passion, manling. I've heard the rumors in the lands of men. They believe you killed someone protected by my favor. You've forced my hand, but for the favors done me, I extend this gift. You killed one of mine, and I killed one of yours. I'll call this thing done, if you will."

Corin strained to catch his breath. A sharp pain stabbed in his left side, near his ribs, but it was nothing to the crushing grief. All the druids' careful plans had come to this. They'd said it wouldn't be enough to kill Ephitel in cold blood. They'd said it needed groundwork, precise preparation, so the tyrant's death would not just leave a power vacuum. There were more than enough among Ephitel's followers to fill his place. No, the beast could not be killed until everything was ready to ensure the act would lead to something truly better.

And until that day, the druids had said, they could not afford to risk losing the one true weapon that might kill him. So the sword *Godslayer* lay hidden in the inner room. And while it waited there unused, while Corin spent his days pretending to be a simple woodsman, Ephitel had not forgotten him. All Corin's slinking, all his patient planning, and still Ephitel had shown up at his door. He'd killed Aemilia.

That thought lit a fire in Corin's breast. In a heartbeat he forgot his caution, forgot all the druids' reasons. He thought only of revenge.

He couldn't bruise the elf, but he could kill it.

Corin struggled to his feet. Ephitel arched an eyebrow at him, perhaps expecting another wild attack, but Corin drew back. Ephitel nodded, satisfied, then turned his attention to a handful of soldiers just now coming from the inner room.

The soldiers' arms were full of Aemilia's things. They had her jewelry chest, her papers, and her outlandish druid artifacts. Of course, Ephitel would want to learn everything he could about the other druids. Corin barely cared. He saw at a glance that none of them had the sword, and that was all he needed now. He darted past them, rushing for the inner room.

The soldiers must have looked to Ephitel for orders, because the elf spoke from his place by the door. "Leave him to his grief. He's paid in full. One life for another."

They didn't interest Corin at all. He'd have killed them to a man if they had stopped him, but the only death he craved was Ephitel's. So he let them take Aemilia's old things, and they let him slip past into the room.

She lay in the corner. He'd almost hoped she wouldn't be there, carted off by some of Ephitel's minions while the others searched her things, but she lay crumpled and motionless beside her desk, beneath the room's only window.

She'd loved that window. She'd loved the view of daisies hanging on despite the autumn chill. She'd loved to stand there watching as he left for work each morning. She'd used its light to read by and its gentle breeze to air the little cottage.

The light bathed her now. Her milky skin almost glowed. Her expression seemed serene despite the bruising near her eyes and on her throat. Corin swallowed hard and tore his gaze away. There was but one thing he could do for her, and weeping over her corpse wasn't it. He dashed across the room without a sound and knelt down on the far side of the bed. That way, he couldn't see her. It helped a little.

In the outer room, Ephitel was speaking with his men. The elf's words carried clearly to Corin, crashing against his stunned grief like the pounding waves of an angry sea. "You searched the room? And this is everything?"

"Yes, my lord. Exactly as you commanded." It was the fervent voice of a worshiper in communion with his god.

"And there was nothing left behind? No hiding places?"

"No, my lord."

Corin's lips peeled back at that. It was not quite a smile. It was the animal grin of a predator prepared to pounce. There on the floor before him was a small trapdoor, barely wider than Corin's palm, but it ran three paces along the wall. It had no lock, just simple hinges, but it was inset at the level of the floor and protected by far more than mechanical artifice.

The trapdoor was invisible to anyone but Corin; the soldiers who'd searched the room would have seen an unbroken floor. Even the druids hadn't found a way to pierce the glamours Corin wove. It was a special kind of magic, a gift given him by a dying god, but Corin spent no time in wonder. After all the waiting, Ephitel now stood in the outer room, and here beneath this panel lay the key to killing him. Corin cast aside the druids' worries. Anything at all would be better than that monster. He destroyed the glamour with a work of will. He ripped up the trapdoor and plunged his hand into the hiding place beneath.

But all he touched was earth. The sword was gone.

The sword was gone.

In the outer room, Ephitel was still speaking with his soldiers. "Deliver all these things into the keeping of my steward; then post a guard upon this place. The girl's companions may show their faces here, and I would have them followed and found out."

"Yes, my lord. And the woodsman?"

Corin blinked. He hadn't moved. He knelt there, dazed, while Aemilia's killers casually discussed how they would deal with him.

"He is no threat to us," Ephitel said. "Leave him to his grief."

"Yes, my lord." The footfalls of a dozen armored men announced their departure, and then the door fell closed behind them. Corin summoned all the strength he had just to force himself upright. He climbed to his feet. His breath came fast and hot, and his heart hammered in his chest. He fixed his eyes on the door into the outer room, just to keep them from touching Aemilia.

And then the door opened. Corin groaned softly as Ephitel himself came through. He'd sent away his soldiers. He was every bit as dismissive of the broken pirate as he had been before. He came alone and undefended into the room, and if only the sword had been waiting in its hiding place, Corin would have stabbed the monster through the heart.

But no. Instead, he watched while Ephitel casually considered the corpse upon the floor, admiring his own handiwork. For how long had Corin hated this creature? All his life he'd despised the wicked ruling family and their tyrant god. And then Corin had stepped into an ancient dream and glimpsed the fiend's true treachery.

And still Corin hadn't hated him. Not the way he'd hated Dave Taker. Or Ethan Blake. Ephitel had always been a distant power, a devastating force of nature. But now, as he stared down at the druid's corpse, Ephitel became something else altogether. He became Corin's enemy. And Corin's enemies had a tendency to end up dead. Corin clenched his fists and struggled hard to breathe.

Oblivious to Corin's rage, Ephitel ran a careful gaze around the outer walls, rapped his knuckles on the desktop, then stepped around the bed, closer to Corin. The elf's eyes found the open trapdoor, and he nodded to himself in satisfaction. "My soldiers performed a thorough search indeed. I hadn't even spotted that before."

Corin didn't answer. He was drowning in the open air.

Ephitel arched an eyebrow. Then he reached out to place one finger under Corin's chin and tilted it up until the two locked gazes. Ephitel shook his head. "I am the lord, your god, Corin Hugh. I do not suffer insults lightly, but neither do I cast away that which can be redeemed. I can always find a use for a deserving man. Will you return unto the light?"

Corin showed his teeth in a parched growl, and Ephitel laughed in answer.

"Very well. Make peace with your grief, my child, and then leave this place forever. If my men find you here when they return, they may not extend my gracious mercy. You might have until sunset."

Then he turned away, leaving Corin to his loss.

(2)

It might have been half an hour later when the door banged open in the outer room. Corin barely registered it. He did raise his head when the bedroom door gave its weary creak, but dropped it again when he saw who had come.

"Wade," he said, his voice flat and thin even to his own ears. "You came too late."

The druid shuffled uncertainly. "I came as quickly as I could, Corin. Aemilia. Is she . . .?"

"She's dead. Ephitel's handiwork."

Wade gasped. "Here? He was here? Good lord, man, get on your feet! We have to run!"

Corin shook his head. "He found us, Wade. He knows we're here. He didn't seem a bit surprised."

"You spoke with him?"

"I fought with him. But aye, he spoke with me. He told his men to post a secret watch for your companions as soon as they return from the village."

Wade frowned. "We have some little time, then." His eyes cut to the still form beneath the window, and he breathed a curse. "Why did you come here, Corin? If you suspected he was here—"

Corin forced a slow breath. "I came to get the sword."

"Ah," Wade said, and in that one word, Corin had his explanation.

The druids had the sword. They'd taken it. Or perhaps Aemilia had given it to them. They'd never wholly trusted Corin, and they knew how precious a thing it was. For the sake of all their clever plans, they'd stolen it away from him and left him empty-handed when Ephitel came to his door.

He couldn't even find the strength to hate them for it. Not anymore. He let his head fall back against the wall and released a moan. "He killed her, Wade, because she was mine. That was all he really cared about. That, and because she was a druid. But not for any true transgression, not even some petty insult in his mind. He killed her as a chore, same as you and me out chopping wood."

Wade rustled as he crossed the room. He didn't answer Corin but rushed to Aemilia's side. Corin fought against a surge of senseless hope. He heard the small sounds as Wade checked for signs of life. He felt for a pulse and listened at her breast, but what was there to find? Ephitel would not have left her alive.

Still Corin hoped. He knew that he would hate himself for leaving her there all this time if the man found the barest trace of life, but still he prayed for it. *Sweet Fortune, let her be alive.*

To Corin's surprise, the druid passed no immediate judgment. While Wade was still fussing over her, Corin struggled to his feet. He had to brace himself against the wall. His ribs stabbed against his innards, and his knees threatened to give out, but he hauled himself upright and then crawled across the bed, a desperate hope burning in his veins.

"There is some sign of life?"

Wade startled at Corin's voice. He flinched away, then sank back on his heels and shook his head sadly. "No. I'm sorry, Corin. She's gone."

"But you're a druid! This is what you are for! It's the only useful thing I've ever seen from your people. Heal her! Use your druid magics, your strange medicines, and make her well!"

"This is beyond our magic, Corin. She's gone."

"But still you were searching—"

"For her tablet," Wade answered, patient as a stone. "She had precious artifacts that we cannot afford to lose."

"Ephitel has them all," Corin said. "He means to hunt the druids down like vermin, now that he has a lead."

Wade nodded. "That might explain why he left you alive. Perhaps he hopes you'll lead him back to us. But we have ways of hiding he cannot hope to overcome."

Corin arched an eyebrow. "Tell me more."

A knock at the door interrupted them. Both men reacted instantly. Corin snatched up a knife from its place beneath his pillow and slipped from the bed to take cover against the far wall. Wade spun in place, still crouching over Aemilia, and drew dartguns in both hands.

Pretty-faced Keelin gave a terrified squeak and dropped to the floor, covering her head with her hands. Aeondra and Noel didn't flinch, but they put on equally disapproving glares for the men. The new arrivals were all druids Corin had met before, though only Aeondra ever came around the cottage. The other two he'd only seen during interrogations in his early days.

All three now crowded into the little bedroom, Noel roughly dragging Wade aside as the other two went to crouch above Aemilia. Corin flinched at the little sounds of horror they made as they saw what had been done to their companion.

"Come away," Wade said, catching Corin's elbow with a little tug. "Come away. Any one of these lovely girls is better suited to tend to Aemilia than I am. All three together . . . if there's any hope, they'll find it."

Corin didn't miss the look of anger Aeondra shot at Wade for that last comment. There was no hope. There'd never been any hope. He understood it, even as the women bent their heads together whispering fiercely.

"Come away," Wade repeated, and Corin followed him into the outer room.

The room was an ungodly shambles. Corin hadn't noticed when he'd first come to the cottage. He'd been far too distracted to consider the state of his home. And then his scuffle with Ephitel had clearly contributed its share to the damage, but as he looked now, he saw broken furniture and scattered possessions.

The curtains had been torn down from the window, the kitchen ransacked. Ephitel had ordered his soldiers to search the place, and they had committed fully to their task. Corin stood staring at the devastation until Wade gave another tug at his elbow to start him moving again. They crossed the living room and slipped out into the garden.

Here too Ephitel's soldiers had done their damage. So many men coming and going, they'd torn up the flowerbeds and made a muddy mess of the lawn. Anger burned hot in Corin's stomach at the memory, but something else sparked too. He remembered Ephitel's warning and the conversation he'd overheard between Ephitel and the soldiers.

He looked in the direction of the village, searching the woods for some sign of the soldiers returning early. Instead, he saw two more druids trotting up, a strange steel litter slung between them. The thing was loaded with small canvas bags packed to bursting, and the two men didn't slow as they jogged past Corin and Wade and into the stricken cottage.

Corin spun after them, then grabbed Wade by the lapels. "What are they about? I already warned you that Ephitel's men are coming back."

Wade nodded. "We have some time left. Time enough to offer Aemilia the end that she deserves."

Corin nodded. "You have some means of hiding from the gods. You mentioned that before. Share it with me, and I will grant her spirit justice."

Wade shook his head. "You misunderstood me. We hide through careful lies. Everyone believes the druids to be disbanded, scattered to the winds, and that alone has kept us safe for hundreds of years. Ephitel believes it too, though he has no way to know for sure. He must suspect. He must worry."

Corin snorted. "You've given him precious little to worry about."

"We've kept the world alive this long. We serve a higher calling than your quest for vengeance."

It was not the first time they'd had this argument, and Corin couldn't find the energy to pursue it yet again. Not when he knew how it ended. He turned his back on Wade and spoke to the encroaching forest. "He will know now, then. He had at least a dozen men, and they carried off everything of Aemilia's they could lay their hands on. They're looking for you."

"They won't find us," Wade said. "Not yet. I've been in contact with Drew and Stibbons, and they're tracking Ephitel's men. We have enough time—just enough."

Corin turned back. "Enough? For what? What are you scheming?"

"I am an honest man; I do not scheme. Right now, my only desire is to bring Aemilia back to the circle."

"You said you couldn't save her."

Wade shook his head. "I can't. But you are not the only one who loved her, Corin Hugh. We must say our good-byes; then we will set her soul to rest."

"Good-byes won't serve her, druid. And they won't save your hide if Ephitel tracks you down. If you want to honor her, then help me grant her vengeance."

Wade shook his head. "The strictures—"

Corin sneered. "That's what I've learned to hate about you all. You'll cling to your strictures like divine law—"

"They *are* divine law," Wade interrupted.

Corin went on, right over him. "—and yet you'll sacrifice *nothing* to improve the world those strictures were meant to protect."

"That isn't fair. We've sacrificed more than you can ever know. Obeying the strictures—even when it means watching someone innocent suffer for it—that is a sacrifice. The strictures are what keeps this world alive."

"And if this world's infected? If it suffers from a cancer your strictures cannot heal?"

Corin said it as a challenge, but Wade nodded as though Corin had just discovered some secret truth. His eyes flashed. "That task must fall to someone else. To someone native of this world. The strictures stay our hands . . ."

"But not mine," Corin said.

"Not yours," the druid conceded.

Corin reeled. He sank down on his heels and steadied himself with a hand on the ground. They *meant* for him to break their laws? They'd wind him up and turn him loose like a dwarven clockwork toy. He'd never guessed they were manipulating him so thoroughly.

There'd been a time, in Oberon's dreams, when Corin flew into a rage at the thought of druids pulling his strings. Now he only thanked sweet Fortune that they would point him in a direction he already meant to go. For their purposes or his own—it didn't matter. He would be glad to see Ephitel put down.

But then a question struck him, and his brow wrinkled. "If that's what you intend, why did you steal the sword from me?"

"Not everyone believes that killing Ephitel is for the greater good. There are some who think you may pose a larger threat to Hurope."

"Give me their names, and I will see the debate resolved."

Wade's eyes grew wide. He shook his head. "It's not so severe as that. But you are opening old wounds and forcing a decision that most had thought unanswerable for . . . ages. Give them time."

"I *gave* them time," Corin said again, "and now Aemilia is dead."

"Killing druids won't bring her back, but bide a while and you'll have your sword again. I'm certain of it. Then we can watch as this world resolves its own problems in accordance with the strictures."

Corin snorted. "You're plotting a mighty complicated course to call that accordance."

"Another little sacrifice. We can't abandon who we are, but protecting the sons and daughters is part of who we are."

Corin sprang to his feet. "Then give me the sword!"

"It isn't mine to give. It's in the safekeeping of the Council until they reach a decision. But you can make your plans. You can set things in motion, so that when they're ready—"

"I have made my plans," Corin said. "All I lack is information and the weapon, and your people have withheld them both."

Wade frowned. "What information?"

"I need to rally the elves to my cause. The loyalists from old Gesoelig who never joined with Ephitel."

"Ah."

That word again. Corin stepped closer. "What do you know? Why won't the Council tell me where to find the elves?"

"It's . . . complicated."

"Then clear it up for me."

Wade sighed. "The elves have all foresworn us through the ages. They will not speak with us, and they will not cooperate with us."

Corin almost asked why, but he saw the answer before he voiced the question. The elves still loyal to Oberon had lost everything in Ephitel's coup, and they had watched the druids hold to their strictures. For how many hundred years had they watched the druids with the same frustration Corin now endured? One by one they'd fallen away.

He'd counted on the elves. He needed them to draw out Ephitel. That was much of why he'd played the druids' game all this time, in hopes that they would hand him an army of elves ready to be stirred up for battle. If they were already too weary of the druids' reticence to even listen, then Corin had wasted his time here.

He growled. "Fine stewards you've been."

"We've done what we could," Wade snapped, defensive again. "And we were not the only ones who faced hard choices."

"Don't ask me for pity there," Corin said. "Life is hard choices. Honest men don't whine about it; they bend their backs to the task and make things right."

Wade rolled his eyes. "Now you'll speak to me of honest men?"

"Brave men, then," Corin said. "Not slinking cowards. I can understand the elves' decision. If your people have thrown away all their goodwill, let me win it back. I'm not one of you, but I'm an honorary one of them. Tell me where to find them—"

"I can't."

"Gods' blood, Wade! All I'm asking—"

"I can't," Wade said again, losing his patience. "We don't know. They've slipped our observation altogether. We have a handful of individuals who still talk to us every decade or so, but only the high seats of the Council even know how to contact those."

"The same Council that can't decide if I'm a greater threat than Ephitel?"

Wade shrugged in answer.

Corin cursed. The energy he'd found drained away again, and he wilted. Corin half-expected a comforting word from Wade, but instead the druid took the opportunity to slip back into the cottage. Corin stared after him, bewildered, but the man was only gone a moment.

"She's prepped," he said. "They have her ready for the journey, but Stibbons says we're out of time. We have to move her now."

The door opened behind him, and Corin fought down an urge to turn and run. He couldn't face the corpse upon its bier. His heart knew Aemilia as sunshine and laughter. He couldn't trade that image for the one of the lifeless corpse they brought him, gray and still.

He would have left them on the doorstep if he could. He knew his heart would find no comfort in good-byes—not in the sort the druids were pursuing. He knew men who believed the gods' lies about a glorious paradise awaiting the righteous in a life after this one. He knew men who believed true warriors might find an endless, glorious war on the other side of death. Men believed all sorts of things.

Corin knew there was only blackness. He had met the god who made this world, and such a creature wasn't wise enough or strong enough to catch the slippery thread of a life extinguished. He certainly could not have fashioned any kind of paradise. No, Corin found more hope in believing that there was rest in death.

But not for him. Not yet. He still had work to do, and to see it done, he required the proper tools. He needed the sword to challenge Ephitel, and the sword was with their Council.

He had no choice. So he licked his lips, set his shoulders, and turned to face the funeral procession as it emerged from the cottage.

Aemilia, forgive me, he thought. *I will remember you as you truly were. I will always remember you alive. And Ephitel will face justice. This I swear. I'll see him dead before I come to join you.*

(3)

The women brought Aemilia out of the cottage, led by the two men who had brought the litter. The druids had prepared her according to their own traditions. She looked odd to Corin, stretched out on the thin steel bed and draped all around with tubes that looked like fine-spun glass but were clearly as flexible as flax. A mask of the same material concealed her mouth, but her eyes were left uncovered.

And then, despite himself, he whispered the cold dread that gripped his heart. "She's dead."

At his side, Wade nodded. "She was a good woman. She will be missed."

Corin blinked against a burning in his eyes and turned away. He didn't try to answer but fell into step behind Aeondra. He had barely gone three paces before Wade caught up and laid a gentle hand on his shoulder. "Perhaps it would be best if you waited here," the druid said. "Weave yourself a glamour and keep an eye on Ephitel's men. I'll speak with the Council and bring you a report."

Corin didn't stop, and Wade was forced to trot along beside him. Corin showed the druid his unmasked grief. "I would prefer to say good-bye. I believe I've earned that much."

Wade pressed his lips together, clearly uncomfortable. Corin only held his gaze, unblinking. At last the druid seemed to wilt. "Give over, Corin. You know the strictures say—"

"None of the sons or daughters may pass into the inner Circle. But I am no longer one of them. I have become something more."

"Perhaps. But I don't have the authority—"

"I do," Corin said, his voice hard as steel. "Who would deny me this? Tell me. When I did everything you asked of me. When I paid such a price."

Those words twisted like a knife in Corin's belly, but they reached the other man as well. Wade winced and tore his gaze away.

Corin pressed the point. "I loved her. That is no secret. She loved me almost as much as she loved this place. Those loves cost Aemilia her life. I have to be there to say good-bye."

Wade could only nod. He squeezed Corin's shoulder once again, but this time it was a gesture of sympathy. Then he dropped his hand and fell into step at Corin's side. They went together, pallbearers to the sleeping beauty.

Somewhere along the way, Drew and Stibbons joined them. They didn't say a word; they simply took up places, one at the head of the procession and one at the tail, both watching the forest intently as they marched. As the sun set on a wicked world, the druids carried Aemilia deep into the woods toward their secret meeting place.

Corin knew the place as soon as he set eyes on it. It was a ring of standing stones perhaps a hundred paces across, each stone immense beyond belief. A quiet energy filled the air around the stones, like a mighty power long restrained. Tendrils of thin gray mist danced in wild currents outside the circle—the same mist that Corin had learned to associate with Oberon's strange magic.

This was a druid circle. Corin had seen the like before in his travels. There was one along the border between the Godlands and heathen Jepta, and Old Grim had told a tale of another just like it deep within the Dehtzlan wood. They only appeared around the far edges of civilization, and most men knew nothing of their purpose.

Nor had Corin until now. He'd only ever seen them empty, apparently abandoned, and in three months working with the druids in this corner of the world, he had never seen this circle until now. The druids had always come to meet him at his cottage.

And now that they had come here, he could not guess why. For all the mystery in those huge gray stones, what purpose could they serve? The circle held an inner ring of smaller stones—and even those stones were each twice as large as a full-grown man—and at the very heart of the place was a huge stone table. Or perhaps it was an altar. Corin shivered at the thought. Was this to be her resting place?

The one thing that still gave him hope was the mist that roiled all around them. It seemed to grow more frantic as their procession drew closer. The first of the druids to approach the circle's edge did so with his tablet held before him. It glowed with an otherworldly light, and arcane symbols danced across its surface. With deft touches on the surface, the druid manipulated them in rapid succession, and half a heartbeat before he reached the circle's edge, a brilliant flash of the same blue-white light burst out of the roiling mists and splashed against the stones' perimeter.

When that light faded, the circle's interior had changed. There was still an inner circle, and beyond it a table of stone, but these seemed to stand at slightly different angles. They were weathered differently. The differences were minor, but Corin had an instinct for spotting such small things.

There were more obvious changes too. The circle held more than a dozen other druids now, half of them dressed in the outlandish garb they never wore around the sons and daughters.

There were artifacts as well: on pedestals and stands throughout the clearing, in open-fronted cabinets, and spread in great number on the broad stone table at the heart of the inner circle. Corin couldn't guess at the uses of them all, but they had the same glass-and-silver look as the dartguns and the tablets he'd seen in druid hands before.

All eyes turned toward the procession when the first of them stepped into the circle, and a handful of men in stark white coats rushed to stand around the stone table. They were expecting the new arrivals, then. Waiting for Aemilia.

Wade tried again to stop Corin. His grip tightened on Corin's shoulder, and he began to speak in a carefully measured voice. Corin ignored him. He tore free and dashed forward, diving through the gap between two standing stones and into the circle's clearing.

A tall man wearing one of the white coats shouted, "Who's this manling? Who brought him here? Someone restrain him, please!"

In answer, Corin drew a dagger in one hand and a sharp-edged knife in the other. He showed his teeth to the first of the druids who started toward him. "I'm Corin Hugh. Perhaps you've heard the name. The first of you who tries to lay a hand on me will lose it."

He spun on his heel and flipped his knife around, ready to throw. "That goes double for anyone who tries to dart me. I know all about your little toys."

It had been barely better than a hunch, but he found himself locking eyes with a white-haired man holding a dartgun half-raised. Corin raised his knife hand higher, threatening, and the druid lowered his gun.

They stood a moment frozen like that, and Corin spent the whole time wondering how many of these men he'd have to stab before they'd let him stay.

Then Endan Wade heaved a great sigh somewhere behind him. He approached cautiously and said, "Put down the knives, Corin. No one's going to make you leave."

"Let's not make any hasty promises," the tall man in the white coat said, finally approaching. He pulled himself up straight and stared down his nose at Corin. "Who gave leave to bring him here?"

Before Wade could answer, Corin pressed forward and met the taller man eye to eye. He tried to suppress his rage, but some hint of it leaked into his tone. "Your god gave me leave. I am the chosen heir of Oberon. And who are *you*?"

The druid raised his eyebrows in surprise. Then he looked right past Corin to Wade and spoke with deep disdain. "This is how you manage your assets, Wade?"

Corin's patience snapped. He dropped his knife, knotted a fist in the druid's lapels, and dragged him down as he brought the dagger flashing up. He lay its blade against the tall man's throat and snarled in his face. "No one manages me, druid. Your people let Ephitel at the woman I love, and your people robbed me of the means to avenge her."

The man's eyes grew wide as Rikkeborh crowns. "Ephitel?" He seemed at last to understand what he had heard before. "You're Corin Hugh? You're speaking of the anomalous sword?"

Vindicated, Corin released his grip on the man's coat. He knelt to retrieve his knife and sheathed both blades; then he smoothed his shirtfront while he took a measure of control.

At last he nodded. "I am speaking of the sword *Godslayer*. It is mine by every right. Return it to me."

"Surely . . . surely this is not the right time. We must focus on Aemilia—"

Corin shook his head. "Aemilia is dead, and her murderer still walks the world. I care nothing for your rituals, and I will not rest until Ephitel pays in blood for what he did to her."

The tall man turned to Wade again, this time pleading. "You must reason with him!"

Wade spread his hands. "I have done everything within my power. No one manages Corin Hugh."

Corin growled. "For three months I did everything your people asked of me. And this is my reward."

He turned away from them to watch as Aemilia's strange bed rolled to a stop beside the huge stone table. Half a dozen druids moved to surround her, with one of those in a white coat supporting her head. That man called out something in an unfamiliar tongue. It was a short, repetitive bark that had the sound of ritual, and on the fourth intonation all the druids moved in perfect synchrony, transferring Aemilia from her litter to the cold stone altar.

Light sprang up across its surface, and strange characters like the ones he'd seen on their handheld tablets. The whole huge slab of stone became an animated slate much like those tablets, and the druids who had brought her there bent over the strange symbols, poking and prodding, manipulating the images while Aemilia rested, still, in the middle of it all.

Slowly, one by one, the men in their white coats turned away, and other men rushed up to take their places. Corin couldn't quite understand the significance of that, but the tall man clearly did.

"Then it is true," he said. "She's lost to us. I cannot imagine Hurope without Aemilia in it." He turned to Corin, and

Corin was surprised to see genuine sympathy in the tall man's eyes. "I understand your pain," the druid said. "I do. But killing Ephitel will not ease it. Go say your good-byes and try to find some peace."

"I . . . can't."

The druid nodded in understanding. "Then watch from here. You'll have a clear enough view. And when it's done, we'll find you a nice comfortable bed for the night. Tomorrow we'll decide what's best for you."

It was everything he'd learned to expect from the druids: shallow comforts and a promise to wrest away more control of his life. He bowed his head in what he hoped they'd take for gratitude, and both men moved away. They left him alone in the bustling outer circle while they went to speak quietly with the men who'd left the table earlier.

Corin couldn't help himself. He drifted closer. He had no desire to see Aemilia, no hope at all to find any sort of peace with what had been done to her. He wanted to avenge her, not grieve his loss.

But she was about to be gone. He could not ignore the fact. She was about to be gone forever, and he had to see her one last time.

So, in spite of himself, he drifted closer to the inner circle even as the druids there were drifting out. They formed a ring, shoulder to shoulder outside the standing stones. Many stood with teary eyes. Some gripped comforting hands. One and all they stared into the inner circle where Aemilia waited on the table all alone.

She looked pretty. Corin couldn't help thinking it. Someone had tied off her hair the way she liked it, out of her face. The strange tubes and mask were gone now, and one by one the glowing symbols on the table flashed and went out. Stillness and starlight settled over the inner circle.

She was lovely on the cold stone slab. He reached out a hand toward her, but he didn't complete the gesture. His throat closed up again, harder this time, and he had to close his eyes and turn away before he could gasp a breath again.

All around him, the druids began to sing. He could not comprehend the words, but he recognized it as an aching dirge. He felt its sadness in his breast. He forced a painful breath, and then another, as the sounds of litany gave voice to his grief. He left the inner circle and pressed through the ring of druids, desperate for air. He broke free of their line and kept walking, faster and faster. He had to get away.

He almost left the outer circle at a sprint, and he wasn't at all certain where he would have ended up. Was this the same circle he had entered in southwest Raentz, or would he find himself in Dehtzlan or Jepta or somewhere else altogether? And would he be able to return?

He didn't have a chance to find out. No sooner had he started toward the standing stones than his eyes fell upon a glass-fronted cabinet filled with the druids' strange artifacts. Though they were not of any design common to Hurope, he instantly recognized them as weapons, firearms from Yesterworld. And there was the sword *Godslayer* in an ill-fitting scabbard, tucked among the otherworldly weapons and looking oh so out of place.

He cast a glance around, but everyone seemed fixed on Aemilia's last rites. He nodded to himself and dashed toward the cabinet, drawing out his lockpicks as he went. This was exactly what he'd come for, and he would grab it now while the druids were distracted, then leave this place and do what needed doing.

But when he reached the cabinet, he could find no lock to pick. The thing glowed here and there with the wicked, artificial light of druid artifacts, and one small panel near the middle of an edge shone in the runes of their language. None of that told Corin how to slip the lock, though.

He stood for a moment, staring in frustration, inches from the thing he wanted most in all the world and stymied by a lock that wasn't there. He tried the door, hoping foolishly that the druids trusted each other insofar as not to lock it, but of course it wouldn't budge. He cast a glance over his shoulder, just to make sure the others were still engrossed in their ceremony.

They were. All but one of them, anyway. A stranger in unaccustomed clothes stood barely three paces from Corin, watching him intently. When he saw Corin glance his way, he answered with a little nod toward the weapons case.

"You could try to break the glass," he said, "but it won't work. You're going to need the combination."

Corin's mouth was suddenly completely dry. He swallowed hard, trying to work moisture into it, then stammered, "W-would you . . . give it to me?"

The other pretended to consider that a moment, then shrugged. "Sure. But only if you promise me you'll kill off Ephitel for good."

Something in that shrug, in the other man's expression and his voice, tugged at Corin's memory. He considered the druid for a long moment and then his jaw dropped.

"Jeff?"

The druid's eyebrows raised, but the corner of his mouth turned down as he nodded in reluctant admission. "In the flesh. You know me?"

"Better than you might believe," Corin said. "Have you not heard my story?"

"I've heard some drivel about time travel, but that's not what interests me. The main thing I keep hearing is that you're anxious to run off and deal with Ephitel instead of waiting for the Council's carefully considered approval."

Corin flashed his teeth. "You've caught me in the act."

"Then get on with it," Jeff said. He leaned past Corin and punched four of the clustered symbols on the glowing panel. Each press elicited a tiny, tortured beep, and on the fourth, the door fell softly open.

The druid's eyebrows rose again when Corin reached past the outlandish weapons and grabbed the longsword's scabbard.

Drawing it out, he clipped it on the belt around his waist. Then he jerked his head toward a distant spot along the circle's outer edge, where a pair of standing chalkboards made a little nook that might offer them a bit of privacy.

As they walked, Jeff asked him, "How'd you know?"

"Know what?"

"That the sword was hidden in the rifle case?"

Corin frowned, uncomprehending for a moment, then he glanced down at the sword hanging from his belt. The thin, almost imperceptible mists of a druid's glamour hung close around it. Corin chuckled to himself and waved a hand, dismissing the disguise with a thought. Jeff choked on his surprise.

"I see through the dream," Corin said. "A gift from Oberon."

"You aren't one of us, then." It was almost a question, if a ludicrous one.

"I am a manling, born in Aepoli. But I did travel into a dream within a dream. I saw the fall of Gesoelig through Oberon's eyes. I met you there. I was in the plaza when you and Delaen rescued Aemilia from Ephitel's prison coach."

Corin watched the doubt in Jeff's eyes die away with every word. By the end of Corin's explanation, he was nodding along.

"Then it's all true?" he asked.

Corin grinned. "Every word of it. I'm a force of nature."

"That would explain how Ephitel found Aemilia."

Corin's grin dissolved. Something sharp and hungry burrowed into his belly. He took a slow breath to fight away the feeling and asked quietly, "What do you mean?"

"It's the puzzle that dragged me here. I'm supposed to be dead, you know."

"Aemilia had hinted at it, but she never said as much outright."

"She never liked to lie. Not where you could catch her at it, anyway. She was a good woman. Is it true you two were an item?"

Corin sighed. "Would they have let me come here otherwise?"

Jeff shrugged. "I haven't understood them for more than a century. But I suppose I see your point. They wouldn't let you do what needs doing, but they would break a dozen strictures for the sake of a forbidden love. That sounds like their style."

Corin blinked at the bitterness in Jeff's tone. He looked the druid up and down, considering his options. A man with such animosity toward the Council might prove useful.

While Corin was still thinking, Jeff picked up the trail of his earlier comments. "I've . . . I guess I've been in hiding for a while. But I keep an eye on things. When I saw the news about Aemilia, I had to check it out. And one question kept nagging at me: How'd he find her? After all this time, what brought Ephitel to one of ours *now*?"

Jeff might as well have punched him in the gut. Corin grunted and dropped his head. "I did. I killed a Vestossi—"

"That's not enough. He didn't need a *motive*, man. He needed a *means*. Ephitel's been gunning for our people ever since he murdered Oberon. We have the resources to evade him."

"And?" Corin asked. "You seemed to think you'd found an answer."

"It never really occurred to me that the time travel stories could be true. But if you've been out of time, then Jessamine could probably track you. You'd be an anomaly of sizable proportions."

"Gods' blood," Corin spat. "What's a Jessamine?"

"A woman," Jeff said, showing the ghost of a smile. It vanished before he continued. "One of ours, actually, until she went over to the other side."

"One of yours? A druid cast her lot with Ephitel?"

"Yep. The only one across more than a thousand years."

"And she can track me?" Corin swallowed hard. Before he had befriended her, Aemilia had certainly shown up a time or two in inconvenient places. She'd had no trouble tracking him across Hurope, thanks to the disturbances created by his use of Oberon's power. It had been bad enough when the druids' Council were the ones keeping track of him. Now he learned Ephitel could do it too? He clenched his fists and asked through gritted teeth, "Why has no one mentioned this before?"

"They don't like to think about her," Jeff said. "Same as me. They like to pretend the world still works according to their strictures. Like Oberon is still running the show." He shook his head in disgust. "Probably never crossed their minds. She's been out of sight for decades now, so they've forgotten all about her."

Corin whipped his head left and right. "Aren't we in danger here, then? If she can track me, I could lead her straight to the circle."

"Not a chance. The megaliths themselves warp reality far beyond anything you can do. You're a needle in a haystack here, but step outside the circle, and you'll be more like a pin on a map. You'll have to watch your back."

The hairs on the back of Corin's neck stood up, but he didn't answer right away. He considered it. He'd been a hunted man all his life, after all. Nimble Fingers learned to keep their wits about them on the run, and pirates thrived on it. He took a deep breath, thinking, then shook his head.

"It's not so bad as that," he said. "I was here three months before she found me. If I keep moving—"

"Do it careful," Jeff said. "Hide in crowds. Mix with other outlanders if you can."

Corin barked a sarcastic little laugh. "You mean like elves?"

"That would be perfect. Know any?"

"I'd hoped the Council would put me in contact with them, but apparently the two sides aren't speaking anymore."

"Then keep on the move. That's all you'll have. And don't tarry. Get to Ephitel as fast as possible and end this. The longer you wait, the worse a threat she'll be."

Corin stared a moment.

Jeff's brows were pinched in a frown. "What?"

"I've discussed these plans with half a dozen others, mostly druids, and you're the first who seems to believe I'll do it."

"I'm the last of us who still believes it can be done. No matter what the others say, they've all given up."

"Not I," Corin said. "I'll die first. He should not have taken Aemilia from me."

"Good," Jeff said, nodding in satisfaction. "But don't die. Kill Ephitel. Your dying wouldn't serve me at all."

Corin chuckled. "I'll remember that."

"Good," Jeff said again, then he stepped closer. "How?"

"I have the sword—"

"No, I understand how you mean to kill him. But how will you find him?"

Corin had considered the matter carefully. He'd spent most of his time working on ways to flush out Ephitel, to draw the monster out where he could take him down, but he thought there might be a better way. He'd never hung much hope on it, but he'd seen more than one myth made real in the last year.

"Will I have to find him?" he asked. "Everyone knows that Ephitel and all the gods live like kings on the highest peak of Mount Attos."

He held his breath, half expecting Jeff to laugh away the notion. Instead, the druid frowned in thought and bobbed his head uncertainly. "In a sense they do," he said at last. "But not . . . not really."

Corin raised an eyebrow. "What are you saying?"

"I'm saying that if a manling climbs that mountain, all he'll find at the top are bare rocks and an icy death."

"I'm no mere manling."

"You're not. I'm convinced of that. But there's strong fairy magic at work there. I'm not convinced New Soelig is even in this dream. It might be back in Faerie proper, with the mountain serving as a crossing point. Can you cross into Faerie?"

"I . . . I don't know."

"Most of the elves cannot. Not at Mount Attos, anyway. Even the ones who've sworn allegiance to Ephitel need an appointed guide to cross over into the high city. Nor can any among the druids. We tried back in the dark days after Gesoelig's fall. We tried, but Ephitel has made New Soelig safe so that only his followers may enter there, and only the most trusted of them may go unescorted."

Corin closed his eyes. "That cannot be the end of it. I will find a way in."

"I'm telling you, there's no way in. For all your strange powers, do you really believe you know more about the ways of Faerie than I do?"

Corin leaned back against one of the standing stones. He didn't answer. Of course he didn't think that. He barely understood the powers he did have.

But he was not about to abandon his quest either. He shrugged and spread his hands. "In all honesty, I never really believed it would be as easy as storming Ephitel's palace in righteous justice. If I cannot go to the mountain, I'll bring Ephitel to me."

"How? Do you mean to pray to him?"

"No, I have a more compelling means than that."

"You think you can provoke the Lord of War?"

"I've done it once before."

Jeff considered him a moment, then he sighed. "Ephitel is arrogant and cruel, but he's no fool. He won't come at your summons, and if he does, he'll come in force. You're lucky to have survived him once."

Corin didn't answer that either. Lucky? Lucky enough to see Aemilia dead. Lucky enough to inherit all the miseries of this broken, worn-out world and its miserable masters.

"I won't rest until he's dead," Corin said softly. "I plan to draw him out and put him down. Are you with me? I could use your skills."

"I'm not a soldier, Corin, but I will fight for you."

"How?"

"Here. I only came to say good-bye to Aemilia. But if you will keep your promise, if you'll commit yourself to ending Ephitel, then I'll abandon mine. I will return to the Council and do everything in my power to sway them in your favor."

Corin shook his head. "I have no desire to wait for that."

"And I wouldn't want you to. I only hope that when you need us, the druids will be ready to stand behind you."

Corin nodded, satisfied. He pushed himself away from the standing stone and caught the edge of his cloak against a sudden gust of wind. He closed his other hand around *Godslayer*'s hilt and nodded to the druid.

"Fortune favor you," Corin said. "While you begin your work, I go hunting for a god."

(5)

Corin stepped through dream and traveled all the way from the Dividing Line in southwest Raentz to the bustling heart of Aerome with just a thought. He had not visited the city often, but he knew well the place he meant to go.

His memory and Oberon's power brought him to a narrow hallway in a rundown apartment complex. The corridor was dark and close, and floorboards creaked even under Corin's careful step. The pirate winced at the noise, but only out of ancient habit; he was not in Aerome for any clandestine purpose. On the contrary—he meant to get caught.

But first he had to lay some plans, and that was why he'd come to this third-story hallway in the least fashionable part of town. He strode forward through the shadows, peering closely at the numbers scratched into the crude doorposts until he found the one he wanted. He rapped on the door.

A woman answered; a pretty little slip of a thing. In itself, that was no surprise at all, but Corin felt a touch of shock when he recognized the girl.

She clearly did not recognize him. She frowned out into the hall, the door opened just a slit. She clutched a linen bedsheet around her, and in her other hand she held a narrow-bladed knife with tracery in gold and silver. Corin raised his eyebrows, admiring, until she gave a quiet growl.

He cleared his throat. "That is quite a piece of handiwork."

"You had *better* mean the knife."

"Oh, I do," he answered earnestly. It was a bauble fit for a prince, but Corin had no doubt it held a perfect edge. Dwarven mastercraft.

"Well," she said, only slightly mollified. She hid a massive yawn behind a delicate fist. By the look of her, she'd been several days without much restful sleep, and the snippy tone in her voice suggested she was most anxious to get back to it. "Do you have some business here, or have you only come to ogle?"

Corin swept a bow. "My dear Lilya, I have come a thousand miles to speak with Master Strunk. Please tell me he is taking visitors."

She pulled the door wider to gain a better view. She frowned at him a moment, then shook her head. "How do you know me?"

He showed her a winning smile. "I have an eye for craftsmanship, my dear, and a good memory for names. More to the point, I will not soon forget the night that Giuliano Vestossi met his end, and you played a noble part in that particular event."

Her eyes shot wide at that. "You know? Oh, but you are him. I didn't recognize you."

"Perhaps the evening didn't register so strongly for you."

Another voice answered Corin, lower in register and lower to the ground. "Perhaps her eyes were full of better men."

Corin grinned. "Or dwarves."

"Or dwarves," the other agreed. He stepped up to the girl's side and slapped her bottom with the same care and precision he had used to make that blade. She gasped, then grinned and blushed by turns, and the rascal dwarf chuckled in reply.

"Might as well find some clothes to keep you warm, darling. I have a feeling Corin here intends to put me to less worthy tasks."

"Alas, I do indeed," Corin said. He tipped his head in a bow to Lilya. "A pleasure meeting you again."

She answered with a curtsy that nearly lost her the bedsheet. "Milord." Then she gave a giggle and scampered off to an inner room.

Ben stood a moment evaluating Corin, then came to himself with a shake of his head and stepped aside. "Come in! Come in. Gods' blood, it's good to see you, Corin!"

Corin stepped past him into the artist's studio. It was a wide, open room divided into four quarters by its furnishings. The nearest corner on Corin's right was lined with low tables that supported potters' wheels and plaster molds, a goldsmith's tools and magnifying lenses. Beyond that stood a mostly empty corner in front of a tiny brick fireplace, but Ben had assembled some strange manner of forge right there on the faded hardwood floor. Wide pipes of copper rose above the forge, then twisted down to empty into the fireplace. Spots of char marred the floor all around the forge, and soot had stained the ceiling and nearest walls in streaks of black despite the makeshift chimney.

The nearby anvil was a small one, topped with a jewelcrafter's delicate tools rather than an armorer's, but two huge quenching barrels stood nearby. There was also a bucket that Corin suspected had been needed more than once to douse a fire started by the indoor forge.

A row of narrow windows in the outer wall lit the other half of the apartment. One corner held a fainting couch, a huge bronze standlamp, and half a dozen easels. The canvases they held all showed the girl Lilya in different poses. Ben had a true talent for painting, and several of these images undermined the noble work of the bedsheet she had borrowed.

The bed and the model both now hid in the back corner, surrounded by tall folding screens. As Corin stepped into the room, he heard the soft sound of the girl snoring delicately behind the screens.

Ben gave a shrug of perfect innocence. "Gods bless her, the poor thing is all worn out."

Corin shook his head. "I can hardly believe you're still playing with Blake's old serving girl."

Ben frowned at him. "You must admit she makes a lovely model."

"Aye. But she belongs to the Vestossis."

A touch of ice entered Ben's tone. "Her affections have shifted. And she never did *belong* to the Vestossis. One does what one must to survive in a city like this."

Corin could appreciate the sentiment—he'd stained his soul at times to survive the streets of Aepoli as a child—but his sympathy was not enough to make him overlook her recent association with his bitterest enemies.

He opened his mouth to say as much, but Ben's flashing eyes suggested the dwarf would not take kindly to further talk in that direction. Corin tried another tack. "Still, it's hardly decent. She's two hundred years too young for you!"

Ben snorted, dismissive. "I've had to learn to count in human years."

"But to a dwarf—"

"She is just as much a woman as she is to you. What can it harm her that I have the perspective to appreciate her charms?"

"Surely—"

"Surely you should bite your tongue, Corin Hugh. You won't win this fight as long as you're still toying with the druid girl. She'd seen a thousand years before I was even born."

Corin grunted. He had not expected Ben to bring her up, and certainly not in such a casual manner. Corin had done his best to force Aemilia to the farthest corners of his mind, but Ben's words brought back a memory of their last adventure together. Ben, Aemilia, and Corin had infiltrated a party at the home of Ethan Blake. That was where Ben had met Lilya. And where Corin had committed the murder that eventually brought Ephitel to their little cottage in the woods.

The memory of it staggered him, and in an instant Ben was at his side, peering up in worry.

"What's caught you, Corin? You look black as midnight. Something I said?"

"Aye," Corin answered. He took a slow breath and shook his head. "Aye, you put your finger on it. Aemilia is dead. Ephitel came for her."

"Gods' blood! How did he find her?"

"I don't quite know. The druids think he might have had the help of one of theirs—a traitor by the name of Jessamine—but all I know is that he came to punish me for killing Blake."

"He came for you? But how—"

Corin shook his head. "He came because of me, but Aemilia was always his target. He *thanked* me for giving him a druid to kill."

"By the rings, Corin, I didn't know. You have my sympathy. Can I do aught to help you?"

Corin glanced toward the back corner of the room, still suspicious of the serving girl, but her gentle snores continued behind the folding screens. Despite them, Corin asked, "Will you take a walk with me? It . . . it would help to clear my head. And we do have much to discuss."

"Aye. Of course."

They left the artist's studio and descended the narrow, creaking stairs of the tenement building. Ben Strunk liked to spend his evenings hobnobbing with the wealthy and the powerful, but he'd always said he preferred to live and work among the poor. There'd been a time when Corin thought it was a careful plan to preserve his artistic hunger, his perspective for the plight of the common man.

One day he'd commented on it, and old Ben had chortled heartily. No, he explained, he preferred to do his work among the poor because his wealthy patrons hated visiting him there. That kept them from interfering in his works in progress. That had been the day Corin and Ben became true friends.

Now they walked in icy silence, leaving the rundown building for an alley just as foul and claustrophobic. Corin set the pace and chose their path. He turned left at the first intersection, then right. Ben only walked along beside him, keeping his pace and holding his tongue. Dwarves were masters when it came to patience and ancient friends with stony silence.

Corin's path might have seemed random at a glance, for he followed no major thoroughfare. In fact, he was aiming for the highest of the city's seven hills, tracking like a bloodhound straight as the ancient, twisting streets would allow him.

They'd left the studio more than a mile behind before Corin finally drew a heavy breath and turned to his companion. "I want justice, Ben."

"I hate to be the one to tell you, but you're in the wrong world for that. There's no justice here. There's just Vestossis."

"I've tried my hand at them," Corin said, casting his voice lower. "They die easy enough. Now I want to aim a little higher."

"I can hardly say I blame you, but it's a fool's errand, boy. Believe me. I've met the man. He won't die easy."

"He'd better not," Corin said. "I want him to die hard and weeping."

"It won't bring her back."

Corin clenched a fist and bit his tongue. Shouting at his friend would do no good. He was not a sentimental child chasing satisfaction. He'd seen more than his share of misery, and he *knew* just how bone-deep wicked Ephitel's Ithale was.

But he was not willing to accept that anymore. The time had come for change. He took a calming breath and answered levelly. "It's not revenge I'm after, Ben. It's justice. Oberon himself gave me this task. You've had a glimpse of the power he gave me, and he gave it to me for this very purpose."

Ben walked several paces in thoughtful silence. He knew the name of Oberon, knew its significance, and he'd heard some portion of Corin's impossible tale. He chewed on Corin's plans awhile, then asked with all the curious care of a master craftsman, "How?"

"Another gift of Oberon's," Corin told him, hesitating over his words. He had told no one but the druids about the sword *Godslayer*. It was his secret weapon, and he hoped to keep it that way.

It was also a tricky thing to carry with him. He had some plans in that direction, but first he had to make sure that Ben was with him. Corin chewed his lip, thinking, then said haltingly, "I have a . . . a means to make Ephitel . . . vulnerable. If I can draw him out to a place and time of my choosing, and if I'm . . . properly prepared . . . then I can strike him down. I can kill him forever. Imagine it, Ben."

"Oh, I've imagined it," Ben said. "My people suffer more than most beneath these current gods' regime. But this sounds like a risky proposition."

Corin stopped walking and turned to his companion. "There's nothing riskier in all the world. I am not blind to that. Even with Fortune and Oberon behind me, there's a thousand ways this could go wrong and only one it could go right. But I can choose no other path."

Ben rubbed his jaw, considering. "I suppose I understand, at that."

"Understand this too," Corin said, trying to find some kindness for his tone. But his thoughts hung too much on Ephitel and all his crimes, and his words came out sharp as *Godslayer's* blade. "I have no other friend in all the world. There are assets and resources and safehouses I could use, but I have no other friend than you. I need you, Ben Strunk, but I cannot ask you to take up my burden. As you said, it is a risky proposition."

Ben shook his head, and his eyes flashed with something like anger. "Ask me. Sand and stone, ask me, Corin, or we're not friends at all!"

Corin licked his lips and looked back in the direction they had come, toward the distant studio where Lilya still slept. "I thought . . . perhaps at last your roving days were over. I thought perhaps the time had come for you to settle down and find some lasting happiness. I can't ask you to give that up for fear and suffering, and almost certain death."

The dwarf peeled back his lips and snarled. "You're a villain, Corin Hugh. I found a pretty plaything for a summer, and you're declaring that my roving days are through? I ought to gut you just for saying that. Now tell me what you have in mind, or I'll start thinking you just want me as an excuse to give up your quest."

Corin spread his hands in apology. And despite himself he smiled. "Forgive me. I meant no offense." He turned northeast again, up the sloping street, and Ben fell in beside him. Corin went on, "As I said, I must draw Ephitel out to a place and time of my choosing. I have some plans for how to do that, but as *you* said, there are risks. When I set my plan in motion, I need someone I can trust who will hang back, somewhere close enough to see what happens but far enough to slip away if things go bad."

"And what about you? I'm just supposed to slink away and let you die?"

Corin showed his teeth in something like a grin. "I won't die easy. Remember the gifts I have from Oberon. If I am captured, if things go wrong, I can always step away through dream. But if we're in the fight together, I cannot guarantee that I could reach you and get us both away."

"Ah," Ben said in reluctant understanding. "Hmph."

Corin clapped him on the shoulder. "Exactly so."

"And what do you need me for at all?"

Corin chewed his lip. Then he shrugged out of the sword belt he'd draped across his chest. It was fashioned to buckle around the waist, and that was how Corin usually wore it, but he'd hung it on his back to help complete the new illusion.

The thin gray mists of a glamour hung about the sword, tracing its golden hilt and leather scabbard to Corin's eyes, but for Ben it would have looked for all the world like a heavy scrollcase. Corin handed it down to Ben, and the dwarf accepted it with a reverence almost befitting the weapon itself.

"And what is this? Some weapon?"

"As I said before, Oberon bestowed on me the means to defeat Ephitel. It rests within this case. If everything goes according to my plan, I will meet up with you and retrieve this package." He hesitated, chewing his lip, then shook his head. "Aye. There should be time for that."

"And if there's not?"

"It doesn't matter," Corin said, more strongly than he intended to. "In truth, this package is more important than I am. I hate to say it, but it's fact. I can risk my life provoking Ephitel. I can even risk facing him and missing the chance to destroy him. But I cannot risk the possibility that something goes wrong, and I deliver this precious artifact into his hands."

The dwarf swallowed hard. "And you would trust this to me?"

"And no one else in all the world," Corin said. "If anything goes wrong—anything at all—you disappear. Leave Aerome as soon as you possibly can, and make your way to western Raentz."

"Raentz? Why?"

Corin walked a moment in silence. They were in a broad piazza now, near the peak of the city's highest hill. Here the men and women on the streets dressed in rich silks and rode in sedans or carriages to go about their errands. These were the nobility that Ben Strunk so often worked for, and more than one of them belonged to the house most favored of Ephitel.

Corin cast his voice in almost a whisper, so even standing at his side the dwarf had to strain to hear him. "Do you remember the woman we delivered there? In western Raentz? We found a farmhouse where she could live quietly?"

The dwarf did not have to consider long to catch Corin's meaning. They had worked together—with the help of the druids and a bare handful of trusted Nimble Fingers—to smuggle Princess Sera Vestossi away from Ithale and into hiding with the man she loved. He nodded once; then he too cast a suspicious glare around the piazza.

No one was close enough to overhear. Corin raised his voice a little and pressed on. "If we are separated and I don't rejoin you immediately, then take the package to that farmhouse and wait for me. I'll meet you there, one way or another."

They left the piazza for a tree-lined boulevard that would take them to another, higher up. Corin left Ben time to consider these instructions, certain he'd have questions, but for a hundred paces he said nothing. As they emerged onto the Piazza Dei, Ben heaved a tired sigh and looked up at Corin. "I don't suppose that you intend to tell me the details of your plan?"

Corin shook his head. "You are a trusted agent of the Vestossis and a respected craftsman throughout Hurope. No one should suspect you in this matter. Anywhere you go, you have honest reasons to be there. Anything you do, and anything you carry, it could be explained."

Ben looked down at the package in his hands and nodded miserably. "You think I will be captured, questioned, and tortured maybe?"

"Perhaps," Corin said. "I don't think it will come to that. But the less you know, the more honest you can be."

"I must admit, you seem to have considered everything. I can see a master's handiwork behind your schemes."

Corin shrugged. It felt haphazard—wild and dangerous— but he could not find the patience or the caution to craft a better plan. It was all he could do to stop himself ripping the sword from its scabbard and charging on ahead to start things now.

But there, at least, he would take care. He tore his eyes from the hazy blade and fixed them on Ben. "I will see justice done."

"I believe you," Ben said. "Just answer one more question."

"Aye?"

"Why have we come to Ephitel's cathedral?"

A mighty bell rang out the call to prayer, tolling in a tower that reared above the piazza where they stood. Ben nodded past Corin toward the cathedral's steps. "And aren't those the royal princes there? Sand and stone, Corin. What do you intend?"

Corin followed the dwarf's gaze and breathed a sigh of relief when he saw the procession just entering the south end of the piazza. Half a dozen armored men marched with them—personal bodyguards of the royal family, not the mismatched riffraff who manned the city guard. These men were hired killers, brutal and efficient. Corin had tangled with their like before, and it had taken all his wits to escape alive.

Behind them came the royal family. King Cosimo, of course, would not attend the holy service; he sat his throne in personal communion with the nation's patron god. But his heirs would lead their countrymen by their example, showing up in pomp and splendor to deliver an opulent offering to Ephitel on his day of feasting.

Ephitel had come to Corin when the pirate tossed an embarrassing cousin from a window. Would he not come when Corin murdered the king's heirs in Ephitel's cathedral on his feast day? A hungry grin tugged at Corin's teeth. He could already taste the blood in the air.

"What's come over you?" Ben asked by his elbow. "I've seen that look on predators before, but never you."

"I have become a predator," Corin answered, distant, but then he tore his gaze from the parading princes and focused on his friend. He caught a calming breath. "I'm steady. I am steady. But we must take our places."

Reluctant though he looked, Ben took a step toward the grand cathedral. Corin caught his shoulder and drew him back.

"Not there," Corin said. "I'll go in there to do what must be done, then I'll slip out here and find some hiding place to wait."

"Out here? On the Piazza Dei?"

"Better than the cathedral itself," Corin said. "I cannot guess what magic that place might hold for Ephitel himself."

"But here on the piazza? You mean to fight him in front of all these witnesses?"

Corin laughed. "Aye! Let the whole world watch as the king of their tyrant gods falls at the hand of a simple manling."

"You've a fever," Ben said. "This has to be some sort of madness. Is it grief?"

"Justice," Corin said, though his voice did sound somewhat feverish. He tempered it with care and spoke again. "I see an alley's mouth beyond that perfumery. It should give you all the vantage you will need." He started hurriedly toward the alley, dragging Ben along behind him, then spun and pointed to another across the way, half a hundred paces from the cathedral doors. "And I will hide in there. That should give us a clear view of each other—and all the vantage I will need to strike when Ephitel arrives."

"Corin," Ben said, then hesitated. He rubbed his chin again. "I know you have your reasons to cling to secrecy, but I must ask this of you: What do you intend? I don't need to know the greater plan. But here and now, when you go into that building, what do you intend?"

Corin didn't answer right away. He closed his eyes and took another calming breath, then worked another glamour. This time he imagined himself as he was—tall and handsome, dark and rugged, dressed in black from head to toe—then carefully replaced that with the image of a minor priest in Ephitel's service.

Ben grunted at the transformation, but Corin barely noticed. His eyes were on the procession as it approached the enormous arching doors of the cathedral. Piero and Giovanni came with their families to pay worship to their patron. These were the heirs to the throne, Princess Sera's elder brothers, and only King Cosimo stood higher in the realm.

Against King Cosimo, Corin could but lay the vaguest accusations. He was a heavy-handed king who owed his throne entirely to Ephitel, but he was no special kind of monster.

But these sons of his were different. Piero commanded all Ithale's regiments, and Corin had seen firsthand his brutal tactics when the Aepoli merchant's guild had protested Cosimo's levy tariff. Piero had besieged his own city and watched near a thousand civilians starve, then hanged every man among the guild leaders before the thing was done.

That had been one small victory in Piero's laurel, but Giovanni had found his fame in the wake of Aepoli's siege. It was he who had united all the slinking spies and cruel henchmen of the Vestossi family into a network of secret police, beholden to no law and committed only to the family's prosperity. They'd turned neighbor against neighbor with the threat of thumbscrews or the promise of a paltry purse, until no one dared to whisper unkind words about the rulers, let alone defy them.

"Justice," Corin said. "I never thought I'd learn to love that word."

"By the rings!" Ben gasped, seeming to understand at last what Corin planned. "I thought you meant to rob them, Corin. Maybe kidnap one! You can't . . . you can't intend to kill a prince!"

"Not one," Corin said. "Not just one. I mean to stick a blade into the heart of this whole family."

"You're serious?"

"Deadly so."

"Corin," Ben said, sincere, "you . . . you don't intend to die today. Do you?"

Corin flashed a grin. "One way or another, this will be a bloody afternoon. But I intend to keep my blood in my veins."

Corin had expected at least a chuckle for that answer, but the dwarf wrung his hands, still staring anxiously toward the distant cathedral. Corin elbowed him. "Does that not satisfy you?"

Ben shook his head, still without looking in Corin's direction. "I am glad to hear it. It's just . . . I wish it could be somewhere else."

"You fear for the priests?"

"Of Ephitel? Hah! No, but you should watch your back with them. They're every bit as wicked as the one they serve."

Corin frowned. "What, then? The royal family?"

At last Ben tore his gaze from the grand cathedral. He stared up at Corin as though the pirate had gone mad. "No! Are you daft? Some of my finest works are on display in the sanctuary."

Corin snorted and clapped his friend on the shoulder. "I'll do everything I can to protect the innocents. But honestly, blood seems a more fitting tribute to this one than precious stones."

Ben considered that a moment, then nodded in agreement. "Paint it red. Paint the whole thing red."

Corin clasped his arm. Then he turned toward the cathedral. In the time Ben and Corin had spent whispering, the Vestossis' grand procession had filed through the doors and disappeared. Corin took one more steadying breath, then ducked his head and dashed across the piazza. He sprinted up the marble stairs and clattered into the sanctuary just as the final echoes of the enormous bells above fell still.

Silks and satin rustled beneath the sound of startled whispers as half a hundred gentlemen and ladies turned to stare in his direction. The sanctuary's central chapel was filled, divided down the central aisle with Piero's family and retainers on the left, and Giovanni's on the right. Even the hired porters turned to stare, now that they'd deposited their heavy chests full of tribute before the golden altar.

Corin bowed his head in mute apology and went on ahead into the room. He still wore the thin gray mist of glamour draped over himself, else the guards who'd turned his way would already be charging forward to dispatch him. All the same, even seeing him as a red-faced cleric late to morning prayers, they watched with narrowed eyes as he proceeded down the aisle toward the altar.

He maintained the disguise by force of will, but it took an effort. Even as it concealed him, the glamour blurred the world around him. Everything felt soft, a touch unreal, and time and space seemed out of joint. It was not enough to cause him any true discomfort—Aemilia had said she barely noticed it—but to a man who'd spent his entire life tripping along the thin line of survival on nothing but his wits and fine-honed instincts, that strangeness was enough to leave him feeling naked and exposed.

He wore it anyway, drifting past the rows of crowded pews, ducking his head as the chief priest came forward to begin his benediction. Corin turned before the altar and chose his first victim on a whim.

Piero had brought the worst of pain to Aepoli. Corin refused him the easy death. He crossed to Giovanni's side of the hall, bowed his head in greeting, then dropped the glamour and slit the bastard's throat.

The princes' soldiers were some of the best, but they had never anticipated an assault on a Vestossi within Ephitel's temple by one of his own priests. They froze in shock for a heartbeat, maybe two, and that was all the time that Corin needed.

The pirate turned and stretched his arm, flipping his knife end over end across the room. The blade flew true, but one of Piero's retainers dove to save his master. The poor man took Corin's knife below his shoulder before collapsing to the marble floor.

Corin had never trusted that one blade to do the job. He dashed toward his second victim, drawing the long-bladed dagger at his side even as the attendant fell. From two paces away he lunged, driving hard, and speared Piero beneath the collarbone. It was not a killing blow, but it was enough to draw a scream from the cold soldier.

Corin grinned at that. Something deep inside him ached to make this man suffer all that Aemilia had suffered—all that Ephitel's countless victims through the ages had suffered—but more than that, he wanted to draw Ephitel to himself. And live to face him.

So Corin withdrew the blade and struck again, this time for the heart. Piero shrank away in terror, and his wife behind him hauled him back, so Corin's blow fell false. Instead of piercing the man's heart, he cut deep into his belly. Black blood flowed. It was still a killing blow, but a slower one. Fitting in its way.

And that was all the time Corin could spare. Already he could hear the hue and cry from the piazza, and half a dozen guards were rushing on him now, recovered from their brief surprise.

Too late. Too late by far. They charged at Corin, but he plunged a hand into an inner pocket and drew out a small paper packet Ben Strunk had procured for him months ago.

Even outside the cathedral and across the wide piazza, Ben would likely get to see the effects of his handiwork. Corin ripped the packet into two and hurled its powdered contents into the air; then he flung himself to the ground. He hid beneath the heavy black cloth of his cloak, and still his eyes seared at the flash of silver light.

Then came the screams. Too much had happened and too quickly for most of those in the princes' retinues to truly comprehend, but at the blinding flash they finally responded. A hundred voices cried out in anger, pain, and grief. Corin dropped his cloak to see the soldiers still charging blindly ahead, arms outstretched before them, roaring as they came like angry bulls.

He dodged them easily, tripping up the first as he went by, then nudging the second just enough that he fell across the first. The rest were farther back, and Corin didn't wait to tangle with them. He wasn't here to kill the hired hands. He'd done what needed doing. The world was less two rich Vestossis; the seed was sown.

But now he had to watch and wait. He had to survive. He sprinted up the aisle, past all the wailing courtiers still in their seats, and straight toward the daylight. There would be chaos already down in the piazza, but chaos favored Corin. He would slip away and hide in his alley, where he'd wait for the vengeful god to come in answer.

A dozen paces from the door, he caught sight of the welcome waiting on the outer stairs. If there was chaos, it waited on the other side of a regiment of halberdiers. Faster than a lightning strike, faster than even Ephitel should have been able to do so, the hapless city guard had somehow caught him in the act.

They'd brought an army, and Corin only had his knives.

He charged them anyway.

(7)

Corin saw the soldiers' eyes widen in surprise, then narrow as they lowered their halberds. They made a fancy formation out there on the marbled stairs, and he knew there was no way he could slip past the long reach of those deadly blades. Instead, he caught the open door in his right hand as he reached it and leaped aside with all his might, slamming it shut in the face of the guardsmen.

He had no time to think. The halberds' blades clanged against the doors, but the soldier's heavy boots would be coming right behind. There was hardly time to hoist the rough-cut bar across the doors, especially with the hostile crowd still in the temple with him.

That thought came just soon enough. Corin fell to the side as a pair of crossbow bolts slammed into the door where he had been, fired from within the sanctuary. The princes' guards.

Corin scrambled up and pressed his back against the door. The soldiers in the street hit it hard, and Corin's boots scraped six inches across the marble floor. The men outside were gathering themselves to hit the door again, and in the temple's heart, the princes' bodyguards were shaking off the last effects of Corin's dwarven powder. Two of them were frantically preparing their crossbows to fire again, and the other two were charging up the aisle with cudgels raised.

Cold sweat beaded Corin's forehead as he tried to judge the timing. He braced himself, ears straining until he heard the pounding footsteps through the door. Then he gulped a heavy breath and dove aside.

The doors slammed open, sudden sunlight dazing the charging bodyguards. The halberdiers were not so slow. They swung their polearms at the charging threat and felled the princes' men with practiced precision. Two crossbow bolts fired in answer and dropped as many of the invading soldiers where they stood.

Corin stared a moment, disbelieving. Cries of anguish and confusion rang out again within the temple, the princes' men beginning to believe the city guard were complicit in their lords' assassination.

Corin slipped into the deeper shadows, farther from the door. The crossbowmen had lost track of him during the excitement, and surely the men outside would hesitate after seeing the first two fall so quickly. He had a moment of confusion on his side.

But how best to use it? He had to get outside. He'd laid this whole plan in an attempt to draw Ephitel, but he had never guessed there might be such a swift reaction. How many men were waiting in the street? More than a dozen, surely. How could they have come so quickly?

Corin shook his head. It didn't matter. He'd summoned Ephitel to face him, and here he was unarmed. He had to get outside. He had to get to Ben, and in this moment of confusion he had a chance. He closed his eyes and wove a glamour, making himself look like a priest of Ephitel again.

Then he dashed through the door. He went through in a flash and then skipped aside, wary of crossbows in the dark behind him. As he went, he held his empty hands high, palms out before him, and cried out in scarcely feigned terror. "Killers in the temple! The princes' bodyguards are killers! Don't let them get away! The king's sons are dead!"

As he went, he got his first close look at the forces in the street. Far too many to have come so soon! There were perhaps three dozen men in arms—crossbowmen with long, neat tabards and officers with rapiers on their hips arrayed among the halberdiers more accustomed to patrolling the city's streets.

Three dozen men, and at Corin's final words, the officers cried, "Charge!" and the whole force pounded up the marble stairs and into the temple's dim interior.

Corin let them go. His eyes were searching still, trying to find the leader of this force. He'd spotted Ben already, but the dwarf could not have known him through his glamour, and Corin had no wish to draw attention to his friend until he had good cause.

But for all the army waiting in the street, Corin saw no sign of Ephitel. He drifted away from the charging column and toward a curious crowd gathered to one side. None of the soldiers moved to stop him, and he thanked his priestly robes for that. But halfway to the safety of the onlookers, a woman stepped in front of him, bringing him to a halt.

She was tall and strong, despite her frail build, and she held herself with a surprising confidence. Long blond hair and smooth, golden skin should have made her a beauty, but ferocity flashed in her green eyes. Corin tried to slip politely past, his eyes lowered, but she dodged right in front of him and stopped him short with hands on his shoulders.

"Please," he said, eyes still downcast, "let me by. I must summon aid."

"Who are you, stranger?" the woman asked, and she spoke with an air to match her powerful stride.

"I am but a humble priest of Ephitel—"

Pain exploded in Corin's jaw, and colors flashed behind his eyes. He reeled a step backward, blinking furiously, and it took a moment before he understood that she'd backhanded him. A powerful woman indeed.

"Do not lie to me again," she said. "Who are you? Why are you here?"

"I am an innocent bystander, caught in the temple when those murderers attacked. I donned a priest's robes in hopes of escaping."

She swung again, but Corin anticipated her this time. He ducked the blow and shrank away, but she knotted her other fist in the fabric of his cloak and held him trapped.

"One more lie, and I will throw you to the crowd. Do you understand? I'll tell them you're the murderer and let them do justice for me."

Corin gaped. How could she know? The second lie had been almost a useless one, suggesting guilt if not confirming it, but it should have been easy to believe. For her to see through it with such confidence, to stop him in the street with such authority—

"You are a justicar," he breathed.

She nodded. "And I'll ask you one last time. Are you the man I seek, or are you the accomplice?"

Fear flared hot and hard behind Corin's breastbone. A justicar in the flesh, and more than that, she knew his secrets. He forced himself to keep his eyes locked on her, not a sideways glance to show her where Ben was hiding, but she already knew he had a helper.

A justicar. Rumor said they could see a man's sins like a living stain upon his garments; that they could taste lies in the air and feel a traitor's plots. They were the enforcers of the gods, blessed with a holy strength to match their unearthly skills, and they were ruthless and unyielding in their hunt.

Corin's sins were dark enough to match his midnight cloak, and he used lies and plots the way a carpenter used hammer and nails. He'd hoped to never meet a justicar at all; worse by far was facing one who knew his name.

Did she know his name? He considered her question and cocked his head. "Who is the one you want?"

"He has a certain sword." Her eyes fell to Corin's side, slipping past the rapier he'd concealed beneath his glamour, but that was not the sword she wanted. She wanted *Godslayer*. She'd come for it, not for the princes' killer. She hadn't known.

But surprise at that revelation betrayed him. Although he'd restrained himself before, when he thought of the sword, his gaze cut toward Ben's hiding place across the plaza. It was only for the barest instant, but for a justicar, that was enough. Her jaw clenched and she nodded.

"The accomplice, then. I'll find him. Captain!"

"Captain?" Corin's heart sank. She called a captain to her aid. She had a little army here, but she was the true force. "Ephitel isn't here? He isn't coming?"

She narrowed her eyes, confused by the question, but still Corin spotted confirmation in her expression. Ephitel had sent a justicar. He had no reason to come in person.

And now Corin found himself in her power. Captains were coming at her call, and she'd consign him to them and then go for Ben. If she put her hands on the sword, then all was lost.

A justicar. He'd never planned to face a justicar. The fear within his breast had turned to anger and frustration, but it still burned just as hot. He tried to tamp it down, to no avail.

"Tell Ephitel I'm coming for him," Corin said. He'd given Ben clear enough instructions; now he had to trust the dwarf to get away. Ben's best chance was for Corin to distract the justicar, to leave her with a puzzle strong enough to slow her down.

She still had one fist knotted in his cloak, holding him at arm's length. He pushed against it to face her nose to nose, and growled at her. "Tell Ephitel I mean to see him dead."

Corin jabbed her with his left fist, hard in the short ribs, and though she gasped, she did not let go. He threw an uppercut that clipped her jaw, sparking anger in her eyes, then barely caught her answering haymaker with a block. He twisted his arm around, trapping hers against his side, then slammed a head butt at her pretty little nose.

She saw it coming and pulled away, but still his forehead split her lip. She spat a curse and released her grip on his shoulder, so she could strike at him.

But before she could do anything, he dove beneath her grasp, rolled back to his feet, and dashed toward the watching crowd. He glanced back once and found her hard on his trail. He also saw Ben slipping out of the alley beyond her, running as hard as his little legs would carry him in the other direction.

Perfect. Corin barreled in among the crowd, spilling spectators to the left and right, tearing away from grasping hands. He'd have faced a challenge to escape them, but he didn't need to. He tangled himself in their midst, just enough to baffle the justicar. Then he closed his eyes and stepped through dream.

He did not go far this time, only to the shadowed depths of the alley Ben was hiding in. That didn't matter much, in his experience. Hopping across a room could cost him moments or days, the same as stepping across the Medgerrad Sea. He'd never found a rhyme or reason to it, or any rules to the twist of time when Oberon's magic was involved, so every step brought the same degree of risk.

This time he could not bring himself to care. He had a war with Ephitel, and if he waged it in the spring or in the fall, in this year or in the next, nothing would change. Aemilia was lost to him, and nothing short of Ephitel's blood would satisfy his vengeance. He'd pay any price at all to see that justice done.

Still . . . it would have been nice to step through dream and end up within arm's reach of Ben. Corin didn't want to lose that sword! The dwarf had his instructions, and Corin could think of no one he would trust more, but everything depended on that blade. Corin opened his eyes upon the darkened alley.

He was alone. Full night had fallen, and whatever furor the day's attack had raised, whatever crowds it had drawn, no sign of them remained at this late hour. Corin spotted a glint of moonlight on steel and the faint shadow of a man across the way—one of the Vestossis' investigators—but there was none close enough to see Corin. He shook his head and sighed. Benny was long gone. Corin raised the deep cowl of his black cloak, another shadow in the night, and slipped out of the alley's mouth and down the road.

Half an hour brought him to the dwarf's workshop, but it was empty. The door was locked, but that did not slow Corin. He had it open in a dozen heartbeats and found the room inside left in its usual disorder, but clearly uninhabited.

Just as he was turning to go, Corin spotted a crumpled scrap of paper fallen from the edge of Ben's worktable. He stooped and grabbed it, smoothed out the wrinkles, and read one word in Ben's tiny, strangely delicate hand:

"A'roving."

Corin nodded. He'd not thought to suggest it, but Ben had left a note. That was good news; it meant he'd escaped the little alley and the justicar's attention. And if she'd somehow followed him here, if she'd read this very note in her investigations, it would have told her nothing. But it told Corin all he needed to know. Ben was on his way to Raentz, to the desperate little farms on its western border, bearing the sword *Godslayer* to the home of the only true hero Corin had ever met among the Godlanders.

High time Corin went that way himself. He licked his lips, weighing the risk, then tossed it aside with a shrug. He closed his eyes and imagined a pretty little farmhouse within sight of the treacherous Dividing Line. It was a simple place, but strongly made, much like the man who lived there. It was a place that spoke of endurance and hope, of warmth and welcome. And Corin had been ordered in no uncertain terms to stay away forever.

But who was he to bow to the whims of a Vestossi princess? A smile tugged at the corner of his mouth. Maybe Ben would be waiting for him there. The princess didn't like the dwarf any better. Corin barked with laughter and stepped through dream.

 **(8)**

Oberon's magic was not enough to overcome Corin's ignorance. Because Sera had never let Corin set foot inside the farmhouse, his step through dream deposited him at the front gate instead. He took advantage of the opportunity to consider this place.

It was not what he would have expected. The only time Corin had ever spent in the countryside had been his recent weeks in hiding with Aemilia. The druid had shown a knack for rural life, but Corin had struggled with it.

By the look of it, Sera had had no such struggles. The pretty little princess had abandoned her family's palaces and estates without so much as an hour's notice, but she'd settled into this three-room farmhouse as though it were home.

It showed in the little touches. The windows boasted lace-trimmed curtains that hadn't hung there when last he'd visited. The front door had a fresh coat of paint, and new flowers in a dozen shades lined the graveled walk to the front door.

Corin let himself through the gate and started up the path. Auric had made his mark as well, though Corin had to look harder to spot it. A pair of muddy leather boots beside the front door sported the worked-silver spurs of a Dehtzlan free lance.

The axe he'd used for splitting firewood—still leaning near the woodpile—had a wicked half-moon blade that had been made for battle. Corin knew from recent experience the importance of a wood axe's shape in its use. Fine though the weapon was, it might require twice the effort to split a log with that thing.

But this farmboy was just the sort to spend that extra effort just to make something harmless—something *useful*, as he would see it—out of a device designed for killing. That was precisely the sort of romantic nonsense the farmboy would go in for.

Corin could use that sentimentality. He'd taken advantage of it once before, when he'd convinced the farmboy to rescue a total stranger against the advice of his more careful friends. That time, Corin had left the man for dead. A week later, he'd tried to impersonate the farmboy to the princess, but even wrapped in Oberon's powerful magic, he'd failed to deceive her. That small deception played some part in her continuing distrust of him. As for the farmboy, Corin could only guess how he'd respond. Corin hadn't shared a word with him since he'd left him for dead.

He squared his shoulders, caught a calming breath, and rapped on the door. Beyond the farmhouse, the sun set.

A voice called something indistinct through the sturdy door, and Corin waited. Then at last the door swung wide.

It wasn't Auric. Princess Sera was a living portrait. Even standing there disheveled—hair tied back and sleeves rolled up, with suds all to her elbows—even standing there disheveled, she looked like oil on canvas. Her hair was gold, her eyes sapphire, her skin a sun-kissed amber.

And though she had despised the darker natures of her name, she still stood proud and angry as any man who ever wore the name Vestossi. She spent one heartbeat on surprise, then threw her shoulders back and glared at Corin down her lovely nose.

"Master Hugh," she said in icy tones.

And then she slammed the door.

Corin grinned and knocked again. She didn't answer. He shouted through the door, "Sera, please! I bring grave tidings and important news!"

But still the door didn't budge. He waited through long minutes, then pounded once again. "I only ask for a moment!" The sound of footsteps answered him this time, and then the door opened to show him the farmboy.

That was the first name Corin had ever heard him called, but looking on him now, it seemed ludicrous. This man was a warrior. He was a hero. He stood head and shoulders taller than Corin, broad of shoulder and sure of stance. His hands and forearms showed the scars of hard years as a free lance, though he could not have seen two dozen summers yet.

Sera lurked in the corner behind him, arms crossed beneath her breasts and an angry pout on her regal lips. Auric threw a nervous look her way.

"Master Hugh," he said by way of greeting. And then, a touch embarrassed, "Perhaps we should speak outside." He squeezed out through the door and pulled it delicately closed behind him.

Corin suppressed a smile. "It is a lovely night."

"It is," Auric said, eyes darting nervously toward the door. He shook his head in apology. "Forgive me, Master Hugh, but Sera—"

He flexed his hands, helpless. Corin could only stare. Here was a man who'd faced death for Corin's actions, a man whom Corin had impersonated to deceive his bride, and a man whose bride had nearly died for Corin's actions as well. And yet Auric was flustered at her honest display of discourtesy. It wasn't in his nature to speak ill of his lady, but neither could he let her rudeness pass without apology.

Corin hid his amusement as he raised a comforting hand to the farmboy's shoulder. "No apologies are needed. I have not always treated her or hers fairly, and she has right to show me some coldness."

Auric chuckled. He wasn't blind to the truth. Then he nodded past the house, away from the village road, and started walking in that direction. Corin fell into step beside him.

"I'm sure you've come to offer explanations and apologies," Auric said. "Sera didn't think you'd come at all, but I've been expecting you ever since we heard the rumors. It will do her well to hear your reasons, I think, but you must understand that it will take her time before she's ready—"

"Rumors?" Corin asked, confused. "Apologies? For what?"

Auric stopped in his tracks and stared down at Corin for a moment. Then a light kindled in his eyes. "You didn't do it?"

"I can't even fathom what *it* is!" Corin said.

Auric grinned and slapped him on the back. "You'd hardly overlook a thing like this." His voice turned grave as he bent closer to Corin's ear. "Someone's attacked her brothers while they were at worship."

"Oh, *that*," Corin said. He frowned harder. "I did that. Is she concerned?"

"They were her brothers!"

"They were awful men!"

"Still, they were her brothers," Auric said. He'd begun to take control of his surprise, and an angry reprimand began to growl beneath his words. "How can you believe she wouldn't grieve over a thing like that?"

Corin spread his hands. "In truth, it never crossed my mind. Vestossis aren't men; they're monsters. I would not have believed the princess loved them. I can scarce believe it now."

"Well . . ." Auric said, hesitating. "Perhaps not 'loved.' She should! Family is family. But in truth, I'd say she's more . . . concerned that you could kill so callously. She doesn't think I should be friends with someone like that."

He sounded concerned himself—like a man afraid he might be on the brink of disappointing his beloved wife. Corin took a glance up at the big man's face and found an expression of nervous concentration. The farmboy was working hard on the puzzle of it.

Corin couldn't wholly hide his grin, but perhaps the night was dark enough. He did conceal the humor in his tone as he asked, "Are we friends, then?"

Auric frowned. "If you make sufficient apologies to Sera—"

Corin shook his head. This was not at all why he'd come here, but seeing the farmboy face to face—and finding him so congenial—Corin found himself overwhelmed with curiosity. He caught Auric's elbow and stopped him in his tracks. "I'm not concerned with Sera. What of you? I left you trapped within the hold of a smuggler's ship beneath a hundred pounds of Dwarven powder."

Auric waved that away as nothing. "I ordered you to leave me."

Corin swallowed hard. Confession was not much in his nature, nor was contrition for that matter, but he'd ached the day he left this noble farmboy to his death. He'd cursed himself and cursed the man who'd put him there, and in all the days that had passed since then, he'd wondered.

"How did you survive?"

Auric cocked his head, considering Corin by moonlight. Then he threw back his head and laughed. "Are you sincerely concerned about that business? I told you at the time that I'd survive."

"Sera told me the same," Corin said. "When I brought her news that you were dead and told her the circumstances, she said you'd escaped from worse than that. I was sure she was just hiding from her grief, but then I heard . . ."

"I lived," Auric said. He laughed again and squeezed Corin's shoulder. "Sun and skies, Corin. I'm an adventurer. I've survived far worse."

"But how?"

The farmboy caught Corin's gaze and held it for a long moment. His answer had no laughter in it. "By the aid of good friends. I've never passed up the chance at a friendship, and those friends have never ever let me down."

Corin hazarded a guess. "Was it Ridgemon? I know he was training to be a wizard."

Auric nodded. "Ridgemon magicked me away before the ship exploded. And he knew where to find me because Longbow led him there. And Longbow was alive because Hartwin never trusted you. He tracked us through the woods that day and watched as Longbow fell. He brought the others back to rescue me, and they succeeded just before the powder blew."

His voice never changed as he explained it all. He sounded fondly reminiscent and grateful for the friends he'd had around.

But that brief narrative revealed a dozen damning secrets Corin had believed secure. He had led Auric into the ambush that left Longbow bleeding out on the sand and the farmboy trapped in the smugglers' hold.

"Longbow lived?" Corin asked, his voice hoarse. He tried not to tense, lest Auric sense it through his friendly grip on Corin's shoulder, but Corin felt an urge to grab for his knives. If the friendly farmboy decided to see justice done—and gods knew he had reason to demand it—he could likely wring Corin's neck before Corin had a chance to flinch.

But Auric only nodded. "He did. He comes from hardy stock, you know. And Tesyn is a wonder with a needle and thread."

"Then he . . . he told you everything?"

"Him and Hartwin, between them." Auric frowned, and then his eyes went wide. "Are you afraid? Corin, none of this is news to me. I learned it all a lifetime ago."

"It's been three months."

"Nearly five now, but that is not my point. We survived the day. That's all that matters. You had your reasons, clear enough, and in the end you saved my Sera from the clutches of her enemies. You brought her out here with me." He released Corin and shrugged his massive shoulders. "I'll call us even just because you rousted her from Ithale. Can't stand the food there, really."

Corin gaped. "You must be mad."

Auric shook his head dismissively. "Don't think so. But ask me sometime how I first came to know Longbow. He tried to kill me. Or Hartwin. He did too. Or Kalad, for that matter! I caught him shoving Ridgemon around when we were all boys. Gave him a bloody nose, and he broke seven bones for me. Best friends ever since."

Corin barked a laugh. "You mean it?"

"All my life, I've never let a good friend pass me by. And they've served me well, no matter how we came to meet."

Corin heard in those words a warped echo of something Ephitel had said when the two had stood face to face in Aemilia's cottage. His awe at Auric's good nature evaporated in the angry heat of that memory.

Auric must have seen the change in Corin's expression because he whipped his head around, searching the deepening night for some sign of danger. He was unarmed, but he flexed his massive hands as though ready to do battle. All of it was instinct, and he spoke in the hoarse whisper of a stalking hunter, "What do you see?"

"Ephitel," Corin said. "Not here, but he may well come hunting us here. He killed Aemilia. He must be stopped."

The farmboy slowly straightened, though he lost nothing of the tension in his frame. He heaved a weary sigh. "Is there nowhere we can escape them?"

"Not until we stand beside their graves."

Auric nodded. "This is grim news indeed. And not the sort of battle I can fight. If you mean to do anything about the gods, you're going to need Sera."

"I know." Corin answered Auric's sigh. "Will she talk to me?"

"I wish I could say."

"Take me to her. Let's find out."

"Gods preserve us both." He caught a deep breath. "Come on, then. And wipe your boots at the door. If you track mud into the house, we're done for."

(9)

He left Corin at the door, and it took more than a moment before he came back. When the door finally did open, it was to Sera, who offered Corin a lovely smile. "Master Hugh," she said, her voice honeyed, "I fear we have already eaten, but will you join us in the sitting room for drinks?"

It was not at all the greeting he'd expected, especially after waiting so long. But she was a princess, after all. And a Vestossi on top of that. She'd been raised on politics and subterfuge. Corin swept a gracious bow in answer. "I would be delighted."

Corin followed her down the short hall to the modest sitting room. Though she moved with a fluid grace, she carried a tension in her shoulders and a rigidness to her fingers that suggested she was fighting an urge to ball her hands in fists.

Corin caught the little details, and they ignited a spark of guilt. He'd spoken truthfully when Auric confronted him about killing Sera's brothers. He'd never seen it as a personal attack, but she could scarce ignore it.

He caught her shoulder at the threshold of the sitting room and lowered his head in contrition. "My lady, please accept my sincere apologies for any harm I've done you."

She raised an eyebrow. "Do you have something particular in mind?"

He licked his lips and shrugged his shoulders. "It was I who slew your brothers in Aerome. I never meant to cause you pain. I only wanted justice for a damage done me."

For a long time she didn't answer. Pain or anger tightened the edges of her eyes, but she showed no other hints at her thoughts.

In the end, she ducked her head. "Auric told me of your loss. You have my sympathy. Aemilia was a good woman."

"And your brothers—"

Her hands did finally close in fists, but still she held her voice under careful strain. "Let us not speak of them. I was never close to either of them, and I am not blind to my family's misdeeds, but I still remember them as boys at play. I cannot easily overlook what you have done."

Corin sighed. "I appreciate your understanding. As soon as I have done with Auric—"

She shook her head. "You are already done with Auric. I can find some way to forgive the things you've done to my blood-stained kin, but I will not have you corrupting Auric's honest nature."

Corin drew himself up tall. "He's not a child, Sera."

"And I am not negotiating. I've spent my life surrounded by your sort—careful, conniving, and hungry for any advantage you can grasp. I love Auric precisely because he is none of those things, and I will not let you prey upon his goodness."

Corin blinked. He'd not expected this. "Auric is a soldier. A mercenary! Even if I'd come to ask him to fight by my side, I wouldn't be the first. And my cause wouldn't be the worst."

"Perhaps. But I believe you may well be the most devious. I fear that you recognize in him a spark that none else ever thought to fan to flame."

Corin grunted. "I begin to see. You love him as the humble farmboy. But he could be so much more."

"I have known men who were more, and none of them were better for it."

"But surely none started from such honest stock."

She dismissed the argument with a shake of her head. "He would make a mighty general and an admirable king, with some able counsel, but I understand the demands that weigh on both sorts of men. Either role might rob me of him as surely as some grievous battlefield."

"Are you so selfish, princess?"

She arched an eyebrow, and Corin understood the words she didn't say. He was at least as selfish in his pursuits, and he acknowledged it with spread hands and a mock bow. But he pressed on.

"I am but a vile rogue. You, however, are gracious and benign. I've seen it. You were far more forgiving the first time we spoke."

She nodded sharply. "I was. But two things have changed since then."

"The first?"

"I have come to know you. I fear I've never met a man so capable of heartless guile and desperate depravity than the one who stands before me."

Corin licked his lips. He could find no answer to that, so he nodded and asked weakly, "And the second?"

"I am with my Auric now. That has taught me a selfishness I never knew before. I am no more a princess. That matters too.

I will cling to him however I must, and the world outside can burn for all I care."

"Then why have you not already sent me on my way?"

"I promised Auric I would hear you out. But I do not want your apologies and I do not want your careful lies. Tell me why you've come here, and then I will send you on your way."

It was not a generous offer, but given the things she'd said, it was more than he should have hoped for. For half a heartbeat he cast about, searching for some clever lie that would gain him her compassion, but in the end he settled on the truth.

"I mean to bring Ephitel to justice."

She sighed. "This is not news to me."

"No. But it is a complicated matter. Among other things, it depends on a certain artifact I discovered in my journeys."

"What artifact?"

"There is a weapon with the power to wound the invulnerable Ephitel."

Sera blinked at that. She covered her shock with the careful decorum of an Ithalian princess, but it showed in the pulse pounding at her temple and the quaver in her voice. "You . . . surely there is not such a thing."

"There is," Corin said. "Aeraculanon's blade, and it can do to Ephitel what it once did to Memnon. The druids know it for what it is."

"And you have this sword?"

"I do."

Her eyes widened, but then she looked him up and down. "Not *with* you, though. I must take your word?"

Corin quickly shook his head. "I don't have it now, but it is coming here."

She laughed. "That is a magic sword indeed."

He fought down a growl of irritation. "I did not know if I could come here unmolested, so I sent it by a trusted messenger. It might be waiting here already. Have you not had a visit from a city dwarf?"

Her eyes narrowed. "You don't mean the silversmith?"

"Aye," Corin said. "I had forgotten you were already friends with dear Benjamin."

"Not friends," she said, "but he has served my family. I am surprised that you can tolerate him."

"I have known him longer than this current engagement, and I have reason enough to trust him. In fact, it helps that he belongs to your family; that should place him above suspicion."

"And you say he has this sword?"

"He does. He brings it here at my direction. When he arrives, you'll know the truth—"

"When he arrives?" she asked. "You expect him on the moment?"

"I cannot say precisely when, but if you've had time to hear news from Aerome, he can't be far behind."

"That could still be days," Sera said with a too sweet smile. "Time enough for you to embroil Auric in some scheme, whether this dwarf ever arrives or not."

"I assure you—"

She shook her head. "You will forgive me, *Captain* Hugh, but I cannot be satisfied with your assurances."

"But you have other evidence. You've seen me working with the druids. You've seen the lengths I've gone already in pursuit of this."

"I've seen you lie to me and risk my life in pursuit of your own agenda. I've seen you kill a cousin and brother."

"All to draw out Ephitel. All in an attempt to bring him within reach of the sword *Godslayer* that I might end his reign."

"And who is to replace him?"

The question surprised Corin. Replace him? An exterminator made no plans to replace the vermin he went out to kill.

But of course it would occur to Sera. The princess had lived all her life surrounded by men clawing for every scrap of power, and murder was not an uncommon means of gaining a position.

Even as he reached that understanding, Sera pressed on. "You? I would not have you for the god of all Ithale."

"Not I," Corin said, with a shudder that he didn't have to feign. "I've no desire to rule. In truth, I'd be best pleased if no one replaced Ephitel at all. Let Ithalians choose the destiny of Ithale. Let the people serve as their own providence. But anyone at all would please me more than Ephitel."

She eyed him for a moment, weighing some possibility. Then she stepped closer and held his gaze. "You mean it to be Auric, don't you?"

Corin laughed harshly. He had no time to consider the ramifications, and he regretted it when Sera's brows came down.

"Why do you scoff? He is as good as any man! Better than most."

Corin raised his hands defensively. "I mean no offense, but the thought had never crossed my mind. I have not the means to elevate a manling to godhood; only the sword that will reduce a god to so much rotting flesh."

She paled at that, disclosing a hint, but only a hint. She had as much to gain from Ephitel's death as Corin did. He pressed closer and held her gaze. "I cannot stop until this thing is done. I've no desire to embroil Auric in it, but I had to get the sword out of Aerome. I had to meet Ben somewhere, and this was the only place I knew."

"That's why you're here? Just to receive the sword?"

"Aye. I'll swear to it."

The princess nodded, satisfied. "Good. Now I've heard you out, in keeping with my promise, and my decision is an easy one. You said the dwarf planned to meet you here?"

"Any day now."

She nodded. "Then I'd invite you to return to Taurb. It's a pleasant little village east along the farmer's road. I know the tavern keeper there, and he is an honest man. He'll board you for a fair rate, and if Master Strunk should darken our door, I give my word I'll send him to meet you there straightaway."

Corin sighed. "Could I at least beg one night's hospitality? I might not find much welcome arriving so late at night."

She hesitated a moment. Corin waited. She heaved a sigh. "Very well. Against my better judgment, I'll offer you a room for the night."

He did not for a moment imagine that he'd won her over. And she was too clever by half to forget her concerns. So he chose to address them directly. He hoped it would make him look straightforward and trustworthy. He met her gaze. "What of your concerns for Auric's innocence?"

She blinked, clearly surprised. After a moment, she bobbed her head. "They remain unchanged. Here is what I would ask of you: Do not entangle him in your schemes. Do not speak with him at all unless I am present also."

"And if he should speak to me?"

She smirked. "You have a dark and brooding nature. Play the part. Your travels must have left you weary. Retire soon, and leave us with the dawn. You should not have much trouble evading him for so short a time."

Corin nodded. "I can do these things. And you are more than gracious for the offer."

"I am," she said. "I am. I try every day to emulate Auric's generous spirit. I pray you don't teach me to regret it."

Corin swallowed hard. For all her dedication to the gentle farmboy, she was still a Vestossi. There was steel behind that pretty mask. Corin worked moisture into his mouth and stammered, "Aye, my lady. You have my word."

"Then get some sleep. There's an empty room right through there. I'll let Auric know you're staying." She took three steps toward the kitchen, then looked back over her shoulder. "And know this for the simple truth: If you do anything to harm my Auric, I'll see you hanged."

She said it with a summer smile and eyes as cold as winter. Corin didn't doubt her for a moment.

10

Sleep should have come easily. Stepping through dream had played havoc with his sense of time, so he could scarcely have guessed how many hours it had been since he'd last slept. Days, at least. A lifetime.

He'd gone to sleep beside Aemilia. That's all he knew for fact. He'd slept an easy sleep and woken to the smells of breakfast frying in the kitchen. He'd gone off to work with the other woodsmen, and he'd put in a hard day's labor.

Since then he'd fought with Ephitel and taken his knocks. He'd argued with the druids, killed two most deserving Vestossis, and even tussled with a justicar. He'd leaped back and forth across a thousand miles and battled wills with half a dozen fierce opponents.

And somewhere in it all, he'd lost his love. The thought leaped out at him, treacherous, and he cursed at the flush of pain it brought. He wasn't equipped to handle pain like that. He'd known unnumbered miseries in his short life, but none of them had cut as deep as this. He forced his breathing to be steady, waited for his heart to stop its hammering, and then gingerly he locked away his thoughts of her. Better far to focus on revenge.

But that course fared him little better. He'd gone off to Aerome with a plan to lure out Ephitel, but that had failed. If the elf knew about the sword *Godslayer*, if he was wise enough to use a justicar instead of answering in person, Corin could not see any obvious way to lure him into a trap. He searched and searched his mind, through all his clever schemes, but he could not find one.

There were other things to fear as well. If Sera's information was accurate, then Ben Strunk was already two days overdue. Was he lost? Captured? Corin scarcely dared consider the possibility that *Godslayer* was lost. Why ever had he let the sword leave his side?

There were no answers for him here. Not now. His mind and body both ached beneath fatigue, and pushing himself harder now would gain him nothing. He fought to slow his breathing more, focusing on his bone-deep weariness, but still it felt like an age before he drifted off to sleep.

And it was no easy sleep. He tossed and turned, awakened more than once by brutal dreams of Ephitel arriving at the farmhouse and doing to Princess Sera what he'd done to Aemilia. Corin dreamed of fighting him in vain. He watched as Auric died a hero's death. He saw Ben as the cruel elf's prisoner, then as his accomplice, won over by the serving girl.

He found no rest in sleep that night, and before dawn had come, he gave up any hope of it.

Muscles still aching and head buzzing with an angry energy, he rose and dressed, pulling on his high black boots. He washed his face and hands in the basin. He went to the window and spent some time staring out over the moonlit yard. The house was utterly quiet, but Corin's shoulders tensed as though there were enemies all around. His hand kept finding the hilt of his dagger and gripping it until his fingers cramped.

He strained his eyes, searching the moonshadows for some threat, but there was none. He snarled at the night. Despite the messages his body was sending him, he *knew* there was no immediate threat here. The threat was larger, spread out—Ephitel might show up anywhere, any time, but until he came, there was nothing Corin could do to fight him.

Corin dropped his forehead against the cool glass of the window. Even if Ephitel came, Corin couldn't fight him. He'd given up the sword. It had made so much sense to keep it safe, but now he'd left himself completely helpless.

And he had come to this wretched cabin. For what? He pounded a fist against the windowpane and felt a touch of surprise that it didn't smash to shards. He spun and kicked the bed that had given him no rest. He glared around the empty room, teeth bared and lungs heaving like some wild beast. He felt an urge to tear this building down around him.

Understanding crashed home then, and he caught a shuddering sigh. Aemilia again. This cottage, this countryside, reminded him too much of the place he'd shared with her. This very room felt like the room they'd slept in. And just there was the corner where he'd found her broken body.

The ache beneath his breastbone sharpened viciously, like a stiletto slipped between his ribs, and he had to gasp for breath. His knees went weak. He caught himself on the windowsill, supporting his whole weight, while a blackness fell across his eyes.

They had been happy together. They had felt safe. For the first time in his life, he'd had a *home*. And like a lightning strike, like a summer storm out of a clear blue sky, he'd lost it all. A pain even stronger than his anger surged up around him, and Corin clenched his jaw to stop a cry of agony. He choked back his sobs and fought his ragged breath until he could hear the total stillness in the cabin once again. His vision cleared, and he found himself staring out the window at the woodpile. At the handsome battleaxe that Auric had used to chop wood.

It called to him. He slung his heavy black cloak around his shoulders and left the room. Nothing stirred within the house. He went with nimble silence across the narrow sitting room and down the hall. Without a sound, he went out into the autumn chill.

He stood a moment, staring down at the chopping block. They'd had one just like it at the cottage—an old stump, shorn of bark by errant swings, scarred across its face from years of punishment. Its naked core, exposed, had turned from a honey color to a dark umber, weathered by the elements and time.

Could he do that? He felt freshly carved now. Could he survive? Could he hold up long enough to wear the scars? To become something useful once again?

He shook his head. Foolish, sentimental thoughts. He hadn't come out here to feel sorry for himself; he'd come out here to accomplish something. He stooped to grab an unsplit log and lifted it into position upright on the chopping block. The motion felt familiar, and he reached automatically for the haft of the heavy axe.

How had this ever become commonplace? He was a vagrant, a thief, a pirate. But for three short months, he'd had a home.

He dashed the thoughts and heaved the axe into the air. Its heft was not familiar. This axe was a thing for killing—brutal and straightforward in a way that Corin had never mastered. Still, as he raised it high, he thought perhaps this served as more than a romantic gesture. He felt a proper headsman, towering above the block, and it was no challenge to imagine the neck that should have been stretched there. He thought of Ephitel, so cruel and gloating at the scene of his great crime. Corin clenched his jaw and swung the axe. It slammed into the solid chunk of wood and split it clean.

It helped. In a tiny way, it helped. He lifted another log into place and struck again. Again. Sweat pricked his brow, and he shed the heavy weight of his familiar black cloak. Then he split another log. And another.

He lost all track of time within the rhythmic motion. The sun rose while he worked, but he barely noticed. He cleared the pile before he stopped, then stood a moment, stunned. His chest heaved, his lungs and arms ached, but his mind felt sharper than it had in days.

"More," he said, his voice raw to his own ears. "I am not finished."

"It's true," another voice answered.

Corin wiped sweat from his brow and turned to find Auric watching. The farmboy's hands were dirty, and a sheen of sweat covered him too. Corin realized there were no split logs around the block. Auric had been clearing them while Corin worked, stacking them neatly on the pile beneath the cabin's eaves. It had to have been more than an hour they'd worked together without him noticing Auric or either man saying a word.

Corin licked dry lips. "True?"

"You're not finished," Auric said, passing Corin a waterskin. "That's clear as day. But I doubt that there are trees enough in all of Raentz to satisfy your need."

Corin took a long, slow drink. Then he nodded his agreement. "No matter how I try, the wood won't bleed."

The farmboy didn't answer right away. He took the axe from Corin and turned it over and over in his hands. Then, with a casual gesture, he tossed it aside. He met Corin's eyes. "That is not the proper tool for your task."

Corin nodded. "A friend is bringing me—"

Auric cut him off with a shake of his head. "Sera told me all about it, but the sword won't do it either—not on its own."

Corin sank down on his heels, still fighting for breath. He was worn out, but he could see the golden light of an autumn morning shining bright. He'd find a way to do what needed doing.

"The sword will serve me well enough," Corin said. "It will spill the blood of Ephitel."

"And what will that gain you?" Auric asked. "Zyphar will only take his place. Or Elsbrit. Or Pellipon. There are gods enough to fill the role, and every one of them is cast from Ephitel's mold."

"So what would you have me do? Forget the wrongs he's done? Grieve for what I've lost and try to find a normal life again?"

Auric shook his head emphatically, and Corin loved him for it. "Don't be a fool. You have to kill him."

"But you said—"

Auric spoke over him. "You're not sufficient to the task. You don't have to be. I tried to tell you so last night."

Corin frowned. "I don't understand."

"You do. You already know precisely what is needed, but you've allowed your grief to blind you. Before you first brought Sera here, you told her that you meant to raise an army."

"Ah," Corin said in sudden understanding. "Last night you spoke to me of good friends. But I have none. My plan required the assistance of the druids."

"I . . . I thought you *were* friendly with the druids."

"The circumstances of that relationship have changed."

Disappointment touched the corners of the farmboy's eyes, but he said nothing of it. He considered this new information a moment, then asked, "What did you need of them?"

"They were to connect me with the elves. But in the end, they could not help me there."

The farmboy ran a hand through his hair and asked with exaggerated care, "Your true goal is to find the ancient elves? Long lost and most forgotten?"

"Aye. They'd be true and powerful enemies of Ephitel if I could but rouse them to the fight. But, alas, even the druids cannot tell me where they've settled."

Auric let loose a mighty laugh. "You see! What did I tell you?"

"What?"

"I have a good friend who is even now setting out on a grand quest to find the elves of lore."

11

Corin's jaw dropped. "You can't be serious."

"I am! He was at the cabin yesterday. You must have passed him on the road. I suspect he's still in town making arrangements for the voyage."

"The voyage?"

"He thinks the elves are living on the Isle of Mists. He thinks they've been hiding there for ages, and all the terrible rumors about the place are contrivances to keep them hidden."

Corin shook his head. "He has the right of it. I heard the plan from Oberon's own lips before it was set in motion. But that was a thousand years gone. Surely by now they've moved elsewhere."

"That was the favorite belief of ancient scholars too, but my friend has uncovered new secrets. He swears they are still there, concealed by some extraordinary power."

Corin fell very still. Some instinct warned him this was too perfect a coincidence, and he wondered how it could have come to pass. Was it some trap of Ephitel's? Or perhaps the druids manipulating events around him? Perhaps it was the work of the very elves that Corin sought. Would that be for good or ill?

Or perhaps it was merely the work of Fortune. She'd always smiled fondly on Corin, in spite of all his sins. Was this another chance, another twist of Oberon's dream to benefit his misfit heir?

More likely by far, it was nothing but an errant venture. The thought rang true, yet he could not entirely shake off the wave of hope that Auric's pronouncement had cast up. "Surely . . . surely he can't have unraveled such an ancient secret on his own."

"Oh, he could," Auric said, grinning. "He is a very clever man. Smarter than the two of us combined. He'll find his way, and I suspect he'd benefit from a sturdy hand and sharp eye to keep him safe. I think you should join him."

Before Corin could find any answers, the farmboy interrupted all his thoughts with a piercing question of his own. Eyes fixed on the ground and voice cast low, Auric asked him, "Did you really mean it?"

Corin shook off his suspicions to focus on his companion. "Mean what?"

"When you were speaking with Sera. You told her you have no plans for Ephitel's succession. Do you honestly believe we could survive without the gods?"

Corin dropped a hand on Auric's shoulder and caught his eyes. "I swear on sea and sky, I think we'd *thrive* if every one of them were dead. These false gods have never served us. We should preserve the dream of the creator and strive to be free men living in a world of wonder, not slaves subject to distant tyrants. This world was made for *us*, Auric. We are all we need."

Auric stared at Corin, stunned, and only then did Corin understand what he had done. He'd grown up a beggar and a thief, hunted by the powers of authority. His own desire for survival had driven him to despise the god that so despised an orphaned child.

Then he had left the Godlands to become a pirate, sailing the seas as a free man in defiance of their laws. Perhaps there were some true believers hidden here and there among the crews Corin had joined, but most of those men hated the gods for all the same reasons Corin had.

And then he'd stepped into Oberon's dream. He'd met Ephitel firsthand and seen the dark dawn of that tyrant's reign. He'd spent his time since then surrounded by the druids who knew all these secret truths.

It had grown so easy to speak of the gods—all the gods—as enemies. He no longer thought of them as myths or legends, but as men. The whole lot of them upon Mount Attos were naught but craven sycophants who'd bent knee to a regicide and traitor.

And certainly the farmboy had never balked when Corin spoke ill of Ephitel. Why would he? Any upright Raentzman hated Ephitel as surely as he hated all Ithalians. It was only proper.

But he would not hate *his* god. Raentzmen honored Pellipon. Most Ithalians made heartfelt sacrifice to Ephitel. It was easy to forget that all across the Godlands, good men and women earnestly worshipped their gods in righteous fear. And none would do so more than an honest, good-hearted farmboy from the remotest corner of Raentz.

Corin raised his hands, prepared to argue his defense. "I meant no offense," he said quickly. "Just the idle musings of a shipless pirate."

But the farmboy did not lash out. Instead, even as Corin watched, a burning hope seemed to dawn in the other man's eyes. It took the place of a fear so old and so familiar that it had become a part of him. Auric rolled his shoulders like a man who had just shed some dreadful burden he'd been carrying for years.

"My mother raised me to love Pellipon," Auric said, his voice still low, but stronger now. "To love Pellipon and hate Ephitel like every man who's good and true. However, in my travels I met Tesyn, and *he* loved Ephitel and hated Pellipon. But he was good and true."

Corin nodded, understanding.

Auric went on. "Then I met Hartwin who worshipped Elsbrit. He didn't murder innocents or wallow in obscenities. He is the most righteous man I know, but he would spit in Pellipon's face if he ever met him."

"I suspect they make us war for sport," Corin said. "You've seen it in the Games. They play our nations off for their amusement, and men die."

Auric nodded. That much most men accepted. After all, the ways of the gods were mysterious and just.

The farmboy continued. "Then I met Longbow. He knows nothing of the gods except their names, and he reserves those as the vilest of curses."

"I remember Longbow," Corin said. "He was good and true."

"I respect the things my parents taught," Auric said slowly, "but my whole *life* since I left Raentz has taught me they were wrong."

"They were wrong," Corin said. "Deceived by the gods they trusted. I have seen the secret face of Ephitel, and he is an elf who killed his king. Everything since then has been a farce at our expense."

The farmboy clenched his massive hands in fists. He took a slow breath, then raised his head and showed Corin a startlingly innocent smile.

"So I suspect it's not enough to bring down Ephitel. We're going to have to kill them all," he finished.

Corin yelped with laughter, startled. Then he clapped a hand on Auric's shoulder. "You know . . . I'm slowly starting to believe you. We could be good friends indeed." He glanced toward the house, remembering his conversation with Sera, and he had a sudden, sinking feeling. She would *not* be pleased at this new conviction.

"Auric, you heard how Sera feels about all this. I've no desire to see you embroiled in my madness."

Auric shook his head. "It isn't your madness, Corin. It's theirs. Ephitel's and Pellipon's and all of theirs. It's wrong, and it must end."

Corin wanted to argue, if only for Sera's sake, but Auric wasn't wrong. Instead, Corin closed his grip tighter on Auric's shoulder. "One thing at a time. First, Ephitel, and then we'll see about the rest."

Auric seemed to waver, and Corin caught his eye. "This is no easy matter. You must see that. It will take careful planning, and we cannot afford to start a war with *all* the gods. Not all at once. Not until we've breached their hull. Once they're foundering, taking on water fast, then we can fall upon them like justice."

Auric still seemed anxious to charge into the fray. "Ephitel is not alone in his tyranny!"

"We will break them, Auric, but not with a direct assault. They will not take any move against them lightly, and they have mighty armies and untold powers at their disposal. Look what Ephitel did to Aemilia just because I struck one of his dandies."

"That isn't right," Auric growled. "It cannot be allowed."

"But if we are to fight such power, we must take every step with care. Think of Sera. She's a target, just as much as Aemilia. She'll be seen as a traitor, and they will not abide that."

Auric blinked. His fervor faded, replaced by a raw fear for her safety. "What do I do?"

Regret clenched Corin's gut. He hadn't meant to scare the man; just to delay him. But now he sought some soothing answer. "For now? Nothing. Keep a careful eye out, watch for any sign of danger, and enjoy your days with Sera."

"All of this I've done. But what if Ephitel comes for her?"

It was a good question, and Corin found his answer. "If you see any of sign danger—or especially if I should disappear without other notice—take Sera and go to the druids. Ask for Jeff. It will be easiest if you can work with him."

Some of the tension drained from the farmboy's expression. "I've dealt with the druids before. They can help me?"

"They will. They helped me bring Sera here in the first place, and they understand the threat. Aemilia was one of theirs, after all."

Auric clapped Corin on the shoulder. "Thank you. Now go and find your allies. You should be able to find my friend in the tavern here in Taurb. Walking, it might take you four hours in good weather."

Corin considered the clear sky and nodded. "I'll make it in three."

"There you have it, then. I know that my friend had planned to stay there while he made all his arrangements. He'd hoped to leave this afternoon, but it might take him until tomorrow."

Corin grinned. He'd planned to wait in the same tavern for Ben's arrival. It could be no great challenge to convince this new companion to wait a day or two. With Fortune's favor, he'd have the sword in hand when he set sail to meet the ancient elves.

He caught Auric's eye. "And how will I know this friend of yours? Has he a name?"

Auric answered the question with a grin. "He does, but I think it only fair that I leave him to tell you. I do assure you, you will know him when you see him."

Corin frowned. "This is scarcely the time for playing games."

Auric only grinned the wider. "I've said all I will say on the matter."

Corin almost pressed him for more, but he could not credit the slightest malice in the farmboy's nature. And more than that, Corin's own good fortunes had won him over. After so long sailing blind, he had a course that he could count on. He felt ready to face anything.

So instead of arguing, he bowed his head to Auric. "Thank you for everything, my friend. Please give Sera my warmest regards and honest gratitude for her hospitality in my darkest hour."

With that, he took his leave. He did not even return to the cottage; everything he owned was in the cloak he caught up from the ground. He clasped Auric's arm in friendship, then followed the graveled path back to the packed earth road.

It took a little more than three hours, even at the brisk pace he set, but he spent the entire time in thought. He considered everything he'd said to Auric and Sera about man's need for gods. He reviewed the secrets he had shared with them, the plans he had revealed, and tried to consider all the ways they might betray him.

He had not forgotten the coincidence he was pursuing now. In all the world, who else might have such an interest in finding the elves of old Gesoelig? How would someone such as he have found friendship with the farmboy? Why would he be here now? And why hadn't Auric given him a name? Was Corin marching straight into a trap?

Corin couldn't credit the man with that much duplicity. He'd have seen more of a hint than just this happenstance. No, if there were some sinister plot afoot, then Auric and Sera both were as much deceived as Corin. But that did not rule out the plot.

Corin puzzled over the question for a mile or two, but in the end he knew it wouldn't stop him. How could he pass up an opportunity—however frail—to find a companion in a quest like this? Especially if it were truly one who had the resources to find what Corin needed.

He touched the hilts of his knife and dagger, unconscious reassurance, and reminded himself that he could slip through dream as easily as thinking. Even a justicar had been unable to stop him.

Gradually, he fought down the buzz of anxiety and set his mind on happier things. It would be a victory to find some familiar face from Oberon's dreams. He'd raise an army such as Hurope had not seen in ages, and he would lead them against their brothers who played at being gods.

While he approached the village of Taurb, he imagined how the fight might go. He'd caught no more than glimpses of the elves in combat, even in the dream, but he could guess from what he'd seen and legends he had heard. Fortune favor, he would *become* a legend if he pulled this off. Bards would sing his tale across the breadth of a Hurope that bowed its knee to no lords but the ones they chose. He could almost hear the ballad now, trilling to the sound of a raucous fiddle.

The music swelled, and Corin chuckled as he realized it was not his imagination at all. The song was coming from the tavern just ahead. It seemed they had a minstrel entertaining despite the early hour. Perhaps that would alleviate the tedium while Corin tried to uncover this mysterious friend of Auric's.

He did not forget his caution, though. He turned aside before he reached the village square, slipping between two houses so he could approach the tavern from the back. A narrow door stood open on the alley, leaking all the warmth and noise of a bustling kitchen out into the autumn morning.

Despite his fears, Corin shoved back his cowl as he slipped through the open door. A kitchen door would often offer welcome to a friendly vagabond, but short shrift to a lurking scoundrel. Presentation was the key.

He caught the elbow of a passing serving boy and tipped his head in greeting. "Morning, sir. Can you summon me the master of the house? I'd have a word with him."

The young man looked Corin up and down, then shrugged and turned to call across the kitchen in his native tongue, "Maître Jacob! Pour vous!"

Corin blinked in surprise as a grizzled old man by the hearth fire climbed to his feet. The old man stood a full hand taller than Corin and was as skinny as a fence post. Corin almost expected to hear a crackling pop every time he moved, or at least a tortured groan, but the man came forward with a surprising agility and caught Corin's hand in a firm grip.

"Jacob Gossler. Pleased to meet you!" He spoke an easy Ithalian, which should not have been a surprise for a tavern keeper, but Corin hadn't hoped for much in such a quiet little village.

"And you," Corin responded. "I hoped you could help me with a delicate matter."

The tavern keeper grinned. "Of course, sir! This is Raentz!"

Corin flashed a smile in answer, then shook his head. "It is a different kind of delicate. I had hoped to meet up with an old companion here in Taurb, but he is late in coming, and I fear missing him. Could I trouble you to watch for him and pass along a message?"

The tavern keeper spread his hands. "I will help you if I can, but will your friend come here looking?"

Corin chuckled. "Do you know another tavern anywhere nearby?"

"Not for more than half a day's journey," Jacob said.

"Then there you have it. Ben would never go so long without a drink. He'll be here."

"And what would you have me tell him?"

Corin hesitated at that. The tavern keeper wore no cheap brass ring on his right hand, or it would have been an easy matter. Though this was not a Nimble Fingers tavern, tavern keepers everywhere observed similar traditions. Attention to details kept them safe, and discretion made them wealthy.

"He is a dwarf who goes by the name of Ben Strunk. If you find him anywhere in the village, send him to me straightaway. He is carrying a package that I dearly need."

"Then you will be staying with us?"

"Aye. If you can spare a room."

"I can indeed. But what if he should pass this way when you are not available?"

Corin hesitated. It was only a practical concern to the tavern keeper, but it rang with the same caution Auric had expressed before, and Corin found himself offering the same answer. "If he should arrive after I have gone, bid him deliver his parcel to the nearest druid he can find. He'll take the meaning of it."

Jacob laughed. "I hope he does, because it sounds like children's tales to me."

"It is a most important matter."

"I can hear that in your voice," the tavern keeper said, growing solemn. "And I will treat it so."

Corin bowed his head, grateful, then he turned his gaze toward the common room. "I am supposed to meet someone else here this afternoon. Would you mind if I lingered in your common room?"

"I'll send a boy out with my finest brandy."

Corin shook his head. "Beer will do. I am a simple man. But I'd accept a crust of bread if you had it to spare."

While they discussed refreshments, the tavern keeper started forward, and Corin followed him out through the door and into the common room. He'd gone perhaps two paces when the music stopped. Then, from the front of the room, someone shouted, "You!" in vicious accusation.

Corin turned in the direction of the voice, then hurled himself to the floor one heartbeat before a finely crafted fiddle smashed itself to splinters on the wall he'd been standing next to.

(12)

Corin rolled away by instinct, but his attacker pounced upon him, raining vicious slashing blows with the fiddle's bow. It was a flimsy weapon, but it cut the air and left welts wherever it found skin.

Confusion cost Corin more than one such injury before he gathered enough control to defend himself. He caught his attacker's ankles in a grip between his own and twisted sharply, dragging the minstrel from his feet even as Corin levered himself upward. He spun and leaped, throwing himself upon his fallen attacker. His left arm swept up high to push the minstrel's arms away and trap them against the tavern's floor. His right hand found the dagger on his belt and whipped it up to press a dimple in the soft skin beneath the other man's jaw.

They lay locked in that position for a moment, Corin's chest heaving from the sudden exertion. He blinked sweat from his eyes and got a good close look at the man who had attacked him.

He spat a curse. "Oh, gods' blood! It's you, isn't it?" He eased the knife away from the man's jaw and rolled aside to stare up at the ceiling beside the person who'd tried to kill him.

"Auric sent me to meet you here," Corin said. "He thinks we should travel together. You're hunting for the elves, right? I have information you will need."

Beside him on the floor, the scholar Tesyn cursed in all the living languages of Hurope. And several dead ones.

A stunned silence had gripped the common room from the moment Tesyn sprang on Corin. The tavern keeper was the first man to recover. While Corin still lay panting for breath, the wiry old man stomped forward, grabbed Tesyn by both shoulders, and lifted the poor scholar bodily from the ground. He held him dangling half a foot above the floor, shouting in a furious Raentzian and shaking Tesyn like a pennant in the wind.

Corin took no hurry climbing to his feet. Tesyn? That was the *last* thing Corin had expected. He'd almost have been happier to find Jessamine waiting here in ambush. At least he might have tortured her for information.

The worst of it was that Auric's plan still made good sense. If there was anyone in the Godlands who might have the knowledge Corin needed, it was likely to be Tesyn. The young scholar *had* provided the map that sent Corin to Gesoelig in the first place. Of course, he hadn't done it willingly. That complicated matters somewhat.

An idea struck Corin, then. Perhaps there was another map to be taken. That would certainly simplify his immediate future. He stepped forward and lay a restraining hand on the old man's shoulder. "What can you tell me of this troublemaker? Has he been here long?"

"He is a stranger. He came here late last night and rented a place beside the fire."

Corin frowned. "Not a room, then? Does he have any belongings with him? Books? Papers? Perhaps a scrollcase?"

The tavern keeper nodded in sudden understanding. "He is a thief? He stole from you?"

Corin considered saying yes. It would have been an easy way to search the scholar's belongings. But if there were no map, he'd have to settle for Tesyn's help. So he shook his head and sighed. "Not precisely. It's a complicated matter. He owns a certain document—"

"I've seen no documents," Jacob answered, apologetic. "He came here with nothing but the clothes on his back and the instrument he attacked you with. But give me half an hour, and I'll find out where it's hidden."

Corin searched the scholar with a glance, then shook his head. "No. None of this is necessary. Release this man. I can settle matters on my own."

The tavern keeper's eyes went wide with indignation. "Master, do forgive. No one assaults respectable gentlemen in my common room. I'll see this dog beaten and *then* I'll deliver him to the gendarmes! They'll find whatever answers you need from him."

Tesyn squawked some frantic defense in fluent Raentzian, but the proprietor silenced him with a vicious shake. Corin suppressed a grin.

"I appreciate your concern," Corin said. "But I'm afraid I must insist. He had his reasons for attacking me, and I have pressing need of him. At liberty."

The proprietor looked doubtful, but Corin held his eye with a steady gaze. After a moment of studying his expression, the tavern keeper nodded and dropped Tesyn to the floor.

Corin offered him a grateful smile. "You have my word there will be no new disturbances." He glanced over his shoulder at the wall where Tesyn's fiddle had shattered on the plaster. "If he's done any damage to your property, add it to his bill. And another round for your patrons. That should make things right."

Tesyn squawked again, but the proprietor nodded in satisfaction and withdrew into the kitchen to see to matters.

Eyes flashing, the scholar rounded on Corin. "You have no right—"

"Be careful," Corin said, his voice steady. "I gave my word there'd be no new disturbances. Control yourself, or you'll have a chance to research the inner workings of a backwoods Raentzian gaol."

Tesyn's eyes popped, but he clamped his jaw shut.

Corin nodded. "Good. Now, Auric tells me you intend to find the ancient elves."

"You've spoken with Auric?"

"Aye. I bore him grim tidings, and he prevailed on me to stay with them the night, but I cannot tarry longer. Grave events are even now unfolding in the world of men, and we must enlist the aid of all the long-forgotten elves, or we are doomed."

Tesyn blinked. "*All* the long-forgotten elves?"

Corin nodded. "A mighty city's worth, dispersed and hiding for the day some willing leader brings them back to reclaim what was stolen from them."

Something like a smile tugged at the corner of the scholar's mouth. "This is your great quest?"

"Aye. The same as yours."

Tesyn shook his head. "There is no great city. There are no elven hordes. But I believe there is a small community of them— perhaps a single one—surviving somewhere lost to the world of mortal men."

"I know that there are more. If you can find me even one, then he can lead me to the people I need."

Tesyn shook his head. "I am forever astonished by the things that you uncover. And you tell me Auric humored you in this—"

Corin grimaced. He understood the laughter in the farm-boy's voice now. "He did. Enough to recommend that I join up with you despite the bad blood we share. This is important."

"I am not helping you," the scholar said. "I have no intention of helping you. It is no hyperbole to say that more than once you've left my life a wretched *shambles*, Corin Hugh. You've robbed me of two fortunes, and now I'm left playing the fiddle in a village inn for some scraps of moldy bread." He sucked a deep breath and shook his head fiercely. "I'd rather sacrifice all of Hurope than assist you in any way."

Corin gaped. The young scholar had always shown a healthy backbone, but Corin had hoped the promise of a grand adventure would be enough to win him over. He tried a different tack.

"I'm not more anxious to endure a journey with a man who hates me so. You summoned guards against me in Jepta, and now you've tried to kill me! But I will set those things aside because Auric asked it of me. He tasked me with protecting you upon your voyage, and—"

"Did he?" Tesyn interrupted. He tapped his chin with an index finger.

"Aye. He said I needed your wisdom and you needed my cunning, and Fortune had clearly cast our lots on the same path for a reason. He bade me watch over you, and assured me you would aid me in kind."

Tesyn considered that a moment. "Auric . . . is generous to a fault. He's patient where lesser men might lash out." Tesyn had the grace to blush at that, but he pressed on. "And he is as forgiving as a hungry priest on Sunday."

Corin remembered something Sera had said. He put on his most earnest expression. "Auric is a model for us all. I try every day to emulate Auric's generous spirit."

Tesyn laughed sardonically. "You do? I'm not so gullible as that. Perhaps good-hearted Auric has forgiven you your crimes, but he's a better man than I. I haven't and I won't. I will not help you, Corin. I'll abandon my own quest first."

Corin fought down an urge to grab the man and shake him as the proprietor had done. He heaved a disappointed sigh instead and glanced back toward the west. "Auric will be disappointed."

"He'll forgive me this petty indulgence," Tesyn said. "That's an advantage of his nature." He brushed at his shirtfront, straightened his tunic, then shook his head and started for the front door.

Corin scrambled after him. "Where are you going?"

"To catch my coach. It was only waiting while I grabbed a bite to eat. But now I find I no longer enjoy the hospitality of this establishment."

"Wait!" Corin snapped, catching at his sleeve, but the scholar ripped his arm free.

"I will not wait. I have a ship waiting for me in Baillon, and I am far more interested in catching her before she sails than I am in staying to chat with you."

He burst out into the noonday sun, and Corin followed close behind. "Baillon, you say?"

"She sails with the morning tide, and I'll be glad to leave you far behind."

"And where from there?" Corin asked as the two men stepped out into the midday brightness. He'd not yet surrendered all his hopes of learning what he needed from Tesyn and making the voyage without him.

But the young scholar seemed to guess at his intentions. He shook his head sternly, even as he left the tavern's threshold and headed west across the green. "My secrets are my own. But fare you well—"

"It's to the Isle of Mists," Corin said hastily. "I know that much."'

Tesyn gaped. "How?"

"I told you: I've been to Gesoelig. I spoke with Oberon himself and came away with secret knowledge that would turn your hair white."

Tesyn weighed the claim for a moment. Then he licked his lips hungrily. "You must tell me everything you know."

Corin raised an eyebrow. "And you will do the same?"

"I . . . no. I'm sorry, no. You have taught me not to trust you, Captain Hugh."

"And how will I trust you? I have no time to go chasing superstition and rumor. Auric seemed to believe you had hard information. A point of contact? A map?"

"Not a map. I've learned the danger of carrying maps." He tapped the side of his head. "It's all in here. The landing place. The ever-forking road. The ghosts!"

"Ghosts?"

"Haven't you heard? The Isle of Mists is haunted by the angry dead."

Corin smiled, amused. "All your careful study, and you still believe that there are ghosts?"

"You asked me for help! If you are unconvinced, I will be happy to continue on my—"

A distant thunder finally registered with Corin, and he moved on instinct. He clapped a hand over Tesyn's mouth and dragged him off the green and around the tavern's corner. Then Corin leaned forward to peek back down the road to the east.

Riders were coming. A lot of riders. At first, Corin took the cloud of dust that they raised for the post coach, but these were horsemen pressing hard, and sunlight glinted here and there off steel armor.

Corin couldn't guess what they intended, but he doubted it was anything positive. He strained his eyes for a better look, but Tesyn shoved him hard in the chest and jerked his head away. "Have you gone mad? Unhand me, sir! Why, I'll—"

Corin slammed him back against the tavern's wall, hard enough to drive the air from his lungs.

He leaned down close in the scholar's face. "I've already told you there are lives in the balance. Those riders mean some trouble, and I can't afford to have you clamoring—"

The scholar looked baffled. "What riders?"

Corin rolled his eyes. He shifted his grip on Tesyn's tunic and spun him around so he could glance past the tavern's edge.

Tesyn spent a moment staring hard toward the eastern road. His head twitched left and right, but he was careful to keep hidden. At last he relaxed in Corin's grasp, and Corin let him go.

The scholar turned back to Corin and spread his hands. "I'll ask again. What riders?"

The sound of their hoof beats rang loudly now, but the scholar's expression was so perfectly earnest that Corin pressed past him to take another look for himself. And then he understood.

They'd come to the very edge of town, but thin tendrils of an unnatural mist hung draped about them. It curled around their horses' hooves and billowed up around their bodies like ethereal cloaks. More glamours. And at this range, Corin had no trouble seeing the figures of the men. At their head rode a pretty young blonde dressed in heavy battle armor.

Ithale's justicar had come to Raentz, and she looked angry.

She should not have been here. It could have been considered an act of war even without the score of soldiers riding at her heel.

Corin spat a curse. "How did she find me?"

Tesyn's face went pale. He peeked again, and though he would have seen nothing there, he whipped back around to Corin and hissed frantically, "Who's there? What does this mean?"

Corin shook his head. "There is no time."

"What's happening?" Tesyn demanded. "What do you see? Are we in danger?" He hesitated a moment, and then his eyes grew even wider. "Or is it someone after Auric and Sera?"

Despite himself, Corin threw a glance toward the little cart path that led west toward the farmboy's home. Corin was nearly certain the justicar hadn't come for them, but if he slipped her grasp here, she would find out where he'd been. She would track him back to the quiet little cabin, and Princess Sera's anonymity would be destroyed. She could easily be dragged back to Aerome in chains.

Corin was lost in worry for the farmboy when Tesyn hauled back and kicked him hard in the shins. That so startled Corin that the scholar was able to wrench free. He kept hidden from the justicar, sprinting along the shadow of the tavern's western wall toward a quiet little stable yard nestled near the back.

Corin cursed and darted after him. He'd been too distracted by the riders out front to notice it before, but now that Corin looked, he saw the carriage waiting there. The stable boys had finished changing out the horses, and now the coach and team stood waiting for their fares. The scholar flew to the carriage door, ripped it open, and shouted for the driver to leave.

"Fortune favor," Corin breathed, still running hard. He threw a quick glance back over his shoulder, but there was no sign of pursuit. The riders hadn't seen them, then. He felt a flash of hope and turned his attention to the coach.

There must not have been other passengers booked for this coach, because the driver complied with Tesyn's orders. He didn't move as swiftly as the scholar had hoped, though. He clucked to the horses, turning them in their traces and pointing the coach toward the tavern's green. He'd just snapped the reins to start them walking forward when he caught sight of Corin, not ten paces off and running hard.

His eyes lit up with the hope of another fare, but Corin had no time to spend on haggling. He leaped toward the driver's seat from two paces distant, landed on the step, caught the rail there with one hand, and brought his other fist smashing down with all the force of his momentum. It clipped the driver just below the ear and sent him sprawling.

"What are you doing?" Tesyn screamed from within the coach.

"For Auric and the princess!" Corin grunted as he jumped down after the driver and heaved him up onto his shoulders. "Open the door!"

In defiance of Corin's instructions, Tesyn grabbed the door and pulled hard against it, keeping it closed. "I'll do no such thing! Not until you tell me what you have planned."

"Are you prepared to miss your ship in Baillon? You need this coach to reach it in time, and I fear the driver won't help you."

For a moment Tesyn said nothing, considering. Then he cursed darkly and twitched aside the curtain. "Have you ruined me again?"

"Not if you open the door!"

The scholar met Corin's eye, suspicious. "Why?" Tesyn demanded. "What are we doing? Do you have some plan?"

"I always have a plan," Corin lied. "But I don't have time. Can you drive a coach?"

Tesyn shook his head.

"Then open the blasted door," Corin said, "and I'll get you to Baillon."

Tesyn did so reluctantly, and as soon as he'd made a large enough gap, Corin hurled the limp driver up into the cabin. Then he shoved the door shut, toppling Tesyn with the sudden motion, and scrambled up to the driver's seat.

Tesyn leaned out the window while Corin was sorting out the reins. "Can *you* drive a coach?"

Corin shrugged. "I'll figure it out as we go."

He snapped the reins. The horses jerked in their traces and started forward, and Corin caught a curse uttered behind him as the scholar tumbled about inside again.

That was enough for Corin. He braced himself against the driver's narrow box and snapped the reins, shouting, "Hah!" to encourage the horses forward.

They took his meaning, dashing forward hard enough to rock the coach behind them. Corin gripped his seat with one hand and snapped the reins once more with his other. "Hyah! Hyah!"

It seemed to do the job. The coach left the inn's little carriage yard like an arrow from a bow. They blasted out onto the highway, and Corin twitched the reins to the right, aiming for the north road out of town.

That sent them right past the tavern green. Corin raised up on his heels and glanced back over his shoulder as they passed. The lovely justicar stood halfway through the tavern's door, one hand on its frame as she turned to investigate the commotion. Her soldiers sat their horses some way off, still packed in tight formation and draped in the clinging mist of their glamour.

The justicar had dropped hers, though. She'd clearly meant to make inquiries here, and Corin dearly wished to keep her from learning where he'd come from.

So he dropped the reins and scrambled up to stand on his seat. The coach pitched and rolled like a boat in the brine, but Corin barely noticed. He threw his cloak out wide with one hand and waved the other overhead.

"Ho, Justicar!" he called above the thunder of the horses' hooves. "I'm moving on! I'm moving on!"

He saw the flash of fury in her eyes. She leaped away from the doorway and toward her horse, and that was all he waited for. He clambered back down to his seat and caught up the reins again.

The coach was not a heavy one, and it had a four-horse team, but ordinarily he would have bet hard on the horsemen catching them inside a mile. His only hope came from the horses' health. This team was fresh and rested. The justicar's mounts all looked hard-pressed, and their riders traveled in heavy armor. They'd have to show some care to keep their animals healthy, and Corin had no fear of killing his team in their traces. He had to get away.

He pushed them hard and made a mile, maybe two, before he dared to look around. When he glanced back, the soldiers chasing him were distant silhouettes, but they were not falling back. He frowned, searching for a plan.

Tesyn interrupted him with a knock on the cabin's wall. Likely irritated at the jostling! Corin pounded on the wall in answer and shouted, "We aren't slowing down. There's a justicar behind us!"

Tesyn's complaint came back muffled by the cabin's walls and drowned beneath noises of the chase. Corin pulled the reins to left and right, steering with the curve of the land, but he half-suspected that the animals knew the route better than he did. He glanced back to check on the justicar again, and the distant figures held in hot pursuit. He cursed and whipped the horses to a frenzy.

As they bolted forward, Tesyn hammered on the cabin's wall again, pounding this time. Corin paid no mind, but a moment later the door flew open, and the scholar stuck his head out above the flashing countryside.

"Corin!" he gasped.

"I'm not slowing down for a pampered nobleman," Corin called back.

Tesyn didn't answer. A moment later the door slammed shut. Then the pounding came again, on the wooden panel right by Corin's head. He spun around, fist raised to pound in answer, when a particularly strong blow from within splintered a gaping hole right through the wall.

In an instant, Corin understood. He leaned closer to the hole, trying to catch a glance inside, and called out, "The driver?"

Tesyn grunted hard, then wheezed for breath and groaned, "Yes, the driver!"

Corin got one clear look inside. There was barely room for Tesyn and the other man standing, and that fact had likely saved the scholar's life. Tesyn had somehow positioned himself behind the bigger man and looped his lace cravat like a delicate garrote around the big man's throat. Tesyn had his shoulder in the small of the driver's back, pulling on the scarf with all his might, but it was not enough. The driver looked red in the face, but none the slower for Tesyn's strangling cord. He flailed his balled fists and stomped hard at Tesyn's instep whenever he saw the chance. It was an ugly fight, and it had an even chance of leaving either of the men dead. Both, if that door fell open again and tumbled them out.

Thinking of the door, Corin found a plan. He popped his head above the coach's roof and found the justicar perhaps ten paces closer. Not close enough to see her clearly, but far too close to shake her.

He dropped back down and leaned close to the splintered gap again. "When I say the word, unleash him and jump out the door."

"What? What?"

"You have to trust me! There's no time to explain, and there's a justicar behind us. In a moment—you'll know when—unhand the driver and jump. *Fast!*"

The young scholar threw a desperate glance toward the front of the carriage, though he couldn't have seen Corin through the gap. Sweat slicked his long hair to his face and neck and stained his pretty shirt. A bruise was growing on his forehead, and he'd have a black eye before dawn. His arms were shaking too, from his grip on the cravat. He wouldn't last much longer, and he knew it.

"Really?" he whimpered, desperate.

"Trust me," Corin said. "Just . . . just trust me."

Then he closed his eyes and wove a glamour. He started with himself, imagining . . . nothing. He'd never tried such a thing before, but the justicar had given him the idea. He replaced his mental image of himself with nothing at all, with an invisible man sitting on the driver's perch. Faint gray mist clouded his vision as the glamour took its hold, and Corin nodded to himself in satisfaction.

Then he did the same for Tesyn, and finally he turned his attention to the driver. He changed the driver into a handsome man of twenty years, dark hair and eyes and dressed all in black.

Inside the carriage, Tesyn gasped. "Corin? What . . . is that your signal?"

"Yes!" Corin shouted. "Jump! Jump *now!*"

The door opened and Corin caught a glimpse of Tesyn as he leaped. The scholar landed hard on the highway's grassy verge and tumbled end over end down the slope and away from the road. Corin took a deep breath, shook his head, and flung himself away as well.

The coach continued down the highway, post horses following the same path they'd followed every week for years. Corin heard them fast receding in the distance, and then he struck the ground. Pain shot through his back and shoulders, and light flashed behind his eyes as he hit the ground rolling. He tucked his elbows to his belly and raised his fists to shield his face while he went tumbling down the slope toward the distant trees.

Somewhere along the way, he heard the drum of hooves passing by above him. They never slowed. He felt a burst of hope in that, even as pain and dizziness crashed like mighty waves inside him. He felt his focus slip, felt the glamours on him and Tesyn unravel, but he poured everything he had into the one he'd laid on the driver. That one had become the most important.

As Corin finally rolled to a stop, he let out a painful sigh and lay a moment, thinking. Victory buoyed him up on the waters of fatigue and pain. He'd fooled her. He'd fooled them all. The justicar and her soldiers were charging down the highway after a carriage that contained a beat-up driver who *looked* an awful lot like Corin Hugh.

They'd catch the coach eventually. Those horses wouldn't keep a killing pace without a driver urging them to it. Then the justicar and her men would fall upon the coach. They'd drag the driver out and put him to the question. Perhaps her patron's blessings would give her some way to see through the glamour. Perhaps she'd figure out what he had done. But that would all take time. The confusion alone would buy him an hour. In the end, she might never uncover a full explanation of what happened on this highway.

Smiling at the thought, Corin levered himself up into a sitting position just in time to receive a full-armed slap from Tesyn. The scholar's right arm hung limply at his side, but he was raising his left again to follow through with a backhand when Corin rolled away and to his feet. He groaned at the protest of new bruises in his left ribs and hip, and then he nearly lost his balance coming up when the soft earth shifted beneath his feet. He caught his footing and ducked away from Tesyn's wild punch. The scholar overbalanced and landed on his knees.

He didn't try to get up. He dropped his chin against his chest and sobbed. "What have you done to me? Gods on Attos, why do you hate me?"

"I've saved our lives," Corin answered. "Perhaps you couldn't see it, but there were a score of Ithalian soldiers on our trail, with a justicar at their head. Do you think they'd have treated us kindly? Do you think they'd have let us catch your boat in Baillon? No. We'd have spent the next three decades in some gruesome prison if they'd let us live that long. And Auric too."

"Why?" Tesyn screamed. "Why would a justicar *care* about me or Auric?"

"Are you mad?" Corin asked. "She's an agent of Ephitel."

"And we're Ithalians! Ephitel's justicars exist to serve us. Gods favor, she owes her loyalty to Sera's family. All we'd have had to do was say her name—"

Corin snorted. "I do forget how noblemen are taught to see the world. But you know about the plots that we contrived in order to steal the princess from Aerome. Don't you see? Sera isn't one of them anymore. She's fled Ithale. She's living with a Raentzian farmboy. I don't know how much they've told you, but she's in *hiding* from her family. And this justicar would love to lay her hands on the misplaced princess. They might even reinstate her—against her will—but they could not allow to live any witnesses to her little embarrassment. Not you. Not me. And certainly not Auric."

Tesyn shook his head, stunned. "They wouldn't go so far."

"They have," Corin said. "Why do you think Auric has shown such faith in me? I've already saved him from one assassination attempt by Sera's family. And Sera from another. I stole the carriage and sent the justicar chasing after it as a diversion, to lead her away from Auric and Sera."

"Then we must go to them! We have to warn them what has happened."

Corin looked south, imagining the distance to the farmhouse. By the roads it would take half a day, but he didn't trust his strange powers to keep him safe from the justicar if she stumbled on him again. Not now that he had shown his hand. They'd have to go cross-country, and that would take a day at least.

He shook his head. "We'd do no good, and risk ourselves besides. No, I've already given Auric instructions for a situation such as this. He should be able to escape her notice with the time we've bought him. But *we* may not be so lucky. We need to move."

"Where? How?"

"Just as you had intended. We press on to Baillon to catch your ship there, then sail for the Isle of Mists. I doubt even a justicar can follow that trail, and if she does, we'll lose her in the wilderness. Meanwhile, Auric and Sera will slip away to safety among the druids, and Ephitel's bloodhound will ultimately return to her master empty-handed."

Tesyn stared. "We'll do all that? We'll best a justicar?"

"All that and more," Corin said. "Don't forget the damsel in distress. Or the ancient elves we plan to meet upon the Isle. They'll write legends about us if we accomplish half so much."

Tesyn shook his head. "I never meant to be a hero."

"It's going to happen anyway," Corin said. He clapped the scholar on the shoulder and drew him to his feet. "Now come! We must get moving before the justicar sends her men to search the countryside."

The scholar paled. "You think she'll do that?"

"I do. But she won't find us." He closed his eyes and rebuilt the glamours that concealed him and Tesyn from prying eyes. The scholar gasped anew at that, but Corin caught his arm and started him moving.

There was no path beneath the verge. The ground was uneven and treacherous, and both men were sorely beaten from their tumble down the hill, so they made slow going. The sun fell half-way to the horizon before they even caught up with the coach.

They came around a wide, slow bend in the terrain, and there before them the highway dipped down into a little dell. The coach stood motionless on the road, its horses loosed to graze and drink from the stream while the justicar and her soldiers stood clustered around the furious, flustered driver.

Tesyn gasped in horror at the sight of them, and Corin breathed a prayer of gratitude to Fortune that the glamour hanging over him would stifle all his little gasps and cries. It was a quiet mercy.

Corin didn't slow. He dragged Tesyn on ahead, though he swung out wide around the spot where the justicar was interviewing the driver. They moved a mile or two in the shadows on the forest's edge, until they'd left the coach and riders far behind. Then they moved right up onto the highway, still hidden from any prying eyes, and pressed harder still along the smooth-packed road.

Even so, it took them half the night to reach the coast, and dawn was breaking when at last they saw the high walls of Baillon. Tesyn whooped in victory, but Corin fixed his gaze upon the waves. An hour yet. Perhaps an hour before the tide turned. How long would a merchant ship wait for passengers when the coach had failed to come? How long would they risk the trade goods in their hold sitting idle? Exhausted though they both were, hungry and dehydrated though the night's journey had made them, he pressed harder still. Behind him, Tesyn almost protested. But then he mumbled, "Heroes in a story," and stomped along behind him.

Corin grinned at that. Perhaps he would make something useful of the scholar after all.

They reached the town as mid-morning prayers were tolling, but to Corin's great surprise, Tesyn's hired ship was still waiting at the dock. Corin let Tesyn's glamour fade away and listened while the scholar spun a brief tale of hardship and woe that smoothed the angry lines from the captain's brow and filled his eyes with sympathy. Still, he was anxious to put off, and Tesyn didn't argue for a moment. They hurried up the gangplank, Corin scampering unseen behind them. Then the sailors cast off lines and pulled hard for open waters.

Corin breathed deeply the salty air, and when he exhaled, he felt an enormous wave of old anxiety ebb away. The water rolled beneath him, deep and patient, unforgiving but also undemanding. The sea had never been his home, but it had always been his freedom, and now he reveled in it like a serpent in the sunlight.

As they slipped out past the breakers, Corin turned and cast a glance back to the port. He saw a score of soldiers darting down the piers, searching ships and sailors while their justicar went straight to find the harbormaster. Too late. She'd come too late. Corin laughed into the ocean breeze and then settled down to rest his aching bones.

He'd made it free and clear. Let her chase him all the way across the world—she wouldn't catch him. Corin Hugh was smart enough to best a justicar.

Now all he had to do was find the elves. And win their favor. And lead them in a war on Ephitel and all the lands of men. He sighed and shut his eyes and started planning.

Corin was not surprised to learn that Tesyn's merchant ship had no intention of carrying them to the haunted Isle of Mists. Instead, the scholar had used this ship to carry his supplies for the expedition and then booked passage from Port Baillon in southwest Raentz to Rauchel in the northwest—one of the closest ports to the Isle. He had assumed that the proximity would make it easier to find a willing captain there.

Along the way, the little merchant ship made excellent time. She coasted in some wild waters, but her captain knew his way. Corin and Tesyn both spent the better part of the four-day voyage sleeping—recovering from their adventure on the Baillon highway—and devouring whatever travel rations Tesyn could demand from the ship's stores.

When they arrived in Port Rauchel, Corin started counting hours. Tesyn's late arrival at the docks—and for a ship he had commissioned back in Aerome—would not have gone unnoticed. The blasted man had *also* made arrangements to take the post carriage to Baillon. It would be a wonder if he hadn't left a hand-drawn map to Auric's cabin with the gendarmes in the village there.

No, Corin had to assume that the justicar had found their trail in Baillon. He counted on it. If not for Auric and Sera, he could have grabbed Tesyn's shoulder and flung them both through dream to the Isle of Mists. He'd considered it back at the tavern, and then again before he'd hurled himself from a racing carriage, but that would leave the justicar without a trail. Her only choice would be to backtrack, and that would inevitably lead her to the farmboy and the princess.

Corin cursed. He'd come to that again and again as he had fashioned and discarded plans, but in the end, he couldn't sacrifice those two. Not yet. Not without a better reason. It was a dicey game he played, but if he could string the justicar along, staying just outside her reach, then everyone might get away clean.

It was a dicey game indeed. And so he counted hours while Tesyn searched for a willing captain in Rauchel. The justicar might have followed them by boat. He'd gotten a good look at all the other ships in harbor there, and he doubted any one of them could have followed close behind the one they'd ridden. A storm had blown up on the second day, just a little thing when they passed through, but it had still been a-brewing then, and anyone more than an hour behind them would have sailed straight into an ugly tempest. That bought him half a day at least—and likely more—if she had come by sea. She might have docked somewhere along the coast to hire a faster ship, but that too would have cost her time. He called it twenty hours on open water.

If she had come by land, things grew somewhat trickier. In her haste to capture Corin in Baillon, she'd risked showing her men openly there. Was that her new intention? Would she risk starting a war between Ithale and Raentz just to capture him? It would certainly slow her down if some minor lord along the way decided to confront her on his own. But even with a glamour hiding them, such a large force would require room and board within a day or two. So keeping them hidden would slow her too. Either way, leading her private army across the length of Raentz would cost her a week. No question.

But she didn't have to bring them. If she left them to find their own way, she could travel quickly. A justicar was never warmly welcomed outside her god's domain, but only a crowned king would dare to challenge her authority in pursuit of a wanted criminal. It was the soldiers that made Jessamine an exception.

If she left the soldiers behind, she could travel fast and light. Without them to slow her, she could hire post horses to carry her from Baillon to Rauchel in four days flat. She wouldn't, though. Not directly. She'd be expecting Corin to try something clever, after all, especially after the trick he'd pulled with the carriage. So she would take the coastal roads instead of the overland highway. She'd stop in every port along the way to make sure he hadn't deviated from the travel plans she'd found in Baillon.

Six days, then. If she pressed her horse and herself she might have made it five. Barely better than the ocean voyage. Either way, he figured twenty hours was the most he dared to spend here before moving on. He had to leave the port before she reached it, but he also had to plant a trail for her here.

So as he trailed Tesyn through the murky sailors' dens, he dropped his glamour too. He let himself be seen, and that was likely all the effort required to keep the justicar on his trail. After all, he was something of a legend here.

He'd been a successful pirate captain, but more importantly, he had been an *interesting* one. Far and wide, they knew the tale of the man who'd led his crew on a three-month expedition into the Jepta desert. No one really knew what had happened there, but they knew the ship's first mate had come back the captain, and Corin Hugh had been left for dead.

Then he had come back with a vengeance. He'd left the traitors' corpses littering the breadth of Hurope, reclaimed Marzelle from his own mutinous crewmen and delivered it back to the Nimble Fingers, and in the process made himself a hero among the very organization that had raised him.

The pirates of Rauchel knew Corin Hugh, and when he showed himself, he caused a stir. He spent an hour being feasted and another hour drinking. He spent an hour telling tales of all his exploits through the years and another hour asking questions. By then the crowd of his admirers had grown large enough to offer a wealth of options—mates and even officers from more than a dozen active crews—and all but Corin had enjoyed enough of beer or rum to get them talking.

By five hours in he had everything he needed. Captain Crowe was not a friendly man, but he knew his way to half the secret grottos that lined the treacherous coasts of the Isle of Mists, and he ran an honorable crew.

It took more time still to convince Crowe to take new passengers, though. His ship was slated for repairs and he'd promised his crew three days' leave while the work was done. He would not deny them that, even for the famous Corin Hugh, so it fell to Corin to track them down, to rouse them from their drinks, and to convince them he was worth the sacrifice.

Somehow he managed that. It took the afternoon and evening, and he'd almost despaired of finding the first mate at all when he discovered the man smoking a quiet pipe in the peaceful solitude of a shady little cemetery.

"I know you've earned your leave," Corin said, "but will you sail for me?"

"There's other ships. There's other crews."

"But none I'd trust to carry me safe out of the clutches of a justicar."

That got the man's attention. He raised his eyebrows and tapped out his pipe, then asked the question. "Whose justicar?"

"Ephitel's. She's tracked me all the way here from Aerome."

The first mate whistled. "I'd call that a lie if you were anyone but Corin Hugh." Then he thought a moment, shrugged, and stuck out his hand. "Honor to serve ye, Captain. How long till we sail?"

"An hour, Fortune favor. If it takes much more than that, your whole crew will get to watch me fight a justicar. It won't be pretty."

He nodded, thoughtful. "No. I think it wouldn't be. But you won't fight that fight alone. There's more'n a few men in Raentz who'd tussle Ephitel himself if they could say they'd fought alongside Corin Hugh."

"I won't forget that," Corin said. "But let's none of us get killed tonight. Just hurry."

"That I will. Have you found everyone?"

"I still need Slade and Joe and Cameron."

"I'll round 'em up. You get back to the ship and hide your face."

"Aye aye." Corin said. "And thank you."

The first mate gave a laugh. "You kiddin'? They'll be buying me beers all winter if I can say I sailed with Corin Hugh. Thank *you*, sir. Thank you."

Somehow he had Slade and Cameron to the ship even before Corin reached it, and it took less than half an hour before the last man showed up. But still they needed to load the ship with rations and equipment for the voyage. Tesyn's chests were brought up from the dock house and loaded in the hold, and then finally the crew piled on the ship and raised the gangplank. Corin threw in beside the other sailors, hauling lines and heaving to like a common deckhand. It was honest work, and it felt good. The clock he'd been counting in his head expired as they slipped into the channel, and Corin went once more to stand at the stern and stare back at the docks, expecting to see the lovely justicar dashing to the end of the pier, shaking her fist at him in anger.

But there was no one. It should have been no surprise. He'd made a thousand guesses to predict when she'd arrive, and this had been the very earliest he'd imagined. She wasn't there. That only proved he'd made good assumptions.

Unless she'd lost his trail. Unless she'd doubled back from Baillon and gone after Auric anyway. He tried not to think about that. He'd made enough of a stir in Rauchel to send rumors to her anywhere in Raentz. That would have to be enough. It had to be.

Still, he couldn't shake the fear. So he found a mop and bucket and started swabbing the deck. He worked himself weary, then finally fell asleep right there on the deck. When he woke at dawn, out in the middle of the open sea, he strained his eyes for some sign of a distant ship trailing in their wake, but they were all alone. No one sailed for the Isle of Mists.

An hour later, while the captain was easing the ship toward a hidden inlet the scholar had described, a mighty wind kicked up and dashed the ship against the rocks. Crushing waves rose up from a still sea and lifted men and debris into the air, then smashed them against each other or dragged them down into the icy depths. Corin and Tesyn were the only two who reached the shore alive.

Alone.

Then the wind began howling while both men lay shivering and exhausted beneath a pale blue sky, and that wind brought the whispers of the dead.

There were worse things than justicars, Corin decided, and all of them were out to kill him.

The Isle of Mists was scarcely more than legend to most, but pirates knew it well. Like the Wildlands further south, it was a haven safe from Godlander authorities. And like the Wildlands, it was an unforgiving place. Fog hung thick and heavy over all its shores, and treacherous currents fought along its rocky coasts.

But the inlands were a mystery. No man who ventured out upon its moors returned alive. Pirates only sheltered in its hidden coves when desperate times demanded it. They'd travel in large groups to fetch timber or fresh water near the shore, and always they went armed to the teeth.

Corin had never been driven to that extreme, but he'd heard all the tales from men who had. Still, no pirate he had ever met could name the dangers of the island. Man or beast, arcane or natural, whatever roamed this land kept hidden in the choking fog and left no survivors to tell its secrets.

But as Corin lay gasping on the rocky beach, he had some clue what lurked there. He'd laughed when Tesyn said the Isle was haunted, but on the howling ocean wind he could hear the sound of ghastly voices. Not just wailing moans, but words in an ancient language. *"Begone from here and leave our shores. No manling's welcome on these moors!"*

Over and over, the ghostly whispers whorled around him. He struggled to his feet, head whipping left and right as he searched for some sign of the threat, but it was just the wind.

The wind and the voices of the elves of old Gesoelig. Corin shuddered. He'd heard those voices once before, when his crew had put Gesoelig's tomb to the torch. The memories of all those elves had gone up in flames, and something in that moment had transported Corin back into Oberon's sad memory.

But though that cavern had contained the record of those lives, this island had become their final refuge. Corin licked his lips and gripped the hilts of his weapons. Would they welcome Oberon's manling scion? He'd never guessed he might end up like the numberless, nameless dead who'd disappeared across the Isle's moors.

He shivered at the thought. This was a dreadful place. The whispering wind still rolled around him, tugging at his cloak and stinging in his eyes. *"Begone from here and leave our shores. No manling's welcome on these moors!" "Begone from here and leave our shores. No manling's welcome on these moors!"*

He drew a ragged breath and answered in their language. "I am the emissary of your rightful king. I am Corin Hugh, the manling out of time. I've come to beg your aid in fighting Ephitel."

The wind went still, and Corin's heartbeat seemed to hammer in the sudden silence. He couldn't breathe. He didn't dare to move. But his eyes darted left and right, searching for some sign of the source of those ancient voices.

Had he stilled them? Had he earned an audience? Or had he merely shouted to the wind?

Farther down the shore, Tesyn stirred. Corin held out a hand to still him, but the scholar didn't notice. He groaned loudly, then rolled up onto his knees. "What was that nonsense?" he called, his voice hoarse. "Something about a king and a diplomat? And Ephitel?" He groaned again and then heaved a stomachful of seawater and bile across the stones.

"Be still!" Corin hissed. "The elves of old Gesoelig are watching us."

The scholar coughed and wiped his mouth before he rose unsteadily to his feet. "And you laughed at me," Tesyn sneered. "You think the ghosts can hear you? You think they'll listen to your lies? You're no diplomat. You're a devil and a rogue!"

As if in answer, the winds sprang up again—not howling this time, but whispering: "A rogue! A devil. Begone from here. Begone."

"He's wrong! He lies," Corin shouted. "I am Oberon's adopted heir. I've seen Gesoelig underneath the mountain. I know the bitter taste of Ephitel's betrayal."

"Betrayal and lies," the ghosts answered, still savage. "Gesoelig lies beneath the mountain. Begone from here and trouble us no more."

Corin turned on Tesyn, brows drawn down, and the young scholar went pale. "You can't believe I had anything to do with that."

"You said this place was haunted, and then you interfered when I had calmed the angry spirits!"

"Angry!" wailed the wind. "Spirits leave this place. Begone!"

Tesyn drew himself up tall and stomped across the rocky beach to Corin. "I didn't do this to us! Your stinking pirates did it. They crashed their ship! What kind of captain crashes into rocks within sight of land?"

"What?" Corin gasped. "Where else would . . . That is no matter now. These are deadly waters, no matter who is at the helm. You should be grateful you're alive."

"Alive," the wind whispered, ominous. *"Begone alive. Or die."*

Corin shook his head, trying to dislodge the voices. They were barely at the edge of hearing. If he focused hard enough on something else, he could forget them altogether. But whenever silence fell, he heard the whispered words, always taunting.

He raised his voice and jabbed a finger at the scholar's chest. "Well? What do we do now?"

"You're asking me?"

"Of course! You said you'd studied this place. You said you knew the way. You knew how to handle the ghosts. You have everything prepared—"

"Indeed I did," Tesyn shouted back. "Would you like to know some of the things that I discovered? It isn't safe to eat any food in this place or accept a gift if offered. That's why I brought so many crates of rations! It isn't safe to stay an hour in darkness, so I brought oil and torches by the dozens. Iron can fend off the angry spirits, and holy water disperses them altogether, so I brought along a hearty stock of both."

Corin rolled his eyes. "All of that is lost."

"Because your stinking pirate captain tried to sail through a pile of rocks! I spent a fortune setting up this expedition, and now we're stranded all alone in the second most godsforsaken place in all Hurope. And you ask me what to do next?"

"Aye," Corin answered. "Aye, and I will ask again. If we had all those precious things, our mission would be easier. But we have just our wits and each other. And everything you know. You claimed you'd memorized your map. If this place is so dangerous, then we cannot afford to waste a moment. Let us find the elves and pray Fortune they'll protect us from the rest."

Tesyn shook his head. "You aren't listening. We won't survive to find the elves. The shrouded city—even if it's real—is easily a hundred miles inland."

"This is your destination, then? There is a place on the Isle called the shrouded city?" A slow grin touched his lips. "A city! I told you there was more than one man here."

"It doesn't matter! We'll never make it there."

"How can you know that?"

"My family spent generations hunting for the ruins of Jezeeli. They chased down more than one false trail in that time, and with the aid of the book you sold to me in Jepta—with some of the language cues it offered—I was able to tease out new meaning from some of my uncle's oldest texts."

"Remarkable," Corin said. "I'd like to see these texts."

"Remarkable? It is our doom. We have to find our way across a hundred miles of this wilderness without supplies! How many hours will we have to spend in darkness? How many angry spirits will we face along the way? What will we eat? It's madness to proceed. We'll have to go back home and start over from the beginning."

Corin thought of Ephitel already hunting him and shook his head. "There is no time to start over. We must press on."

"It's suicide! Perhaps you have heard tales, but I'm the one who's read all the literature there is concerning this island, and I assure you that if we leave this beach, we're dead men."

"And what would you suggest? Wait here and hope some passing vessel puts in at this lovely quay?"

"Don't be a fool. I think we should light a signal fire."

Corin smiled, though it didn't touch his eyes. "A signal fire. To summon aid?"

"Just so."

"And have you forgotten the righteous fury hunting us?"

"The what?"

"The justicar! She's hunting for our hides. If we wait here, there is no one in the world more likely to discover us than her. I'd rather take my chances with the ghosts."

"But . . . we lost her. I saw her on the pier in Baillon. She can't have followed us this far."

Corin laughed. "What do you think a justicar is for? She'll track her target past the edges of the world if it's required. She certainly would not give up on us because we left a port just as she was arriving."

Tesyn stared. "You think she's still on our trail?"

"I'm counting on it," Corin said. "If she didn't follow us, then she went back to that miserable little village, because that was her last solid lead."

"Gods on Attos," Tesyn breathed.

"Aye," Corin said. "She followed us. I'd stake your life on it. The harbormaster must have known where your merchant ship was heading, and I made our intentions loud and clear across Rauchel."

"You did?" Tesyn snapped. "Why?"

"To keep her on our trail," Corin said. "For Auric's sake. After all, we had all the secret wisdom necessary to survive the horrors of the Isle. I hoped that if she dared to follow us this far, she'd disappear forever on the moors."

"A grim thing to hope."

Corin barked a laugh. "Unlikely too. She seems far too smart to take the risk. Instead, she'll search out our beachhead and drop anchor somewhere safe offshore, then wait for us to leave."

Tesyn whistled in appreciation. "You have a devious mind, Corin Hugh."

"It's why I'm still alive."

"And how will we escape her?"

"With the assistance of the elves," Corin said. He had another option up his sleeve—he could step through dream and return to Raentz or Aerome, and leave the justicar fixated on an empty stretch of beach—but now he'd come this far, he wanted to find the elves. He laid a hand on Tesyn's shoulder and caught his eye. "It's time to venture out upon the moors."

Tesyn whimpered, a low, animal sound, but Corin squeezed his shoulder in comfort and said more strongly, "It's time to have a grand adventure."

"I don't have adventures," Tesyn mumbled. "I only tell about them."

"You explored the Wildlands with Auric!"

"Twelve days! Twelve days I camped with him and his mad followers, and they were some of the most terrifying days of my life." He looked Corin up and down dismissively. "And at least then I traveled with a hero."

Corin clapped him on the shoulder. "Today *you* are the hero. If we linger here, we're dead men, sure as sunshine. But if you can find us a way across the moors, we will be legends."

Still Tesyn hesitated. Corin felt an urge to slap him, but instead he displayed all the genuine sincerity he could muster and asked, "Would Auric falter now? Can you truly bear to disappoint him?"

That did the trick. The scholar recoiled as though he'd been hit, but then he shook himself. He straightened his spine and stared Corin in the eye.

"I'm not a coward!"

"You'll be a hero," Corin said. "The farmboy will tell the world *your* tale."

Tesyn laughed at that, but it was in amusement. He still stood tall, and now he turned his gaze toward the distant hills.

Corin stepped up beside him. "You know the way?"

"I know the beginning of the way," Tesyn answered. "Pray the gods that is enough."

Even without the eerie voices of the dead, without the fear of unknown terrors lurking in every shadow, every twist of the land, it still would have been a taxing journey. The pirate and the scholar moved from a rocky beach into a fetid march. The plants there looked fat and greasy, overripe and sharp with thorns. The marsh sucked at their boots and burped up noxious gasses in their wake. An icy wind blew through it all, not strong enough to dispel the odor, but sharp enough to cut through cloak and clothes and steal a body's heat.

Long, curling tendrils of mist rolled across the land like breakers, endless waves rising up from the beach behind them and crashing against the distant highlands. The tendrils seemed almost alive, twin to the unreal mist that Corin ever saw in the presence of Oberon's strange magic. But if these mists bespoke some vast enchantment cloaking this whole land, he could not readily determine its purpose. It was nothing immediate, nothing obvious, but an otherworldly malevolence lay thick and heavy everywhere across this land.

Corin watched and waited, hopeful that at need he would be able to thwart this spell as he had done with others. In the meantime, he did everything he could to ignore the itch it placed between his shoulder blades. He toiled ever onward, pressing hard for higher ground, but every pace he went wore at him. And those voices never once relented. *"Begone! Foul manling, leave our shores! We've seen enough of senseless wars."*

Corin shook his head at that and muttered to himself, "This one is different. This time we will win. I swear by Fortune and by Oberon, I'll find a way."

That marsh cost them hours, but Corin took some comfort in the trackless ground. It would leave no trail for the justicar to follow. She'd find hints enough that they had left the beach, but naught to tell her where they'd traveled through this sodden land.

And then near midday they finally broke free. They left the marsh for higher ground, but that was its own struggle. The hills that bordered the wetlands rose up high and steep, smooth but for the occasional boulder on their sides. Tired as his aching legs were, Corin bent near double and tried to scramble up the slope, catching fistfuls of damp grass when he could brace himself again a stone. Three times he went too fast and lost his footing. Each time he slipped a dozen paces down the slope and had to recover what he'd lost before he could press on.

At last they reached the top, and from there they saw what seemed the whole of the Isle spread before them. It was a vast and changing land—an island nearly as large as all of Raentz—but everywhere below these peaks, the fog that gave the Isle its name lay thick and roiling. If Corin strained his eyes, he could just make out the shape of distant hills, the shadow of a sprawling forest, and the slow, sinuous brown curves of a lazy river.

"There," Tesyn shouted, pointing to the river. "Across the bogs and to the highlands, then down the moors to river's side. Retrace her path into the heartland, where sun and moon almost collide."

Corin frowned. "Your map is a bit of verse?"

"It helps me remember," Tesyn said. "And there is more, lest you're thinking you can leave me behind."

Corin shook his head. "What would I gain from that? At this point, you're near as likely to save my hide as you are to put it in danger. Tell me another verse, and maybe I can help you choose an easier path for the next leg of our journey."

Tesyn sighed. "There is no easy path. I've pieced together fragmentary maps drawn by men who'd made it this far before. There's no more detail in all the library at Rikkeborh than you can see at a glance from here."

"But you said you had read some ancient text—"

"From my uncle's private library. It was set down in a time before this place was called the Isle of Mists, so no one had ever made the connection before."

Corin stared. "It told you all the secrets of this place?"

Tesyn shook his head. "Alas. No. It was also before this place became the nightmare that it is now. In fact, it said little of the land itself, but it made mention of the shrouded city, and I have pieced together everything I could from the fragmentary maps."

"And you know how to get us there?"

"I . . . well, I know how to get us close enough to find it. If we survive the moors. But everything I've read suggests we won't. Not without our supplies. And seeing this . . ."

"Aye?"

"It's worse than I believed. It's everything they said it was. I think we should go back and search for some wreckage from the ship."

"You can search until you die of thirst, or until the justicar finds you. That's the best you could hope for."

"We washed ashore!" Tesyn cried. "Surely some of the wreckage did too. There must be *something* we could salvage."

"We didn't wash ashore. I dragged us ashore, against one of the most fearsome rip currents I've ever seen. I cannot guess how far away the wreckage might have landed."

The scholar's shoulders slumped. "Then we are doomed. Everything I've ever read suggests this terrain is worse than anything the Wildlands can boast."

"Aye. I've heard much the same from other pirates." Corin clapped Tesyn on the shoulder. "Still, we've come this far. We might as well see what we can discover before we die, eh? You say we're heading for the river and then tracking it back north?"

Tesyn nodded, mute.

Corin nodded back. "Then I recommend we start out slightly to the west"—he waved toward the distant shadow of the woods— "and do our best to avoid that forest altogether."

"Why?"

Corin shook his head. It was no more than instinct, but he feared the close confines and creeping shadows of a forest. He'd have preferred the clean cobblestones of a city's streets or the open waves of a sea, but even the rolling moors seemed less sinister than the forest.

Somehow, he couldn't bring himself to admit any of that to the scholar, so he shrugged one shoulder and answered, "Predators."

Tesyn considered it a moment, before nodding. "Very well. I'd planned to join the river as far downstream as possible and track it up, since this vantage doesn't tell us where on its length the shrouded city lies. But I can't believe it's that far downstream, or someone would have found it long before. So we will go northwest as you've suggested, and then bend back to the east as soon as we have passed the woods."

It seemed a solid plan, so they set out. They left the highland ridges for the fog-shrouded moors. And here, despite everything Tesyn had said, they at last found easy going. The wind still whispered vicious threats of murder in their ears, but the earth was smooth and solid, the grass soft and springy underfoot. Here and there, low-lying flowers bloomed, white or pale purple. Corin set a hard pace, taking advantage of the easy terrain, and Tesyn gave no complaint. They hurried north and west, deep into the heart of this strange land.

For hours they trekked across the earth and through the swirling mists. The sun was no more than an angry orange patch off to their left, the sky a slightly darker shade of gray, the world around them roiling fog in all directions.

Then Corin understood the true danger of this land. He drew his knife and slung its tip into the earth a pace ahead of him—at his best guess for north—then he turned in a slow circle, searching the horizon for the hills they'd left before.

But there was no horizon. He turned in the direction he thought was east and strained his eyes, but he could not discern the distant shadow of the woods. Everything was fog.

Sometimes ships lost were at sea in much the same conditions. No ordinary fog would even give a sailor pause, but on rare occasions a fog bank might rise up so thick, a steersman couldn't tell his up from down, let alone his east from west. A man's best hope in times like that was often to spread full sails and pull the oars and hold a steady course straight on, and hope to clear the fog before he drifted too far from his plot. Before he ran aground. Guessing could betray a man in fog like this, and instincts could mislead. Rumors told of crews who'd starved to death, sailing in circles for days and never more than hours from land. But they had lost their bearings.

Corin had never quite believed those tales. The sea was not so fickle a thing as that. Northward had a feel like falling, if a man grew still enough within himself. And east was like a yearning. Even in the densest fog, Corin had never lost his way at sea.

But here . . . here he could imagine it. Here there was no end to the fog bank. There was no escape. He and Tesyn might blunder right into those knotting woods at any moment. Or step into another bog and drown beneath the sucking earth. He'd heard that on the highlands there were chasms, unpredictable and sudden, that might swallow a man whole.

He trembled as he came full circle, grateful for the knife still quivering in the turf. Tesyn was watching him, confused, but Corin couldn't find the words to express this fear.

He looked toward the smear of red that marked the sunset. It was too wide, too uneven to give a pinpoint west, but it might be enough to keep them from blundering in circles. Small hope, that, but it was all he had.

"We stop at dusk," he commanded. "The moment we can't mark the sun's position, we stop moving. And we don't begin again until it shows us east. You understand? If there comes a storm, we wait it out. We never move unless the sun is shining."

The scholar frowned, his gaze fixed on something faraway, almost forgotten. "May I ask you why?"

Corin licked his lips. "The fog. It could kill us if we lose our way. You understand?"

Tesyn thought a moment and nodded. "It clarifies a thing or two. But how do you intend to wait out a storm? We have no food. We have no water. It's barely been an hour since we passed the last stream, and I'm already parched."

"We'll find a way," Corin said. "Perhaps tomorrow we'll get a little better sunlight. Perhaps we'll find some high ground where we can rise above the fog. If nothing else, we'll lay some snares and hope for coneys."

"That's not much of a plan," Tesyn said. There was no accusation in it, and Corin couldn't bring himself to disagree.

"I'll have something better by tomorrow. But come. We've no more than an hour left, and I mean to make headway while we may."

He retrieved his knife and pressed on in the same direction. North, or something like it. They made perhaps another mile—it felt like a mile by the aching in his back—and by then Corin was glancing to his left at almost every other step, and always wondering if there was *really* sunlight there, or if he was imagining it. The fog played games with light sometimes.

He opened his mouth to call the halt, and ran hard into the trunk of a tall oak. It hurt. He staggered back, cursing, and ran into Tesyn. He pulled himself away, fighting for his balance, and bumped into something else.

It swayed away from him, swinging gently on a tether, but not before he heard the ghastly rattle. Not before he saw the bleached-white skull.

A skeleton suspended from a higher limb. Corin drew a calming breath and caught the corpse as it came swinging back. He knew the pattern on the dead man's bandolier, rotted though it was. Only one crew on the Medgerrad had ever worn the slavers' brand as a badge of honor. Corin had learned the trade on Old Grim's ship. He'd worn that bandolier for years, before he'd risen to his own command. And now he found a comrade swinging from a tree on this haunted island.

"What's happening?" The scholar asked behind him, leaning on Corin's shoulder and stretching on his toes to look for himself.

"Worse and worse," Corin muttered, as he recognized the hair-thin cord that had been used to tie a noose. "I was wrong," he answered, louder. Only the elves had ever made such cord. He prayed Fortune they would give him a chance to plead his case. "The fog is not the only thing to fear. Brace yourself, Tesyn. We have a long, dark night ahead."

(**16**)

Corin had hoped to find some stream or pool to camp by, and he certainly had no wish to sleep beneath a hanging tree, but he could see no real alternatives. He could not even pretend to find the sunset now, and with that light gone and all the stars obscured, true dark was falling fast.

"Four paces straight ahead," he told Tesyn over his shoulder. "You'll find the trunk of a tall tree. Walk to it and make a mark with your belt knife at eye level."

"What?"

"Do what I'm telling you," Corin said. "Walk to the tree, mark it, then try to find a comfortable position within reach of it to pass the night."

"That's no answer to my question," Tesyn said. "I heard your yelp."

"I didn't yelp!"

"Your cry of warning, then," Tesyn said, patronizing. "Tell me what you discovered in the mist."

Corin swallowed hard and turned his back on the corpse he'd found. "Another tree," he lied. "And when I strained my eyes, I could see still more, all around us. Despite our best efforts, it seems we've blundered right into the forest we'd hoped to avoid."

"Gods on Attos," Tesyn grumbled. "Who can guess what horrors might await in a place like that?"

Corin didn't answer. An eddy in the swirling mist revealed another form not far beyond the scholar. Tesyn was walking the other way so he didn't notice, but Corin saw the way the figure swayed so gently on the breeze.

He turned away. There was nothing he could do for them, and nothing they could do to him. Gruesome though it was, this tree would make as good a shelter as any other, and it was all they had. He only hoped that he could keep the scholar from discovering their grim companions. The nobleman's frail courage might shatter altogether if he discovered what surrounded them.

Despite his care, Corin almost lost himself again. He'd gone three paces past the tree, arms outstretched and searching, when Tesyn called from behind him, "Corin? Do you plan on scouting? I don't think that's wise."

"No," Corin answered, turning toward the voice. He took a step and his right hand brushed against the oak. The form of Tesyn resolved near his feet, and Corin sank down on his heels to speak with him.

"I anticipate three problems," Corin said, thinking aloud. "We have no supplies, so there's a risk of exposure. There's a risk of starvation. And there's a risk of dehydration."

Tesyn nodded, a shifted shadow not far from Corin's knee. "And don't forget the ghosts." Something went *scritch-scratch* on the ground beside him, but the scholar didn't seem concerned.

"I'm not as worried over ghosts as I am about the elements. By all accounts, this is a temperamental land. If we lose our way, if we blunder blindly forward, we could wander aimlessly until our strength gives out."

"I see," Tesyn said, though he was paying no attention. He had his head bent away, and he was staring down in the direction of that scratching sound. Corin leaned closer, but he could see almost nothing through the fog.

"What's there?" he whispered.

"Hmm?"

"What has your attention?"

Tesyn looked up suddenly, and they were nose to nose. The scholar blinked and frowned at Corin. "What do you think it is? An angry spirit come to haunt us in the night? Or perhaps one of your pirate friends, slipped free of his aging noose."

Corin pulled away and dropped his gaze. "You spotted them?"

"It would have been hard to miss them. I counted half a dozen, but there might well be a man for every limb on this majestic oak. They're pirates, right?"

"Aye. Who else would dare to come here?"

"Who else would provoke so unfriendly a reception?" Tesyn asked in answer. "Why would the elves greet visitors in any other way, if the only visitors they ever see are brigands?"

"Not all pirates are vicious men," Corin said. "The Godlander authorities reserve a special kind of justice for the orphaned, for the homeless and the poor."

Tesyn raised his chin. "Whatever made them outlaws, it's a cruel life, and it makes cruel men."

"Hah! You've missed a cruel point. The elves are outlaws too. They chose this place and use it as a refuge for the selfsame reason pirates do."

"Fascinating," Tesyn said. He turned away, and Corin heard the scratching sound again.

Corin gasped. "You're taking notes?"

"Shouldn't I? What other chance will I ever have to experience this place? If only someone else had thought to document these things, then you and I would not have come here blind."

"But . . . but how? It's dark as sin already."

Tesyn gave a condescending chuckle. "I forget not everyone can write in darkness. I owe my gratitude to a professor at the University who requires all his students to master the skill. He gave every lecture in an unlit cellar room. And yet, somehow, he kept a perfect record of attendance."

Corin stared a moment, though the scholar was no more than a darker shadow in the darkness now. "You . . ." he began, and then he shook his head. "You and I have lived very different lives. But where did you find paper?"

"I have a little book for just this purpose," Tesyn said. "And a case with ink and pen, though I fear the ink will not last long. I do wish I had a grinding bowl."

Corin rolled his eyes. "That's what you wish for? But where'd you keep the book and pen?"

"I wear a little oilskin pouch beneath my tunic," Tesyn said. "I never travel anywhere without a book for notes."

"And food?" Corin asked. "Surely if you thought that far ahead—"

Tesyn heaved a weary sigh. "I *did* think so far ahead, you will recall. I brought food enough to feed us for a month. But all of that is lost beneath the sea."

"And yet you have a pen and ink."

"Indeed. Fortune showed her favor, eh?"

"Oh, aye! It's fortunate that you have the means to record your fancies while I'm trying to find some way to keep us both alive."

"My *deductions*—"

"Are nothing of the sort!" Corin snapped. "You are inventing support for the things you already believed."

"What? How so?"

"This fantasy about the elves all hating pirates! You've written that down as some discovery, but you have no evidence."

"We are surrounded by the evidence!" Tesyn shouted. "Can't you see the significance of all those corpses?"

"I see no proof its elven handiwork," Corin lied. The scholar's theories rattled him, and despite the cord he'd seen, he found himself still anxious to dismiss them. If elves had ever lived here, some more recent traveler might have found the cord and put it to such a grim use. He tried his hardest to believe it, and offered the scholar another explanation. "It could easily be the result of a failed mutiny."

Tesyn paused on the point of a rejoinder. And then a moment later, he snapped his mouth shut with a click. Another moment passed, and then he said, "Or a successful one."

Corin didn't like the thought of that any better. He'd seen a successful mutiny firsthand, and under similar circumstances. If a pirate captain had led his crew to a wandering doom in this godsforsaken fog, he might well have found his end—along with any loyal supporters—hanging from those trees.

"You see?" Corin asked, voice suddenly hoarse. "There's no need to assume it was the elves or to imagine they feel about pirates the way you do."

"I have good reason!"

"You do," Corin said, mollifying him. "But we must set that aside for now and make our plans. As I was saying, exposure and starvation seem the greatest risks, so I intend to find some firewood to keep us through the night."

Tesyn heaved a sigh and levered himself up. "No. You stay here. It should be me."

Corin chuckled. "I trust my sense of direction more than yours, and still I have my fears."

"And I trust my fears more than yours. You've proven useful. I'll give you that. But if you stumble on an elf while you are hunting for firewood, they'll kill you right away, whereas I might have a chance to beg some aid."

Corin flung his hands up. "The ancient elves do not hate pirates!"

A cold, deep voice rang out in answer some way off. "In that, I fear, you are entirely wrong."

Tesyn yelped and called, "Who goes there?" But Corin needed no introduction. He recognized that voice.

The new arrival answered anyway. He came forward, steps soundless even on the bed of dry leaves, but his voice grew louder in the air. "Lay down your arms and abase yourselves. You've met the ghosts of old Gesoelig."

"Kellen," Corin breathed, astonished.

The elf stopped. It was not a sound, but a change in the air. Then he spoke a word in the elven tongue, and fire flared up all around them, cold and blue. It seared away the creeping mists and bathed the canopy beneath the tree in stark relief.

The one who stood before them was a fearsome sight. He stood head and shoulders taller than a man, lithe but with an air of springs compressed.

He was not the same man Corin had encountered in Oberon's dream. That man had died, but it had been a dream within a dream, a half-remembered fantasy.

Here before him was the Kellen who had lived, and time had made a martyr of him. His left arm ended just below the elbow, and a sterling patch hid his right eye. A vicious scar passed beneath the patch as well, running from his hairline to his jaw.

But time and injury hadn't dulled him any. He held himself prepared for battle. Menace hung about him like a winter robe, and judgment was his crown.

"I'll say again, lay down your arms, or I will take them from you."

Corin took a step toward him. "Kellen. You have changed, but I would know you anywhere."

Before Corin had gone a pace, Kellen's sword was in his hand and hovering between them. It didn't waver.

"I do not know you, manling, and I've no wish to. Take your companion and leave these shores forever, or you may decorate our trees. There is no other option."

Corin held his gaze, unwavering. How best to proceed? He might win the warrior's respect by fighting, though he had no hope he could best Kellen Strong. He might persuade the kindhearted man he'd known in Oberon's dream, but perhaps the long years after Gesoelig's fall had scoured away that gentleness.

While Corin was still scheming, Tesyn dashed forward and threw himself down in the dirt at Kellen's feet. "Hang him! He's the dreaded pirate captain Corin Hugh, and he brought me here against my will! Hang him, but I beg you, show me mercy."

Something cold and deadly settled on the elf's expression, and Corin saw his doom written in those eyes.

"Tesyn," Corin said levelly, "I'm going to make you pay for that."

Then Kellen charged.

(17)

Corin had already decided not to fight, and he held to that. He sprang aside from Kellen's charge, rolling as he hit the ground, and came up with the scholar positioned between them. It only bought him a moment, and though Corin's hands itched to draw his blades, if only in defense, he didn't touch them. Instead, he raised his voice.

"I am not a pirate anymore. I'm Oberon's chosen emissary. I beg you for an audience."

Kellen started right, and Corin shifted to keep Tesyn between them, but the elf anticipated that. He'd feinted right and came back left faster than even Corin would have guessed. His blade licked out, passing within a hair of Tesyn. The scholar let out a terrified scream, though it was Corin who took the wound. The blade's tip took a long, shallow gouge from Corin's forearm.

He spun away, gaining distance, and tried to ignore the searing pain of the injury. "I've seen Gesoelig underneath the mountain," Corin cried. "I know what happened there. I know Oberon named you mayor for your valor in fighting Ephitel and tasked you with protecting the survivors."

"You know too much by far," the elf snarled. He came forward again, slashing hard, and Corin chose to try his luck. He stood his ground, unarmed and defenseless, and stared the charging warrior in the eye.

"I want justice for the traitor Ephitel. I need your help!"

That last came out a squeak, despite Corin's best efforts, as the warrior's blade slashed straight and true toward his neck.

It stopped against his flesh. It didn't cut, but the blade lay cold and sharp beneath his jaw.

For a long moment, the elf only stood there breathing. Corin held his gaze.

Tesyn came forward, shaking his head. "You cannot possibly believe him."

"Gods' blood," Corin snarled. "Hold your tongue or I'll have it out!"

The blade's pressure at his throat increased, and Corin clicked his teeth shut. Still he didn't yield.

That seemed to earn some measure of respect from the elf. "You will make no more threats upon this manling while you're on my soil. Do you understand?"

Corin didn't dare nod, so he answered, "Aye."

The elf turned his head to answer Tesyn. "I am afraid I do believe him, until he convinces me otherwise. He knows too much of things he shouldn't know."

"He's a scoundrel!" Tesyn snapped. "He knows his way around a library, but he is *not* to be trusted. String him up or send him away. It's me you'll want to talk to."

Corin didn't answer. He held Kellen's gaze, and after a moment the warrior nodded to him and removed his blade.

"I'll hear your tale, pirate."

"What?" Tesyn cried. "No! At least hear mine first. He's going to trick you."

"No easy feat," the elf said, dismissive.

"Please," Tesyn cried. "I cannot tell you how many great projects he has ruined! But now I have this chance—"

He cut off sharp as the elf's sword swung his way. Kellen stared the scholar down. "You'll hold your tongue or lose it. I keep my own counsel when it comes to prisoners. I don't need your advice."

Tesyn nodded mutely, then shrank away from the sword's point. In truth, Corin admired the scholar's steady nerve as he withdrew three paces, then took his seat upon the trunk of a fallen tree.

Corin turned back to Kellen and found the old warrior waiting. "You have your audience," Kellen said coldly. "Now plead your case."

Corin told him everything. He started with the excavation into Jepta and the buried wall filled with ancient carvings they'd uncovered. He told how he and his old crew had found Gesoelig's tomb, how his men had betrayed him and put the city to the torch, and how Oberon himself had plucked Corin out of the midst of that inferno and dragged him back to relive the tragic history.

Kellen listened patiently. He asked no questions and offered no responses. Corin told Kellen how they'd met within the dream, and everything he'd seen of Kellen's transformation during those dark hours. He spoke of Avery as well, and Maurelle his sister, and named the druids he had met. His voice caught when he named Aemilia, but the elf showed no sign he'd noticed. Still, at each of these names Kellen nodded once in recognition, and Corin took that for confirmation of his tale.

Then at the end, he told how Oberon had cast him from the dream, sending him back to his own time with all the secret knowledge that he'd gained. And also with a sword, stolen from the dream, that had the power to strike down immortal Ephitel.

"I have the sword *Godslayer*," he repeated, emphasizing the name. "And I intend to use it. But I will need your help, and the help of all the loyal elves. Will you aid me, Kellen Strong? Will you right an ancient wrong and help pull down the fiend who killed your rightful liege? Will you gather all your brothers to aid me in my war?"

Heart hammering, he stood waiting for Kellen's answer. At last the old elf tipped his head and wet his lips. And then he answered, "No."

"No?"

The elf nodded. "I have seen too much of that war. My people are no more. Those who haven't left this world are scattered to the winds, and there is nothing left of Oberon but memory. I can no longer even feel joy at the once dear names you've mentioned. You're speaking of a dream that is no more."

"Joy?" Corin snapped. "That's not what I expect of you. I feel no joy at them. I feel pain and anger and a vicious thirst for blood. Those of them that Ephitel has not yet killed, he's driven into hiding. I'll make him pay for what he's done."

"You'll try," Kellen said, his voice infuriatingly calm. "And you will fail. Ephitel has secured his throne. It will take more than some magic sword to end him."

"Aye! That's why I've come to you. You were the most loyal of all Oberon's guards, even when Ephitel was your commander. You made yourself a hero, and in honor of that day, Oberon tasked you with overseeing the rest of his loyal followers. Now is the time to rise to that honor. Summon them to war, and we will avenge your fallen king."

Kellen only shook his head. "I've lost too much to Ephitel. I'm sorry, pirate. You'll have no aid from me."

He turned his back and started for the circle's edge, for the distant darkness beyond the cold blue flames. Somehow Corin knew that if the elf disappeared into that darkness, Corin would never find him again.

"I remember a time when you were wrongly called Kellen the Coward, but somewhere through the ages you have rightly earned the title."

That cut too close to home. In a blink the elf's sword was clear of its scabbard and hovering at Corin's collarbone again. Corin didn't flinch this time; he sneered.

"You'll spill my blood, but not the blood of honest villains? I'll say it again: You've made yourself a coward."

"I cannot so casually throw away the lives of men."

"On the day you first made that choice, Ephitel won his war."

"You're a fool. He won that war the day we started it. Aren't you listening? For how many hundred years did we fight him? It didn't matter. He won every engagement."

"And yet he had no victory. As long as you challenged him, he was a vile usurper. It didn't matter how many of your men he killed, he couldn't win. But the moment you stopped fighting, his victory became complete."

Kellen shook his head. "Sometimes you have to choose your battles."

"Is there a more important contest in all this broken dream than thwarting Ephitel? To the last breath, I'll fight him. If the price for challenging his tyranny is the blood of men, I'll pay in full and never regret a drop."

Kellen scoffed. "The lives of other men may not weigh heavy on your soul—"

Corin shook his head in sharp denial. "Not just other men. I placed my own life in the balance long ago. From the moment I saw old Gesoelig all in flames by Ephitel's actions. I'll pay with my life and any other lives I can claim, if it means bringing down that traitor."

Kellen considered him a moment, then turned away. "Then go ahead. May Fortune grant you long enough a life to see how bad a choice you're making. I made the same for three hundred years, and now I have regretted it for twice as long. Go in peace, noble pirate, and trouble me no more."

"Kellen, listen to me. The tide has turned in our favor. Oberon himself granted me a gift that changes everything. This time—"

"You will have to fight your war without me," Kellen said again. "I will not leave these shores again until I return to Faerie."

Corin couldn't quite conceal a sneer. "Why not go on now? What could possibly keep you here? It can't be hope. It can't be a thirst for vengeance. Because I have brought you both upon a platter."

Kellen almost didn't answer. Perhaps it was Corin's clear contempt that moved him. In the end he stalked across the clearing to jab a vicious finger at Corin's chest.

"I have watched the death of hope and nearly drowned in my own thirst for vengeance. Everyone I loved, every name I ever knew, all burned to ash centuries ago in this mad war you are so hungry for. One friend still remains. I only wait for him to see what I have seen." He turned away, staring south and east toward the mainland, and after a moment he heaved a weary sigh. "Perhaps I cannot wait for him much longer."

Corin frowned. It could be anyone, but some spark of desperate hope whispered that this friend might prove a better opportunity even than Kellen himself. He cocked his head. "This friend—"

"He has no more patience for your war than I do," Kellen said. "He distracts himself with foolish games, and he courts death in the very shadow of our enemy. All for a pair of pretty eyes. The fool."

"Avery," Corin said. "Avery of House Violets. Fortune favor, you know where I can find him."

Kellen's eyes narrowed. "You speak well and listen poorly. I have no interest in aiding you, and certainly none in setting you upon a friend."

"But if I can find him," Corin cried, "if I can convince him to join me in my fight, surely you would fight beside him."

Another man might have missed the hesitation, the wounded wince that glanced across the elf's expression, but Corin caught it. It happened in half a heartbeat, and then the elf mastered himself. He tilted back his head and fixed a frigid stare on Corin. "I have said all I mean to say to you. Go in peace, and may Ephitel forget your name forever."

Corin was still searching for some answer, some new approach, when a footstep from the forest drew his attention. He turned in place, prepared to chastise Tesyn for the interruption.

But the scholar still lurked at the far edge of the clearing. By the look of things, he'd spent the whole interview crouched on the fallen log, scribbling in his precious book.

But now the book lay open on the ground, his inkwell spilled in dark black splotches on the bark of the fallen tree. Tesyn was standing with a stranger's arm across his throat and a meaty hand clapped over his mouth.

A dozen other bruisers like the one who held Tesyn stood around the clearing, spread out to make a neat perimeter. And at their head came the golden-haired justicar who had stalked Corin across two nations. She glowed with a divine light despite the failing dusk. Trusting her men to guard the trap, she alone came forward, empty-handed, to challenge Kellen and Corin both.

"I am afraid he cannot simply go in peace," she said. "And I'll make sure Ephitel knows both your names by heart."

18

Run, Corin!" Kellen shouted. "She's a justicar. *Run!*"

He shoved Corin hard to get him started, then raised his sword and threw a cut toward her neck. She moved faster than a mortal should have been capable of. Corin breathed a curse as he watched her duck the expert slash, withdraw half a step, and draw her own blade fast enough to meet his on the counterswing.

The justicar's heavy blade tolled like a bell from the force of the elven warrior's blow, but neither arm yielded and neither blade would break. She rolled her point around his rapier twice and then beat once at his blade and chopped toward his head.

Kellen had no choice but to withdraw himself. He yielded a single step, but that bought her all the time she needed.

Corin had not been idle, but the whole exchange had taken mere moments. He had his dagger drawn and slashed at her back, but as Kellen retreated, the justicar spun in place, twisting her wrists, and the heavy blade lashed out toward his knees. He had to fling himself aside in an awkward leap to avoid the strike, and that left her time enough to catch her breath.

She used it to shout an order. "Kill the elf!" Corin felt a flash of sadness as the dozen soldiers charged the clearing, but his own fear drove it from his mind as the justicar came charging after him.

Her heavy armor should have slowed her. That monstrous blade should have cost her speed and accuracy. It didn't, as far as he could tell. She lunged at him while he was still falling, and he barely dodged the stabbing point. He crashed down on the ground and threw himself into a roll just in time to escape her. The blade whispered as it cut the air behind him.

His roll slammed him hard against the same fallen trunk the scholar had used for a seat. The impact bruised his shoulder blades and drove the air from his lungs, but he didn't dare hesitate for a heartbeat. Gasping for breath, he dove forward off his knees, narrowly dodging another strike. As he landed, he closed his fist around the fallen inkwell. He rolled onto his back and hurled the bottle with practiced precision straight at her eyes.

A snake could not strike as fast as that woman moved. She flicked the heavy broadsword like it was a courtier's fan and intercepted his projectile in its flight.

She had not anticipated that it was made of glass. Tough though the little bottle was, it shattered beneath the force of her sword's cut, and the sharp-edged shards continued in their flight. She had to flinch away, to close her eyes against the tiny splinters, and one of the large pieces carved a gash along her left cheekbone as it passed by.

More importantly, it distracted her for half a heartbeat. Time enough, at least for Corin to find his feet and draw his little blades. He wasn't sure how much success he could hope for against that mighty sword, but he could do more standing than scurrying in the dirt.

She blinked twice and then took her guard. Heedless of the wound that fanned bright red blood down her pale cheek, she advanced on Corin once again. He retreated slowly, careful of his footing, staying just outside the reach of her deadly blade.

To his surprise, she spoke. "I have a great deal of authority," she said. Her voice came even, unstrained by all her exertion, and it showed no hint of the emotion that had driven her to execute him. "I do not have to kill you here, you understand. For the first time in centuries, I have been asked to eliminate a threat to my master. Killing you would probably suffice, but I would prefer to secure that sword. Give it to me, and I will let you live."

Corin leaped back to avoid a vicious cut, then narrowly parried another with the edge of his dagger. Even in passing, the shock of her swing slammed up his arm and left it numb below the elbow.

He suppressed a curse and even forced a weak smile. "I had not heard of justicars being so forgiving."

"You have proven yourself a nuisance, and without the sword you're harmless." She seemed to think a moment, and then she shrugged. "Dead you're harmless too."

She came on with a renewed vigor then, and it was everything he could do to retreat. She knocked the dagger from his grip when he tried to parry another blow, and smashed the knife from his left hand with her counterstroke. She clipped his thigh, and hot blood washed down his leg, slicking his pants to his skin. Another strike caught him just above the knee, and though the cut was shallower, it hurt like thunder. Both injuries slowed him too. She had every advantage over him. He couldn't beat her. He could barely keep his feet, and with every slash of her sword she came closer to gutting him.

Even as that crossed his mind, she lunged forward, feinted high, then chopped low faster than he could react. She turned the blade so it caught him with the flat, but it crashed into the side of his left knee with all her force behind it. The knee buckled instantly, and Corin spilled onto his back. She brought the sword around to rest its heavy tip against his breastbone. The weight of it was a threat. All she had to do was relax and the blade would pin him to the earth.

She watched until she saw that understanding in his eyes. Then she nodded to herself. "I'll only ask you once," she said. "Give me the anomalous sword. Now."

She thought he had it here? Corin's mind raced while he tried to put the pieces together. Jeff had said that Jessamine could find anomalies. Wasn't that how Ephitel had found the cottage in the woods? And this justicar was Ephitel's bloodhound. Was she somehow in communication with him now? Was he passing along the druid's information so that this creature could track him even here, far beyond the Godlands' boundaries?

And then an inspiration struck him, and he was astonished it hadn't occurred to him before. He blinked up at her and cocked his head. "Oh! You're Jessamine."

She showed her teeth. "Charmed, I'm sure. Now, where's the sword?"

He licked his lips, searching for some way to at least gain more information. But he was badly hurt and fading fast, and she was something from a nightmare. He couldn't touch her. He would have to disappear through dream again. It meant leaving Tesyn and Kellen in the justicar's power. It meant all the effort

Corin had spent to come here was wasted. But he would gain nothing dying here upon her blade, and he could see no way to overcome her. He cursed inside his head and tried to think of somewhere worth escaping to.

She seemed to know he wasn't going to answer her. She tipped her head in something like a shrug and shifted her grip upon the heavy sword, tensing to drive it home.

And then a rock the size of Corin's fist slammed into the side of her head. She staggered sideways, dragging the sword limply across Corin's chest. It took her just a moment before she came to herself and raised the sword, but that was long enough to leave a searing, jagged furrow in his flesh.

Even as she raised her weapon, Kellen met her in combat. His rapier rang against her blade and then dipped to cut beneath it. She retreated. He feinted, again and again, then drove forward in a sudden lunge that sent her reeling backward out of reach. As fast as she had been, the elf was faster. Now that he had his feet beneath him, he was the better swordsman.

Corin had no time to glory in the thought. Even as it struck him, he picked up other tiny details. The elf's dark clothes stuck to him in half a dozen places, slick with blood. His eyes were tight around the corners, pinched with pain. His left foot dragged a bit as he repositioned. He was fast and furious as a winter windstorm, but he was also almost spent.

Corin glanced toward the clearing, and he was unsurprised to see all twelve of Jessamine's soldiers on the ground. The elf had overwhelmed them all, but he had paid a price for it. And now, weakened, he went against the justicar alone.

Corin climbed to his knees. His wounds burned fiercely. His bones ached. If Kellen was weakened, Corin was very nearly undone. But he had to find some way to help his ally.

He was searching for his fallen blades when Kellen stopped beside him. "I thought I told you to run." He wore sweat like a mask across his face.

Corin flashed him a smile. "I could hardly leave you here."

"Go!" Kellen shouted, unamused. "I'll hold her off."

Corin spotted his dagger three paces away and scrambled forward, but Kellen kicked him in the side hard enough to knock him over. "I said go!"

"You can't take her alone."

Jessamine sneered. "You both belong to Ephitel. No one's leaving unless it's on my leash."

As she said the words, the gentle light that hung around her began to pulse. It grew sharper, brighter, until it was almost painful to behold. Shining like the sun, she charged for Kellen.

The ancient warrior cursed beneath his breath and then closed his eyes. Something hard as steel smashed into Corin and drove him back. That familiar gray mist came washing in, but it was not the thin cloud Corin had seen so often, nor the wildly questing tendrils. It was a flood. It poured past Corin and welled up around Kellen and Jessamine just as the two clashed in battle once again.

Corin scrambled to his feet. He snatched his knife up off the ground and dashed into the mist. It didn't yield. He slammed against empty air that had become solid as a wall of stone, and Corin crumpled to the ground again. No light penetrated the roiling fog, but he could hear the distant ringing sound of steel. He pounded the knife's hilt against the fog, but it refused to yield. The distant sounds grew more intense, almost frenzied, and someone cried in pain.

Desperate, Corin closed his eyes and fixed his mind on the area within that dome. He focused on the ink-stained trunk and stepped through dream.

His mind slammed against the barrier as surely as his body had. Lights flashed behind his eyes, and he groaned at the sudden pain. Kellen was in there, dying.

He'd done all of this for Corin. After everything he'd said, all his fierce refusals, he'd chosen to sacrifice his life so Corin could escape. It was just what Corin would have expected of the man he met in Oberon's strange dream.

And he had called the man a coward. He staggered to his feet and tried one more time to go to Kellen's aid. He pressed a hand against the wall of mist.

And now it yielded. Corin grunted in surprise and threw his weight against the wall. It held for half a heartbeat; then it melted around him, and he stumbled forward into the dome.

Corin raised his knife, ready to throw, but even as he scanned the empty clearing, all the mist dissolved. The ground showed the clear signs of Kellen's struggle with Jessamine, but elf and justicar alike were gone.

Her guards still littered the ground, unmoving. Corin noticed with some small distaste that Tesyn was still there as well, crouched against the tree where he'd been held. Blood in great quantity stained the shoulder of his fine white shirt, but it was not his own. One glance showed Corin that the guard who had held him prisoner now lay behind him on the ground, pierced through the heart by Kellen's rapier. It had probably been done before the fight with Jessamine, and all this time the scholar had cowered there, watching.

Corin fell to one knee. For a long time he only knelt there, gasping for breath. Fortune favor, what had happened here? He stared down at the forest floor, searching for some hint in the damage made by boots and blades. He saw no blood but his own.

The scratch across his chest no longer seared. It throbbed now, slow and hot, like a forge fire beneath the bellows. He knew that for a bad sign, but he could scarcely attend to it now. A step through dream might take him to the druids, but he could not guess what welcome he might find there. Surely they wouldn't let him die. But they would not allow him any liberty either.

The Nimble Fingers might have the skills to save him. They would certainly provide a place to hide. And while he convalesced, he could make use of their spy network. He was not yet sure *how* that might lead him to Ephitel, but it was the last resource remaining to him.

Something tugged at his memory. Something about the Nimble Fingers? Something Kellen had been saying? But his thoughts seemed heavy for some reason. Sluggish. He frowned and tried to trace the thread of memory, but it slipped from his grasp.

Something about Kellen? No. He'd lost it. The Nimble Fingers, though. They could help him. Corin closed his eyes and fixed his mind upon a bustling common room richly dressed in pure black velvet, but before he could step through the dream, someone spoke his name.

"Corin? You're alive?" The scholar's voice rang with surprise and just a touch of disappointment. "I'd thought for sure I watched her stab you. Isn't that what set the elf in such a fury?"

Corin almost left. He'd come to hate the bright-eyed nobleman for more than just his social class. But Corin had made a promise to Auric, and he might still need the farmboy's special talents. Repeating that within his head, he exhaled heavily and opened his eyes.

The scholar was just now rising. He looked more than a little unsteady on his feet as he brushed himself down, but he showed no signs of injury. That same old curious sparkle danced in his eyes despite everything that had happened here.

Corin dragged himself to his feet so he could face the man standing. He clenched his jaw against the pain and answered. "The elf was trying to protect me. He gave his life for my freedom. Surely now you'll recognize how important a role it is I play."

The corner of the scholar's mouth turned down; he was clearly thinking hard, but then he shook his head. "No. I just don't see it. It was remarkable to watch him fight, though, wasn't it? And then to catch a glimpse of Faerie!"

"Of what?"

"Of Faerie. Where'd you think they went? The mad old elf tore a hole right through reality and left a gaping window into the land beyond."

Corin's shoulders slumped. "He said he meant to wait for Avery." How many souls would he have to send to the next world? So far all of them had been for nothing. Would that ever change?

Tesyn came forward, eyes glowing with excitement. "I think he did it to counter her magic. Did you see the way she glowed? I've never seen a justicar all full of righteous fury before. Not like that. It was giving her an edge, but then he tore the world apart and kicked her through into Faerie, and the light whipped out like a candle in the wind. You should have seen the shock in her eyes."

"You mean he won? He killed her?"

The scholar shrugged. "I couldn't say. The world closed up behind them, and then you were here and they were not." He fixed Corin with a disapproving glare. "You promised I would have a chance to speak with him."

Corin arched an eyebrow. "You blame me for this?"

"Who else is there to blame? She knew your name. She said she was here for you. And what is this anomalous sword she mentioned?"

"Nothing you should concern yourself about. Now come, we must tend our wounds and then make plans to get you home."

The scholar frowned, skeptical. "I don't believe I am prepared to dress battle injuries. That will have to fall to someone else."

Corin looked around the battlefield. There was no one else but corpses. He met the scholar's eyes. "A bandage will do the job for now. But don't you know the hidden secrets of the world? Herb lore? Surely at the University you learned to make a poultice to cure any wounds. A potion to restore vigor?"

"Not really. Sorry. I mostly learned the names of dead men."

"In seven languages."

"Oh. Sure. That part's important too."

Corin groaned. "I hate to inconvenience you, but I am sorely wounded."

"*You* are sorely wounded?" Tesyn asked. "All you've lost is blood. You cannot guess how much of my life I spent on this mission—how many months I searched for clues to find the last of the ancient residents of Jezeeli. I brought you here against my better judgment—"

"You begged Kellen to string me up."

"And with good reason! But then he didn't. He talked to you like an equal, and for a moment I dared to believe we might salvage this venture. I thought perhaps when you were done bickering with him, you might introduce me, perhaps convince him to speak freely, and that might at last have undone some small measure of the injury you did when you stole my family's ancient map."

"I have, in fact, apologized for that," Corin said.

"No. No, you haven't."

"Well . . . I considered it."

Tesyn gaped. A moment later he waved it away. "After all of this, I thought perhaps you had redeemed yourself. And then you picked a fight with him over your mad schemes and brought an angry justicar down upon us."

"I am trying to undo the ancient wrong of Jezeeli's fall! I'm trying to break the power of a tyrant god. It's not just some mad scheme!"

The scholar shrugged. "Well? What has come of it? Nothing at all. Now we've wasted all this time, and it will take another age for us to return to civilization, and weeks more after that to get to Aerome."

"Aerome?" Corin asked. "Why Aerome?"

The scholar blinked. "Don't you ever listen? The elf told you of his companion. This Avery."

"Somewhere in the Godlands. That's all he said."

"No! He said it was in the very shadow of their enemy. Where could he mean but Aerome? Where else would a man go to taunt the tyrant god?"

Corin stared, stunned. It's where he himself had gone. And everything he knew, he'd learned from the Nimble Fingers— Avery's own organization. Could it be so simple?

He barked out a laugh. Aerome, where all of this had started. Aerome, where he would find the richest Nimble Fingers in the world. He took an unsteady step closed to scholar and tapped him on the chest.

"You know," he said, "in some ways, you're a very clever lad."

The scholar frowned, wondering what was coming next.

Corin withdrew a step and spread his hands. He closed his eyes and offered a slow smile. "In other ways, you aren't very smart at all."

Then he fixed his mind upon Aerome, and left the scholar in the woods alone.

19

Corin always liked to make a splashy entrance, but this proved one of his best. He arrived within the busy common room of Aerome's Nimble Fingers just at midnight—the tavern's busiest hour—in tattered clothes and soaked with blood.

He drew himself up tall despite the pain that wracked his body and proclaimed to the room at large, "Aerome! Your hero has returned. No accolades required, but I could dearly use a bed. And someone be so kind as to summon me the elf named Avery. I would have a word with him."

Then he swept a stern, imperious gaze around the hall and collapsed upon the floor.

Corin regained consciousness in an unfamiliar chamber. It took him a moment to recall the circumstances of his arrival, but when he did, it only sharpened his confusion, because he knew at a glance that this was not one of the guest rooms at the shady tavern.

His hands were not tied. That was promising. And he was still alive.

He lifted himself upright and succeeded without any great difficulty, though the skin across his chest began to itch fiercely. He felt the tension of a bandage tight enough to hold his ribs together, which seemed a bit too much for a flesh wound. But as he rose, his vision washed dizzily. Perhaps it had been a graver injury than he imagined.

His knee too still throbbed slow and hot, but he could feel the familiar weight of a poultice there, wrapped tight as well. He tried to keep that leg still as he adjusted on his bed and looked around.

It was not a prison cell, though the size was right. And the quality of furniture. He shifted uncomfortably on the thin, hard mattress. A dressing table stood beside the bed, backed by an enormous mirror that must have cost at least as much as all the room's other contents combined. Three wig stands on the dressing table held three wigs in very different colors, and a fourth stood bare. More than a dozen jewelry pots in outlandish colors stood before the mirror, all arranged in careful rows.

He worked some moisture into a painfully parched throat, then tried his voice. "Hello? Am I alone?"

His wounds still ached, and a vicious hunger worried at his belly. Whatever sleep he'd gotten had been spent repairing all his injuries. He felt weak and weary still.

"Hello?" he tried again. "Who brought me here?"

A young lady peeked in at the outer door; then she nodded to herself and came in. "Thought I heard something," she said, offering him a smile. "I'm glad you're awake. The physician said it might be weeks."

Corin felt a stab of fear. "Physician?" He looked beneath his sheets to confirm he still had all his limbs, but still couldn't shake the quiet anxiety that word always sparked in him.

She laughed. "Don't worry. He's a careful man. And discreet."

"That sounds expensive."

"Very." She turned up her smile. "I hope you're worth it."

Corin looked around the room again. "There aren't many actresses who can afford such services."

"You of all people should know better than to judge by first appearances."

Corin arched an eyebrow. "Oh? You know me so well?"

"You have quite the reputation. Born a pauper, turned a pirate, and raised to a captain before you'd seen twenty years."

"I like to keep my feet moving."

She smirked. "I'd say so. Because in the last year you have discovered some new magic, made friends with the ancient druids, become a hero of the Nimble Fingers, murdered poor Giuliano in his own house—"

"Technically," Corin corrected her, "it was just outside the house."

She laughed. "And now you've spat in Ephitel's face, it seems, and blackened the eye of his favorite justicar."

Corin whistled low. "You are well informed."

She preened. "I try to be."

She was dangerous. Beautiful too, but deadly things were often beautiful. She wore her long black hair tied back, showing off a pixie face of pale skin and huge, innocent eyes above the most mischievous smile he'd ever seen.

He blinked in sudden recognition. "I know you!" He'd met this girl before, though she had not made such a strong impression then. He'd needed a small favor following the Ethan Blake affair, to help keep Auric and the princess safe from scheming Vestossis, and this was the girl who had procured the document he needed. "You went by the name of Jane."

"You remember!" She clapped her hands, the picture of a child delighted at a bit of recognition. But her eyes were sharp and measuring.

Corin shook his head. "I'd never thought to make a Nimble Finger of an actress, but I begin to see the value."

She gave a performer's bow, then dropped the act. Her stance relaxed, but her expression only grew sharper. "Not an actress myself," she said, coming over by the bed, "but some of my best friends are."

"But you *are* of the Nimble Fingers?"

She hesitated half a heartbeat before nodding. "I am," she said. "In heart, at least, I am."

That answer did not surprise him. There weren't many women in the organization, though Corin had never truly understood the reason. Some of the most deadly folks he'd ever known were women, and certainly some of the cleverest. But membership required a sponsor, and some old habits had proven hard to break. Few men chose to take female protégés.

But somehow—without the support of the Nimble Fingers behind her—this girl had stolen from the paranoid and powerful Vestossis a document of great value to them. Such a feat could not go long overlooked. And she could not have done that on a lark. She must have had someone teaching her.

"Keep trying," Corin said. "You'll find a place someday."

"Hah! I will be leading them someday. But that's not why you're here."

"Oh?" Corin asked, a sudden chill chasing up his spine. "Why am I here? I went to the Nimble Fingers, trusting them to hide me away somewhere safe while I recuperated."

"I did already mention the very expensive physician, didn't I?"

"You did," Corin said. "And now you want some favor from me in return?"

She grinned. "You *are* as clever as they say."

"I'm sorry," Corin said. "You've earned a debt from me, but I am caught up in events of huge importance. I don't have time to train you up and sponsor you."

She cocked her head, considering him for a moment. "Training me? Unless you've been skulking in the shadows on your poop deck, you are half a decade out of practice. When was the last time you picked a lock?"

More than a thousand years ago, Corin thought, though he didn't say so. He'd had to brush off rusty skills to survive his time in Oberon's strange dream. But if it wasn't that, what did she want him for?

"Do you mean to hand me to Ephitel?" he asked.

She rolled her eyes. "I mean to ask you questions. Nothing more. I want to know what you know about Avery."

He blinked. "You . . . what?"

She sank down on her knees beside his bed. For the first time since she'd entered the room, she looked entirely unguarded. She licked her lips and clasped her hands together. "You announced to the Nimble Fingers common room that you were looking for an elf named Avery. I've invested a small fortune seeking any hint of information on an elf of the same name, and then the newest legend of the Nimble Fingers appears within reach of the table where I'm eating and announces that he knows the man. I *need* to know what you know."

"You know an elf named Avery?"

She looked away. "I am trying to, but he wears secrets like a second skin."

Corin nodded to himself. Kellen had said that Avery had a project keeping him around. This girl could well have been enough to trap the old elf's heart here in Hurope. That would explain where she had learned her trade without the Nimble Fingers to support her.

And by the expression on her face, Avery's was not the only heart affected.

"I need his aid," Corin said, measuring his words. "The future of this world might well depend on his goodwill for me. Do you understand?"

She thought a moment, then shook her head. "No. But I will listen."

"I might know some portion of the secrets you demand. I don't know them all, but I likely know a few."

Her eyes lit up at that, and Corin laid a consoling hand on her shoulder. "But if Avery has kept it from you, how can I risk his ire? I need him, Jane. I can't afford to betray his confidences."

"Surely you can tell me something."

Corin's heart went out to her. She had him wholly in her power and deeply in her debt, but she'd forgotten all of that. Or she was too kind of heart to use it. Instead, she begged him. What sort of hold did this Avery have over her?

It didn't matter. Corin was not so blinded, and he was certainly not softhearted. He saw his opportunity and took it.

"I can see a way," he said, his voice warm with sincere encouragement. "Take me to Avery. Convince him to hear me out, and I'll gain his permission to tell you what I know."

She sighed and shook her head. "You won't. He guards his secrets like an ancient treasure."

Corin considered her a moment. He had another card to play, but it was a greater gamble. How good an actress was she? How sincere were these lovesick sighs?

He chose to trust in them. He looked left and right, then leaned closer and lowered his voice. "There is another way. Help me gain the aid I need from him, and then I will be willing to endure his wrath. I'll tell you anything that won't endanger him."

"I'd never hurt him," Jane insisted.

"I believe you, but he's beset by enemies you can't begin to comprehend. Everything he does, he does from desperate need."

That only added to the man's romantic mystique. Corin saw the fire kindle hotter in the lady's eyes, and he knew he'd judged well.

He squeezed her shoulder. "Help me in this, and I promise I'll help you in return."

"Upon your name?"

He shook his head. "I have no name, but I will swear it on sweet Fortune's favor. May I never win another gamble if I let you down."

She dropped her head against his knees at that, a penitent in benediction, and whispered quietly, "Thank you. Thank you. Thank you."

A pang of guilt twisted in his stomach, but he ignored it. He patted her head and asked her softly. "When? How soon can you arrange it?"

"I . . . you won't be fit to walk the streets for days yet. But I can bring him here. I'll . . . I don't know when. But I will make it happen soon."

"And he will listen to me?"

"I'll do everything I can." She scrambled to her feet, eyes wide with excitement. "He does not exactly come when I call, but I should have him here within a day or two. In the meantime, get some rest and eat whatever Mary brings you. Understood?"

"Understood. But can you carry a message to the Nimble Fingers tavern keeper?"

She hesitated, frowning. "I would prefer to keep your secret close."

"I'll tell him nothing. But I have great need of information."

"Ask me, and I'll provide it. I have resources of my own."

Corin could hardly doubt that. She was friends with Avery, and she had casually discussed the fortune she'd laid out to gather rumors. Then there was the physician, and this girl had spoken of Guiliano Vestossi with a casual familiarity. Unless Corin missed his guest, she was gentry born and bred. This Jane came well connected, and she would prove a mighty useful asset if he could just secure her.

That process always started with a show of trust. Corin bit his lip. How much did he dare reveal? He stared into her coal-black eyes, and she met his gaze unflinching.

"I need to know the date," he said at last. "How much time have I lost?"

She nodded to herself as though she had expected that very question. "You've been in my care for half a week," she said, "but I don't think that's what you're asking. It's April 1st tomorrow. You were seen in Rauchel, Raentz, in late November, and then you disappeared completely for three months." She caught her breath, before asking him in a halting voice, "How long has it been for you?"

"Thirty hours," Corin said. "Thirty hours, more or less. And I have lost the winter."

She nodded, unsurprised. "Jessamine hasn't. She's been busy." Corin's surprise must have shown in his expression, and some hint of the questions that flooded his mind, because Jane leaned forward and nodded encouragingly. "You see? I can help you. And I won't waste your time begging for explanations or doubting the things you claim."

Corin shook his head. "You are remarkably informed."

"Then ask me what you need to know."

Corin's mind buzzed with questions about the justicar. She hadn't lost the winter. She'd been busy. The thought made Corin cold. She'd survived her trip to Faerie, then. Poor Kellen. And how had she spent her time, when he was nowhere to be found?

He shook his head. There would be time enough to dwell on that later. If he were in any imminent danger here, Jane would have told him so already. Better to focus on the things he could control first. So he bowed his head and prepared his list. "I need to learn the whereabouts of a dwarf named Ben Strunk. Last I saw him, he was leaving Aerome for Raentz, and he might have had that justicar on his trail."

Jane shook her head. "Then pray the gods show mercy to his soul, because there won't be much left of his body."

"I'm not sure she even knows he exists, and I'd put my money on the dwarf either way. He has a knack for surviving. See what you can discover."

"I will."

"Good. And ask after Princess Sera. She has been missing for a while now, but I can't believe the Vestossis have given up the search. Find out how much they know."

"Do you mean her harm?"

"Would it trouble you if I did?"

The girl gave a shrug. "I only met her once. She mostly made me sad for her. I don't suppose you could do much worse to her than her family's already done."

"I couldn't," Corin agreed. "And I won't. No, I mean her well, but I need to know how much her enemies know."

"I'll find that out for you. Anything else?"

"You've spoken more than once about that justicar. Pretty little slip of a thing? Blonde?"

"Your information may be out of date. She's lost an eye and half an arm, and she's become a raving killer. I doubt you'd find her pretty now."

Well. Kellen hadn't died without a fight. Corin nodded. "I begin to think you know more about my life than I do. I'll need a full report on the justicar."

She nodded. "I'll get the latest for you and tell you everything at once. Until then, just focus on recovering. You're going to need your strength."

She hesitated in the doorway and threw one last glance back behind her. "It's bad," she said. "It's . . . it's very bad."

Jane did not return that day, though Mary did check in on him. Mary proved to be the actress—both the one whose room he'd stolen and the one whom Jane had called her dearest friend. Mary seemed almost worshipful of Jane, and she kept insisting she wasn't at all bothered to lend her room to Corin for a few days. Not at all. Good for Jane.

It took Corin longer than he'd have cared to admit before he realized what Mary was assuming. She mistook Corin for Jane's gentleman caller, and more than once he caught her looking him up and down, nodding to herself, and muttering beneath her breath, "Good for Jane. Good girl."

He couldn't guess whether Mary's belief came from her own suspicions or from a cover story Jane had invented, and he didn't dare jeopardize it in the latter case. So he held his tongue and tolerated the attention.

Apart from that, she was not bad company. The girl was easy on the eye, a redhead when she went without a wig, and playful with a sort of barmaid charm. Twice a day she brought him meals—beans and bread, or barley stew or something of the like, hearty and filling fare for the poor convalescent.

And in truth, he needed it. He began to suspect that he'd suffered some malingering infection, because the wounds he'd suffered held him to his bed for days.

For all the woman's charms, she still sparked a silent curse in Corin every time she peeked through the door. He wanted Jane back. He wanted her information. And even more than that, he wanted her to bring him Avery.

Three days he had to wait before she finally returned, and when she did, she was alone. She'd asked after Ben Strunk, but all she'd really learned was that he'd gone to Raentz. Bourgonne, some said, or Rauchel or Ris. Some said he was now the protégé of the Raentzian king. But there was nothing certain, nothing Corin could use.

"Keep trying," he insisted. "Trace the rumors, track them down, *find out where he is.*"

"Why is this dwarf so important?" Jane asked. "From everything I've heard, he's something of a knave. Perhaps barely better than a dandy, and I don't think that's ever been said of a dwarf before."

"He is no common dwarf," Corin agreed. "It doesn't matter what you've heard. If we cannot find him, everything is lost."

"Then we'll find him," Jane said. "No matter what, he doesn't seem to be in hiding. There are rumors everywhere. We only have to find the truest ones, and we will find your dwarf."

Corin smiled at that. She was nearly quoting Nimble Fingers dogma there, and that dogma had been written down by Avery himself. It gave him hope that she was everything she claimed to be.

"I've faith in you," he said. "I only pray that you'll be swift about it."

"My best resources are at work."

"And Avery?"

She frowned at that and turned away. "He . . . I haven't heard from him. Not yet. He isn't often gone so long."

"These are trying times," Corin said, as much for his own comfort as for hers.

But she only looked more stricken. "Then you've heard."

"Heard?" Corin hadn't meant to, but he'd broached the subject he'd been dwelling on for days. Her final words as she had left him, and she'd left this for the last now that she'd finally returned. What had become of Jessamine, that it troubled this young woman so?

Corin shook his head and sighed. "I have heard nothing."

"I haven't had the heart to tell you," Jane said, sinking down beside him on the bed. "I'd really hoped that I could find some good news to bring you first, something to balance out the rest. But there's been nothing, and I could hardly leave you stewing."

Corin swallowed his sarcastic answer. Three days had certainly felt like stewing. Instead, he offered her an understanding smile. "I've seen hard times before. What are we facing now?"

"Jessamine," Jane said, "has gone to war against the Nimble Fingers."

Of all the bad news Corin had imagined—very bad, Jane had said—this possibility had never crossed his mind. He blinked up at Jane, his jaw hanging open, and finally he asked her, "What?"

"Jessamine has gone to war against the Nimble Fingers. She's roused the armed authority of all the civilized nations in the name of Ephitel and called on them to stamp out the organization in every corner of Hurope."

"Impossible," Corin breathed. No one would attack the Nimble Fingers. But he could recall the feverish look in her pale green eyes. He could recall the threats she'd made against him. And if she had survived her trip to Faerie, if she had wrung some information from Kellen there, it would have pointed her to the organization like a hound after a hare.

"Unreasonable," Jane said, "but all too possible. And effective. Every city has its shady tavern, and they are not close-kept secrets. The first raid was right here in Aerome, on a Saturday at midnight. Jessamine came herself, leading a contingent of the city guard. She'd sent a dozen investigators to infiltrate the place beforehand, and as soon as the guards came dashing through the door, the investigators were already waiting with a list of names."

Corin shook his head, imagining the raid. The Nimble Fingers was an open secret, a tool at least as useful to local nobility as to its members. That utility had been their aegis through the years, far more than anonymity. But if the reigning powers turned against them, it would be a bloodbath.

Corin shuddered. "What became of them? The ones she took away?"

"Questioned," Jane said. "Extensively. Then all but one or two were hanged in public squares."

"Gods' blood!" Corin spat.

"That's been the pattern," Jane said, her voice cold. "All across Hurope. Everywhere she's gone, she has taken our best men and put them to the question, then put them to the sword."

Corin didn't want to ask the question, but he had to know the answer. "How many?"

She shrugged. "It's hard to say precisely. Two hundred at the low end, but it could be near a thousand now."

Corin covered his eyes and drew a heavy breath. "This is all because of me. A thousand men have paid because of me."

It took a moment before she answered, but in the end she said, "Nobody blames you. You're more a hero to them now than ever."

Corin dropped his hands to meet her gaze. "That doesn't mean I'm wrong."

"No."

"What is she asking? When she questions them, what does she want to know?"

Jane raised a hand and ticked off the questions on her fingers. "Where is Corin Hugh hiding? What does Corin Hugh intend? How many men does Corin Hugh command? Who is the liaison between the Nimble Fingers and the druids? What has the Nimble Fingers done with Princess Sera? And finally, where is the anomalous sword?"

Corin's heart seemed to ring like a struck gong at every question. No one she had captured could have answered all those questions—or likely any of them—but it still cut him to his core to hear laid out all the secret, hidden pieces of his plans. Of course she knew about the sword and the druids. That had begun with Aemilia. And perhaps it was Kellen who had pointed her to the Nimble Fingers, or perhaps she'd discovered it somewhere in Corin's history. Either way, she knew. She knew everything but where to find him, and even that never seemed to take her long.

Eventually it struck him that neither he nor Jane had said a word for a quite a long time. He'd nearly forgotten how to breathe, but this whole time she'd sat unmoving, holding his gaze with hers and waiting patiently.

"What?" he asked, though he already knew.

"I want to know the answers," Jane said.

"It isn't safe," he tried. But of course she already knew that. And she'd asked anyway. She didn't even bother saying so. She just raised her eyebrows.

"Those secrets are my life," he said. "They are my purpose. They are everything that I have left."

"And I already know the only one that matters," Jane said. "I'm the only person in Aerome who knows you're here. Mary thinks you're some pretty boy I rescued from a fight down by the docks. The tavern keeper thinks I've smuggled you away to some family estates near Rikkeborh. And no one else could even guess that I'm involved."

She leaned closer and tapped his chest with a manicured fingernail. "I know where you are, Corin Hugh, and if I ever do betray you, you lose everything anyway."

"No," he said. "Even if she kills me, she won't have Princess Sera. She won't have Ben or Auric. Not if I can prevent it."

Jane stared him down for a long time, but he refused to flinch. In the end, she smiled. "You will protect the princess. I'm glad to hear it."

She drew up her legs to sit cross-legged on the bed and relaxed a bit. "I can accept your reservations," she said conversationally. "Even admire them. So don't tell me any names. That still leaves two very interesting questions. What do you intend, Corin Hugh?"

He weighed his choices in an instant. She hadn't thought to press her advantages before—not when Avery's secrets were on the line—but Corin had already carefully considered them. She had the upper hand, and he needed her assistance. More than that, he needed her trust.

So now he met her eyes and answered her question honestly. "I intend to kill the false god Ephitel. Before I can do that, I must draw him out to meet me. And when we meet, I must have with me the means to finish him."

She grinned. "Then you have also answered the other question. The anomalous sword must be the thing you mean, and from the things you said before, I must conclude that it is in the hands of Ben Strunk."

Corin concealed a flinch at that. He hadn't meant to tell her quite so much, though it scarcely mattered. She now knew everything. The only thing left to do was wait and see how she would use this information.

He watched her eyes. That would tell him more honestly than anything she said. He watched her eyes and held his own expression as blank and innocent as he could manage.

She grinned. "I had hoped those were your answers," she said. "I truly did. Otherwise, I'd feel a fool for investing as many resources as I have in tracking down those rumors about Ben."

It was an ominous pronouncement, but he still saw no warning in her eyes. He kept his voice level. "You've found him, then?"

She shook her head. "No. I told you everything I know. But when you asked about him, I suspected he must be some connection to Jessamine's mysterious sword—he is a craftsman, after all—and so I started on follow-up before I even brought the news to you."

"Of course," Corin said. "And to the rest?"

"To what?"

"I told you what I intend to use it for," Corin said. "You don't seem surprised."

She measured him a moment, and then she blushed and dropped her eyes. "The only reason I am not surprised is because Avery assured me that must be your plan. He even thinks he knows the sword's true name."

"*Godslayer,*" Corin told her. "It was forged by Aeraculanon two millennia ago."

"Gods' blood," she sighed, exasperated. "I hate that he is always right."

"Then you *have* spoken with him."

She nodded. "He insisted on this test."

"And I have passed?"

"You passed. Avery will visit you at dusk." She hesitated, clearly weighing something, and then she met Corin's eyes. "He does not mean to support you in your plans."

Corin's eyes grew wide. "He didn't bid you tell me that."

"No," she said. "He will hear you out, but he has no intention of tangling with Ephitel."

"Then I must be convincing," Corin said. "It will not be the gravest challenge I have faced." At least he shared a heart with Avery. He'd tried his best with Kellen, and it had gained him nothing.

Corin breathed a silent prayer to Fortune for the poor elf's soul. Had he survived as well? Or had she left his corpse back in that other world? Corin hated to imagine it. However obstinate the ages had made him, Corin still remembered the bright-eyed hero who had stood by him in battle back in old Gesoelig.

Jane still lingered in his room, some distant thoughts heavy in her eyes, and Corin hoped that she meant to feed him other clues. In the end, she only shook her head and slipped away, leaving him alone again.

Jane's news had proven bad indeed. A thousand dead within the Nimble Fingers? He could scarce believe it. The organization had been almost a family to him, a refuge, a promise of safety within a vicious world. Now this Jessamine had torn all that to shreds.

He'd known enough to fear her when she came hunting him in Raentz. He'd known some tragedy could follow if he left her without a clear trail. He'd only feared for Auric and the princess then, and his efforts had apparently been sufficient to protect them. But he'd never guessed she would strike against the Nimble Fingers.

He shuddered at the thought. They weren't heroes. They weren't soldiers. They were the poor and desperate, the ones forgotten by the gods' cruel justice. They were his brothers, and he had unleashed a fury upon them. Worst of all, he had no clue how to help them. He'd fought her once, and it had left him crippled in this bed.

The only spot of hope that he could find in Jane's report was Jessamine's question concerning Princess Sera. He'd never doubted that Ephitel would make the connection between Giuliano's murder and the princess's disappearance. But if his justicar was still hunting information, then she did not yet know where to find them. That ploy, at least, had been successful. He'd bought time enough for Auric to find refuge among the elves.

And in the process, he'd led Jessamine straight to Kellen. But how? How had she found him so quickly on the Isle of Mists? In that strange place, she'd come directly to him almost immediately after Kellen appeared.

An inspiration struck cold and crushing around Corin's heart. She'd found him once before, when he'd come to Aerome to kill the princes. He'd thought at the time that Ephitel's response to the deed had come too quickly, but perhaps the murders hadn't been the cause. To bring so many soldiers ready for a fight, she must have started gathering them before he'd even set foot inside the cathedral.

No. She'd detected his arrival in the city. Corin couldn't guess how, but Jeff had warned him of the possibility. She could sense anomalies, he'd said, and though Corin wasn't enough of one on his own, when he was near the sword, she could feel it.

And he'd said the sword was not the only catalyst. He'd warned Corin to avoid anyone or anything that might have had an echo in old Gesoelig.

So she had found him once he reunited with the elf. She must have been already on the island, or perhaps she'd used some justicar magic to transport herself, but clearly she had needed that extra reference point to find him.

"Gods' blood," Corin groaned, as a new fear washed over him. "Avery!" She'd sense them together. Corin had to postpone that meeting, perhaps conduct it at a distance, with Jane as an intermediary. He'd lose some advantage there, but he could not afford to lure Jessamine to him here. Not in this condition.

He sprang from his bed, hoping he might still catch Jane on the stairs outside, but a dizziness spun his vision, and a weakness in his legs made him stagger. He grasped at the dressing table to steady himself, but it was too far away.

Still, he didn't fall. Strong hands caught him by the shoulders and steadied him on his feet. Corin spun his head and groaned at the way the world washed around him, but finally his eyes fixed on the helpful stranger.

Avery was there. The room had been empty moments earlier, and Corin knew no one had entered by the door. The sole, sad window looked painted shut, and it sat an inch above the bed Corin had just left. He could not imagine how the elf had appeared there in the room.

But this was Avery, the founder of the Nimble Fingers, who'd pilfered palaces and robbed the very gods. This was not the bumbling nobleman Corin had met in Oberon's dream, but the legend, the hero Corin had worshipped as a child.

The years had darkened him much as they had Kellen, though in slightly different ways. He had no scars, no missing limbs, but his eyes were cold and guarded. He held himself like a cornered beast, ready to fight or flee on a moment's notice. There was no laughter left to him. He was a killing grief, right down to the bone.

"Avery," Corin whispered, trying to pull himself together. "You shouldn't be here."

"You invited me."

"It was a mistake," Corin said. "Go. Now. I'll explain later. Send Jane."

Before Avery could comply or question, the door slammed open. Corin leaped away, grabbing for the bundled clothes that hid his knives, but Avery held fast to his shoulders, and Corin couldn't budge.

The moment's panic passed, and Corin's vision cleared enough to show him Jane—not Jessamine—entering at the door. He felt a flush touch his cheeks and gulped a calming breath. Perhaps it did a bit of good.

Then Jane slammed the door behind her. She snatched up the same bundle Corin had been reaching for and shoved it into his arms. Her eyes danced with the same panic Corin had felt a moment before.

"It's Jessamine," she said. "She's coming now. She's here."

(**21**)

The room fell very still following Jane's announcement. Then Avery nodded in sudden certainty. "It's true. She is quite near."

A cold fist closed around Corin's heart at those words. He glanced out the smoky window, but Avery could not have seen the street from where he stood.

As if in answer to the thought, the elf shook his head. "I feel her like an itch beneath my skin. She must be close indeed. Perhaps within the building."

Corin unfolded the bundle Jane had given him. He buckled on his blades then shrugged into his shirt. As he was reaching for his cloak, Jane stepped toward the door, but Avery stopped her.

"Are you sure?" he asked. "You're positive it's Jessamine?"

Corin frowned. "But you just said—"

"It is a justicar," Avery said. "I can feel the way they warp the world. And I can't imagine why another would have come here at this time."

"Why would Jessamine?" Jane asked. "How could she have found us?"

Corin ground his teeth. "It's me. Me and Avery together. One of the druids warned me, but it slipped my mind."

Avery rounded him, and his voice came out a roar. "It slipped your mind? Blasted knave, you've doomed us all!"

"Oh, hush!" Jane snapped. "The both of you. It doesn't matter how she found us. It only matters that we deal with her and somehow escape alive. We'll sort out the blame sometime later."

Avery composed himself, then turned to Jane. "You are, of course, correct. Can you scale the wall beneath the window? If not, I'll try to draw her down the hall, so you can slip past."

"No," Corin said, making a rapid inventory of his cloak's many pockets. He would have given much for even a pinch of dwarven powder, but he had used it all to kill the princes. He'd have to trust his skill with knives.

"I'll fight her," Corin said. "Avery is right. She's here because of me, and you two owe me nothing. On the contrary, I'm greatly in your debt. Avery, take Jane and slip away. The justicar is after me anyway. I can't imagine she'll try too hard to stop you."

Jane gave a dramatic sigh. "Oh, Fortune save us all from noble gentlemen. You're fools, the both of you. Do you think I'd have brought Corin here without an escape plan, Avery? Do you think I'm such a twit as that?"

She didn't wait for his answer. She dragged the rickety dressing table in front of the door then dashed across the room to the inn's back wall. She knelt down smoothly, hands tracing the cracked plaster in something almost like a caress, until she found the spot she wanted. Then she slammed her shoulder against the wall with surprising force. It was enough to draw a cry of pain from her, and one of worry from the elf, but it also revealed what she intended.

New knife-edge cracks within the plaster revealed a panel, three-feet square. She planted her palm against one edge and shoved it hard. Muscles corded on her arm and across her shoulders before the panel budged. After that, it scraped back into the darkness beyond with a sluggishness that spoke of some great weight.

That caught Corin by surprise. He moved to help her in her efforts, but there was no room for him, and she didn't yield her place. Instead, she repositioned, planted her feet, and shoved hard enough with both hands to force the panel all the way back. Then she scampered through. Avery dove forward before Corin could even move, and slithered through the gap like a wisp of smoke. Corin followed close behind.

The room beyond was dark and musty with disuse. Jane and Avery hadn't moved; they waited just beyond the wall. As soon as Corin was through, Jane put her shoulder to the slab again, shoving it back closed.

"Leave it," Avery said, his voice touched with concern for the girl. "It won't fool her long anyway, now that it's been disturbed. We should already be running."

"No!" Jane snapped over her shoulder. "I will not spend my life running from Cosimo's justicar."

Avery laid a hand on her shoulder. "You've trained hard, girl, but you cannot hope to beat her in battle. She's a justicar."

"And I'm a Nimble Finger," Jane said. "I don't intend to fight her. I intend to punish her for all the good men she's killed."

She flicked a quick look up to Avery's face, then snapped her attention back to the other room. It lasted half a heartbeat, but it was all Corin needed to understand. She was doing all of this for Avery.

Corin blinked in sudden clarity. As much as Jessamine's rampage had shaken Corin—who had always thought of the Nimble Fingers as his brothers—it must have hurt Avery far, far worse. He'd founded the organization. He'd set down their rules and taught everyone who followed after him *how* to be a noble outlaw. The whole organization was his masterpiece, his work of art.

And for months now he'd been forced to watch while that shrew wrought her vendetta against his people.

Corin caught his arm and said softly, "Avery . . . I'm sorry. I apologize for everything I've brought upon your people."

Avery held Corin's gaze for a long moment; then he raised his chin. "Your apology solves nothing, manling. How many more will die?"

Corin flinched at that. "Have you heard from Kellen?"

The elf's eyes narrowed dangerously. "What have you done to Kellen?"

"I approached him on the Isle of Mists. I thought perhaps Jane would have told you."

"We knew you'd gone there. I never guessed you might have found something."

Corin bowed his head. "I found Kellen. I asked him to join me in this quest, and he told me he would stand beside me if I could but convince you to join us."

"Now!" The elf snarled. "You would ask this of me now? When you have brought ruin upon us all?"

Corin shook his head. "I will add it to my apology. While I was meeting with Kellen, the justicar found us. He killed a dozen men, fought her to a standstill, and dragged her into Faerie for my sake. I know not what happened next."

"But she returned from Faerie," Avery snarled. "Your shadows falls across my miserable life like a killing blight."

"Hush, the both of you," Jane whispered fiercely. "I think she's here!"

Corin frowned toward the tiny gap Jane was still peeking through. Avery crowded closer to the young woman, but only she could see into the other room.

"It's her!" She breathed, exultant. She heaved with her shoulder, shoving the heavy slab back into place, then turned aside. Following her motion, Corin spotted what looked very much like the butt end of a flintlock pistol sticking out from the wall. It was cocked and primed, and even as Corin recognized it, Jane closed her hand around the grip and pulled the trigger.

From the other room came not the sharp report of a fired gun, but instead the heavy, percussive boom of a thunderclap. It seemed to shake the building, and it jarred the panel Jane had been so careful to restore. The new gap thus created exhaled a thick, choking stream of acrid smoke and showed a hint of angry red and orange.

For a long moment, no one moved. No one spoke. Corin and Avery met eyes, equally astonished and confused, then both men turned to Jane for some explanation.

She was still kneeling by the wall, her right hand locked in a death grip around the pistol's stock. Her other hand was shaking almost convulsively, and her mouth hung open in shock.

Slowly, like a mighty warship coming around, she turned her eyes to Avery. She looked pale and afraid. She raised her trembling hand to brush her hair back from her face and said almost reverently, "It worked. It really worked."

Avery went to her like a huntsman approaching a wounded animal. He reached out a hand ahead of him and touched her ever so slightly. "What was it? What have you done?"

"I destroyed her. Gods and princes, I'm going to have to buy Mary a whole new wardrobe. It worked. I don't think I believed it would. I never really thought I'd have to use it." A shiver chased up and down her spine, and then another that set her teeth chattering, and then she was shaking uncontrollably. "Gods on Attos, Avery, it w-w-worked. What . . . what have I done?"

Avery scooped the poor young woman into his arms, crushing her against his chest, but he looked past her at Corin. His expression showed more fear than it had when he'd announced that Jessamine was coming. For all his ancient ages, he had no clue how to handle the emotions that gripped the girl.

Corin recognized them, though. He cleared his throat and stepped closer. "Do you perchance recall a time before the fall of Gesoelig when you and Kellen fell into Ephitel's power? He imprisoned you within his deepest dungeon. Desperate to escape and warn King Oberon, you sought a plan to overwhelm the guards. You struck first, throwing a knife—"

"I remember well," Avery shuddered at the memory, and Jane moaned softly against his shoulder.

"It was the first time you killed a man," Corin said.

Avery's head jerked around, his gaze fixing on the tiny stream of black smoke. Then he hugged Jane more tightly and whispered something soothing in her ear.

"We need to move," Corin said. "Even if the justicar is dead, she must have reinforcements nearby. And either way, that blast must have started quite a fire. I won't be surprised if this whole quarter burns before it's done."

Jane shook her head, sniffling. "No. There shouldn't be much fire damage."

Corin tried to hide his doubt. "I know the scent of dwarven powder. How much did you detonate within that room?"

"About a barrelful, all told," Jane said. Corin's stomach rolled at the thought, but Jane's voice only grew steadier. "I lined the walls with potter's clay. The floor and ceiling too. It cost a little fortune and killed my back, but unless I grossly misjudged something, the fire should be small."

"Gods' blood," Corin breathed, admiring. "You made the room into a kiln."

The girl seemed to perk up at Corin's tone. She raised her chin and nodded. "I thought someday there might be need. Avery always said there's no room for mistakes."

"If you must strike, strike clean," Corin quoted. "You did well, Jane."

"Indeed," Avery said. He stroked her hair for a moment, then very deliberately unwrapped his arms around her and withdrew a pace. "You did admirably. The foresight and the planning that went into this escape do you great honor, and it does not detract from it at all that Jessamine escaped."

Corin and Jane both turned to him, astonished, and then the girl shook her head. "If you're just saying this to make me feel better—"

The elf rubbed his upper arms as though soothing an itch. "No, it's true. I can feel her still twisting the world around her. She yet lives, though I cannot say how. I saw that device you fixed upon the door."

Jane nodded. "It should have let the door open once, then sealed it so even you could not force it. No, she must have used the window."

"It is not a short fall, but somehow she survived. Justicars are hard to kill."

"Then it's true? She lives?"

Avery nodded, and Jane answered with a dainty curse. "She must have noticed when I closed the panel. I didn't want to risk hurting someone else."

"You did the right thing," Avery said. "You bought us time."

"How much?" Corin asked. "If she knows where we escaped to—"

Avery shook his head. "She's not stopping off downstairs to confer with her soldiers. That makes me doubt she brought any. Perhaps she only meant to confirm we were here, but now she's running."

"It doesn't matter," Jane said. "This building is connected to the next via a crawlspace in the basement, and the next used to be some sort of church, because *its* basement offers access to the catacombs. From there, we can travel anywhere between the rivers."

Avery's eyebrows rose at that. "Oh, well done indeed."

She beamed at his approval, then hastily she put her plan in motion. From a dilapidated wardrobe in the corner, she produced a bull's-eye lantern and a shiny copper key. She checked the door, but it revealed an empty corridor where undisturbed dust coated the floor. They made no effort to conceal their passage there, for Jessamine had clearly seen how they escaped the actress's room.

A servant's stairwell at the end of that long hall twisted down and down into the distant depths. At the final landing, Jane's key opened the door's rusty lock, and once she'd lit the lantern, she led them on a twisting path among the long-forgotten relics of an unused lodging house. The passage to the church's basement was a narrow crawl space, close and cramped. Corin breathed his thanks to Fortune that the girl had thought to bring a lantern.

On the other side, they crossed two empty rooms before they found the wide stone staircase leading further down into the depths. At the bottom of the steps, the twisting catacombs stretched off to right and left. Corin took one step out into the way and spotted the tiny charcoal markings on the pillars to his right. To anyone else they might have looked like smoke-stained smudges, but to a member of the Nimble Fingers, they were clear as a scribe's tracery. This way led north toward the Piazza Dei; that way south, toward the palace.

Corin turned to Jane in quiet awe. "You've planned this perfectly. But now we should split up lest Jessamine find us again the same way she did before. I can find my way from here."

Avery turned to Corin, his expression now stern. "That is not the only reason. I told Jane already, I do not intend to work with you."

"But surely after what this justicar has done to the Nimble Fingers—"

"That is no objection; that's the very reason. I endorse your war on Ephitel, but you have initiated it with insufficient resources and insufficient care, and now the entire organization pays for your impatience."

Corin swallowed hard. "I could not have known—"

"Jane could not have known she'd have to escape a justicar, and yet she'd planned. She's been my student for less than a year. Meanwhile, you've spent more than a decade among the Nimble Fingers, *and* you seem to have found some secret knowledge of your own. But still you cannot protect the innocent bystanders caught within your scheme. That is a betrayal of everything I stand for."

For a moment, Corin couldn't breathe. He struggled to put words around some answer to the accusation—Jane's actions today would almost certainly bring harsh consequences to poor Mary, for one—but some treacherous corner of his mind agreed with Avery. The Nimble Fingers weren't the only bystanders he'd endangered, nor were these two. What of Auric and Sera? What of Kellen? What of Aemilia who'd paid for Corin's recklessness with her life?

He clenched his fists and fought the stinging tears that sprang to his eyes. His voice came out harsher than he truly meant it to. "I only strive to undo the wrong your people failed to answer. With scant resources, information, or worthy allies, how much can you ask of me? Every war has casualties."

"And I will not be one this time."

Corin clenched his jaw. "We can't afford to stand here arguing. I do hope you'll change your mind. I will to head to southwest Raentz. I have some friends among the druids there. If you reconsider, if you choose to help me *end* Ephitel's reign, then the persecution of your people will die with him. I leave that to you."

He turned away, but Jane caught his elbow. "How do you plan to travel?" she asked quietly.

He didn't answer. Avery was right. He hadn't thought that far ahead.

Avery raised his voice. "What she means to say is, will you disappear again for months and leave the Nimble Fingers to crumble?"

The elf knew some measure of the flaw in Oberon's strange power. That did explain how Jane had so easily understood his concern with time before. Now, it only reminded him of his limitations. He didn't dare sacrifice the time, nor did he know if stepping through the dream might paint as clear a target on him for Jessamine as it had for the druid Council before.

Corin looked back over his shoulder. "No. But I cannot fight Jessamine in her seat of power. Spread the word among the Nimble Fingers. If she asks where I have gone, tell her the truth. I've fled the Godlands altogether and taken refuge with the druids."

Avery smiled, cold and condemning. "So you will spare the Nimble Fingers and sacrifice the druids instead?"

"They are better prepared to deal with her," he said. "But no. I mean to disappear where she can't find me. I'll gather my resources there, then lay a trap that Ephitel cannot ignore. Alone, if I must."

"And if she finds you first?"

"I'll kill her, or I'll pay for all my sins," Corin said. "Either way, some justice will be done."

Sympathy and disbelief shone in Jane's eyes at those words, but Avery only showed approval. "That is as it should be."

Corin licked his lips. "I wish we had met under better terms this time. We could have done much good together, if you would call me friend."

"Perhaps. But you are not my friend. You have become another tragedy in a life beset by them." He almost turned away, but then he bowed his head. "I hope you succeed. Kill Jessamine and Ephitel, and I will call you friend."

"That's no small task."

The elf shrugged. "They're no small sins that you must atone for. Go in peace, manling, and Fortune favor."

He turned his back on Corin then, though Jane still lingered. She came closer, worry creasing her brow. "You shouldn't leave on such terms as these."

Corin shook his head. "I killed his closest friend and endangered the woman he loves. He will not soon forgive those things."

Her eyes widened when Corin mentioned the elf's feelings for her, and a soft red blush touched her ivory cheeks. "You still owe me a great many secrets. I have done my part."

"You have. But I would ask another favor of you yet. Help him discover what became of Kellen. I have only guesswork and conjecture, but he deserves to know the truth of it."

She frowned, thinking hard. "How does that serve you?"

"It doesn't," Corin said. "It is for his sake alone. But he deserves that much of peace."

"And you deserve your vengeance," Jane said softly. "And we all deserve freedom from the monsters you defy. If I can sway his heart in any way, I'll send him after you."

Corin blinked, remembering how fiercely Sera had defied him. He glanced toward the stiff-backed elf five paces off. "You don't fear losing him?"

"I have never had him. And I don't think I ever will until the man who killed his sister faces justice. Then he'll at last decide whether he will drift off into Faerie or embrace a life here. With me."

Those last words came out in a rush. She blinked against the tears that threatened in her eyes, then leaned forward to brush a kiss on Corin's cheek.

Behind her, Avery cleared his throat meaningfully. "Keep safe," she whispered, fervent. "And cling to hope. We aren't finished yet."

Then she went to Avery, who never once glanced back at Corin. Instead, he took Jane's hand and pulled her gently away down the path toward the Piazza Dei. Corin watched them go, watched the light of Jane's only lantern bob away into the distance. The darkness that engulfed him seemed the perfect echo of the one that filled his thoughts.

Rejected by both Avery and Kellen. He'd lost the druids' aid, failed to win the elves, and couldn't make himself ask more of the Nimble Fingers. For all of Jane's kind words, he couldn't find a shred of hope that Avery might forgive him. He was alone. Ever since he'd met Aemilia, he'd planned to gather allies to stand against the gods. And now, for all his efforts, he was more alone than ever.

But there was no time to consider it. He was not half a block from the place where Jane had tried to cook the justicar, and they'd left tracks enough to point her to this cellar. He had to move. Relying on his memory and touch, he turned south—away from Jane and Avery—and set off through the pitch-black catacombs searching for an exit.

22

Though Corin didn't know the catacombs here in Aerome, he'd spent much of his childhood exploring Aepoli's. Drowning there in total darkness, ancient instincts surged up to his rescue. He advanced down the tunnel path in a stuttering half step, almost like a dance, tracing the path ahead with a searching toe and then testing the footing with his heel before he shifted his whole weight onto it. And then again with the other foot.

As he went, he trailed the fingertips of his left hand against the wall. He had to shift up and down around the cavities of ossuaries, and when he passed an opening of any sort—a side tunnel or a stairway to the surface, or even a natural pocket on the limestone bed beneath the city—a quiet dread always settled over him until his fingers found the wall again.

But at those passageways he found hope too. He'd almost forgotten all about them, until his fingers touched the notches chipped from stone just before the first stairs up. A crude triangle told him to avoid the stairs. Keep going.

These were not the intricate designs of the Nimble Fingers' secret language. These were the markings made by desperate urchins. But in their way, they were just as useful. Here they told him that the stairway led to a locked door; there they warned of a vigilant guard on the building's cellars. The worst were those that indicated there were hungry guard dogs waiting for a careless intruder.

Every exit from the catacombs was marked. Corin passed by the ones that promised a sympathetic almer or hot meals for the hungry. Generosity toward a starving child wouldn't necessarily extend to a grown man appearing unexpectedly from the dark.

Still, in a city vast and ancient as Aerome, it didn't take him long to find three vertical strokes. Then he turned aside and left the catacombs for a long-forgotten cellar in what turned out to be a wholly abandoned building. He strained his ears at every step, but there was no one waiting for him as he emerged into the light. He climbed old stairs that creaked frighteningly beneath each step, then crossed a corridor, littered with the detritus of several seasons, to an open door that looked out into an empty stable yard. He lurked in the shadows of the doorway for a while, thinking.

How *was* he going to fight Ephitel without the elves? The pirates? No. His name did hold some fame, but pirates were straightforward souls. They sailed for profit, not for pride or noble purpose. They'd scatter at the first sign of danger, and he needed a more reliable and sustained plan to draw out Ephitel.

That didn't leave him much. He thought of the farmboy—pure charisma dressed up like an adventurer of old—but even a living hero wouldn't be enough without an army at his back.

The druids, though . . . they might be enough. Ephitel had expressed his hatred for them when he'd come for Aemilia. They were no mighty power, but they held all the secrets of this world.

They would not lightly forgive Corin's last act toward them, but they could not easily reject him either. They needed him almost as much as he needed them.

Yes. The druids were his only answer. And his best shot at finding them would also lead him to the farmboy. But he would have to take great care in his travel plans. Justicars were masterful thief-catchers, even without Jessamine's strange sense for anomalies.

But Corin was himself a masterful thief. He'd spent his whole life practicing that kind of care, and he had new tricks to aid him now. Before he left the doorway, he dressed himself in the glamour of some northern farmer. Then he picked his way down to the docks and convinced a friendly captain to grant him passage all the way to Marzelle, where he claimed to have family.

Corin disappeared that night when the ship put in at Ginoe for supplies. After all, if she asked enough questions of the harbormaster, Jessamine could be waiting for him at the docks there in Marzelle.

Nor did he stay the night in Ginoe. He wove a different glamour, stole a horse, and headed north along the highway. He rode hard, and before dawn he crossed the border into Raentz.

The horse began to falter after sunrise, and Corin had no wish to slow his journey. So he changed his disguise again and stole another horse—and with it, this time, a loaf of bread and four winter-stunted apples. Then he chose a course that took him wide of Marzelle, and pressed hard west, racing the sun.

Even so, he was riding yet another horse beneath the silver light of the moon before he reached territory he recognized. A dark foreboding fell upon him as he neared the little village where he'd fled from Jessamine. He dismounted and left the road to pass Taurb by. He led the horse between two rows of corn; then at the far end, he followed a split-log fence most of a mile to the cart path that led west to Auric's place.

He should not have been surprised to find it dark, but he was. As he approached the gate to the farmboy's property, he strained his eyes for some light from the farmhouse, but there was none. That should have been encouraging. After all, he'd warned Auric to get away; the farmboy was much safer gone.

Even so, a dark disquiet hung over him as he passed through the gate. He'd gone halfway up the path before the cause struck him: There *was* light from the direction of the farmhouse. Starlight.

There was no structure to interrupt the far horizon. For a while he convinced himself this was some nervous fear, that the footpath was longer than he'd remembered, but then his boot struck the cracked stone step that had marked the threshold. There to his right he made out the tall, spindly statue of the stone chimney standing all alone.

He had to strain his eyes to pick out the charred timbers, the littered remnants of a burned-down home. He knelt and felt with his fingertips the raw, exposed edges of the stone foundation.

The house was gone. He could not believe this was some accident. Had Jessamine done this? Had she found them? Or had it been the villagers when they'd learned about Corin's antics? It could not have been too hard for them to figure out where he had come from.

Cursing himself for being seven kinds of fool, he sprinted back along the path and scrambled up into the saddle of the rundown animal. Corin hauled its reins back around to set the horse and himself on the path and kicked the beast up to a gallop.

He dashed straight to the tavern's door and leaped down from the saddle. He'd long since lost the mental discipline to hold his glamour, but he no longer cared. He dashed through the door into the common room and bellowed, "Jacob! Where's that blasted innkeeper? Jacob Gossler! Come out here!"

This time of night in a little village tavern, Corin would have expected the modest common room to be packed with tired farmhands resting from a long day's work. Instead, it was mostly empty, and those few who had come out tonight were gathered in small clusters, heads huddled together and the hoods of their cloaks pulled up despite the early spring warmth.

Some of those hoods swiveled his way when Corin started shouting, but none lingered long. No one showed his face, and no one answered Corin's bellow. He watched the door to the kitchen, and a balding, skinny man did peek through the gap, but it was not the proprietor Corin had spoken with before.

Then a quiet voice spoke from a dark corner. "You won't find him here."

Corin turned that way, searching, and he found the thin, clinging mist of a glamour roiling around the man who sat alone there. A man he recognized. Corin threw another gaze around the common room, but no one wanted to be seen noticing anything unusual. That suited Corin well enough. He settled his cloak around his shoulders and went to join the druid in the corner.

"What have you done with him?" Corin asked.

Jeff arched an eyebrow. "Which one? The innkeeper? Nothing. He left on his own."

"And the farmboy?"

"We've relocated him somewhere safe."

Corin shook his head. "It isn't safe enough. Jessamine is hunting the princess now. She knows they're involved. We need to move them outside the Godlands altogether."

"Think so?" There was a hint of laughter in the druid's tone, though it didn't touch his eyes. "And where would you suggest?"

"The Wildlands," Corin said.

Surprise raised both the druid's eyebrows this time, but Corin leaned forward, intense. "It's better than anything you can offer. I know it's dangerous, but that should work against whoever they send against him too. And he has experience there. I'll go with him, and together we can work out what to do next."

Jeff leaned back, lacing his fingers behind his head. "You think the druids are prepared to listen to your advice?"

"I think that if they don't, they're going to lose this war."

Jeff sighed, and his shoulders slumped. "They don't yet want a war. They're furious that you've provoked a justicar—"

"Call her by her name," Corin snapped. "She's one of yours, after all. And now she's murdering the Nimble Fingers."

"I'd heard. I'm sorry."

"So am I, but that doesn't stop her. We have to end this."

"And you have a plan?"

Corin hesitated. He didn't have a full plan. Not yet. He'd been patching something together ever since his confrontation with Avery, but now that Jeff had asked him right out . . .

"Aye," Corin said, and in his mind all the pieces fell into place. "Aye. We'll fortify some blighted hole in the Wildlands, and then we'll let her find us. I've already laid the start for that."

"You think we can defeat her?"

"Any one of us alone, no. Kellen couldn't take her, and neither could a firebomb. But with the druids' aid? With the farmboy's heroism? Sure. We will end her reign of terror, and then we'll hang her corpse out as a lure for Ephitel."

Jeff pulled back at that. "He'll come in force."

"Let him try," Corin said. "There are mountain passes in the Wildlands that a dozen men could hold against an army. And there are monsters there who'd harry any force they sent against us. We could hold, and eventually Ephitel will tire of waiting for his vengeance, and he'll come against us in person."

"He has a nation full of soldiers to hurl against you. How can you believe he'd be so foolish as to come in person?"

"Because it's exactly what I'd do. What I've been doing. And that much we both have in common. This is personal, and he will not wait long for satisfaction."

"You're sure of it?"

"I'm sure."

"And then you will behead him with *Godslayer*?"

Corin dropped his eyes. The sword. Where was the sword? Jessamine was searching for it, so Ben was still at large. But where? Corin had hoped the innkeeper could at least tell him whether Ben had ever been through here.

"What do you know about the innkeeper?" Corin asked. "You said I wouldn't find him here."

"I was referring to . . . to the farmboy. But no, you won't find the innkeeper—or half the locals who lived in this town two months ago."

"Why?"

"Jessamine came here. After she lost track of you in the Isle of Mists, she came back here. She was much the worse for wear—"

"That was Kellen's doing," Corin interrupted.

Jeff nodded. "—and angry for it. She took that anger out on the townsfolk here, but they couldn't help her any. Auric and Sera were already six days gone by then, and we'd tracked down everyone who knew anything significant and convinced them to leave town for a little while. That notion caught on among the others too, and most of them have made it a good long while. No one wants to live in a town that's angered the gods."

"She's moved on," Corin said. "She's working on the Nimble Fingers now."

"And when she's done with them, she'll come for the druids," Jeff said dismissively.

Corin blinked. "You've already heard?"

"Heard what?"

"The druids. You said she'd come for the druids now."

Jeff stared at Corin for a while, saying nothing, then nodded in sudden understanding. "You told them to point her our way."

"Aye. I thought you could handle it. Better than the Nimble Fingers, anyway, and—"

"No," Jeff said, raising his hands. "No, you were right. The Council won't see it that way, but I don't feel inclined to tell them. It would have happened eventually, regardless, and this way probably saves some lives."

Corin leaned back, relaxing a little, and nodded. "What will the druids do?"

"If I have my way, they'll do precisely what you have suggested. Fortifying some stronghold in the Wildlands seems as good a plan as any I have heard."

"Then I will need your help," Corin said. "We must choose a fitting spot and move Auric and Sera there. And you must find me Ben Strunk. And Jacob, the innkeeper. I need to speak with him."

"Why do you need them?"

"Some secrets I must keep close," Corin said.

"If I knew the significance of your assets, I could better help you manage them."

Corin considered the druid for a moment. Then he sighed. "They've accepted you back into the Council, then?"

He cocked his head. "How'd you know?"

"You're already talking like them. The honest truth is that Ben is my friend, and I entangled him in all of this. He's not an asset, but Jessamine will see him the same way you do. I want you to find him just so I can know he's safe."

Corin felt a touch of remorse at the shame that reddened the druid's cheeks. But just a touch. Ben would not expect any honest sentiment from the pirate, no matter how close their friendship. They were not that sort of men.

More importantly, Corin could ill afford to let the Council discover that he'd lost the sword. Whatever ploy he had to use to prevent that, it was worth the cost.

So he sat patiently through Jeff's apologies. Then, dismissing them with a gracious word, he changed the subject. "And of my other request?"

"Which was?"

"The princess and the farmboy," Corin said. "I want to see them hidden somewhere safe within the Wildlands."

"Preposterous as the concept is," Jeff said, "it's something I can offer. What else do you need?"

Corin blinked. "That's it? No arguing? No wheedling? You'll make that happen?"

"Without delay!" Jeff said. "If you have a horse that can make the journey, I'll take you there tonight."

"And the others?"

Jeff grinned. "They're already waiting. I'll send word ahead for the princess to set an extra place for breakfast. She's a surprisingly good cook."

23

While Jeff was settling his tab with the new innkeeper, Corin slipped out to the stable, donning the glamour of one of the men he'd seen inside, before he stepped out into the night.

In the end, the effort wasn't necessary. The stable hands seemed to have been as caught up in the fear as everyone else, so only one remained on duty. That one was snoring softly in the hay, wrapped protectively around an empty bottle.

Corin left him sleeping, saddled a horse, and led it off into the shadows while he waited for Jeff. The druid came along soon after, and shortly the two men were riding west along the same cart path that passed the burned-out farmhouse.

Corin couldn't help looking in that direction as he rode past. "I came by the farmhouse first," Corin said, his voice raw and thin. "I didn't know what had happened. I thought—"

His throat closed up, his collarbone aching, and Corin tried to shake it off. The very memory of that dread overwhelmed him.

Beside him, the druid tsked. "You've my apologies for that. No, no harm befell those two. After you raised such a ruckus in the village square, Auric brought me your instructions, and we saw them off to safety right away."

"Then what . . . what happened to the house?"

"We did that. In case Jessamine followed the trail back to here. Stirred up some locals and convinced them to put the place to the torch. They're not really violent folks, and I don't think it sits well with them, what they did. But it certainly convinced Jessamine that the farmboy you had visited is well and truly gone. And this way she could find no evidence that the family here was in any way related to the missing princess."

"Clever," Corin said dully. It *was* clever. It was precisely the kind of plan he liked. But at that moment, the thought of them torching Auric and Sera's home—however temporary that home had been—lay on his chest almost as heavily as his fear for the people themselves.

He remembered how he'd felt that morning when he woke up in their cabin. The memory of home had hit him like a crushing wave, and the grief of losing that, and now he felt some echo of that loss on the princess's behalf.

"Gods' blood," he muttered. "I need to see this matter settled so I can breathe again."

He hadn't meant much by the comment, but Jeff fell into a contemplative silence for a while. Then, without looking Corin's way, the druid said, "It won't work."

Corin looked up sharply. "What?"

"Killing Ephitel. It won't solve your problem."

Corin snorted. "It'll certainly help."

"I was a doctor in another life. That's not the same as a counselor, but sometimes I had to fill that role. And *this* is something I have seen before. You need to grieve, Corin. You need to say good-bye. That's the only way you'll ever be able to breathe easy again."

"Stormy seas, they've got you good and deep," Corin said.

"This is not the Council talking."

"There was a time when you were the only person in the world encouraging me to do what needed doing."

"And I still do," Jeff insisted. "If avenging Aemilia is the only reason you have to kill Ephitel, then cling to that reason. It's the end I care about, not the means."

"Then what—"

"I just want you to understand," Jeff said. "It might improve the world to make him dead, but it won't fix what's broken inside you. There's not enough hatred in the world to take the place of missing love. Got it?"

"I . . ." Corin couldn't find any words. Pain and anger burned like twin forgefires in his breast. He wanted to lash out at the druid, but he could find neither the strength nor the words.

Jeff nodded with an infuriating understanding. "I told you, I've seen this before. Hell, I've lived it more than once. I know what I'm talking about."

Corin forced the emotions back. He buried anew the pain of his loss, crushing the sharp-edged memory, until at last he could speak.

"It's all I've got." His words were thin and parched, as though he hadn't tasted water in days. "Hate's enough to do the job."

"And afterward?" Jeff asked.

Corin rode in silence for a while, feeding the last vestiges of his pain into the inferno of his rage. It boiled hot and wild down in his belly, but when he spoke now, his voice carried an eerie calm.

"Afterward," he said, "belongs to you. Let the druids fix the world. I only do the breaking."

They rode in silence after that. Corin's body ached from hard days in the saddle. He felt bone weary too, despite the week he'd spent in bed. He followed blindly when the druid led him off the cart path and into a fallow field. They pressed through tall grass for a while, with forest to the left and right, and mountains up ahead. Southwest, then, toward the Dividing Line. Jeff pushed the horses hard, and Corin was glad of it. He was ready to be done with this journey, ready to start the next step. Ready to face Jessamine and right that wrong, at least. Or fall to her and join Aemilia in death.

The druid rode straight for the Dividing Line. Farther north, the forest grew right up to its edge, but here there was only open, rolling plains. This land would have been prize farmland any-where else in Raentz, but no one wanted to live so close to the Wildlands. For miles, there was only wild grassland.

Corin looked back over his shoulder. The sun was rising, red and angry, staining the whole horizon pink. How far had they come?

He turned forward again, and shied his horse away from the edge. From his vantage on the horse's back, Corin caught a glimpse thirty paces down to the Spinola lowlands.

The Dividing Line made the border between Raentz and ancient Spinola—better known as the Wildlands, and rightly so. The Dividing Line was said to be the edge of the gods' domain. It was a sheer cliff, some thirty paces high, that ran straight as a knife's edge from the Endless Ocean to the Medgerrad Sea.

Sheer everywhere except at Reconciliation. Such was the poetic name of the half-mile stretch where a gentle slope inter-rupted the Dividing Line. To north and south, the cliffs made a lethal fall, but at Reconciliation, a child could stroll across the border between civilization and wilderness.

It was said that in the ancient days, when Spinola boasted law and prosperity and bustling cities, that the grandest and most prosperous had been right here at Reconciliation. It certainly had been one of the most important markets in all Hurope.

Now no remnant of that place remained. Corin hadn't entirely believed in the slope, either, but he saw it now before him—wide and green and gentle. Even the lowland plains beyond looked safe and inviting, but Corin knew better. He'd spent a day ashore in Spinola, when he'd first met Auric, and the things he'd *heard* in those few hours had been enough to convince him he never wanted to come back.

But now, despite himself, he heeled his horse forward beside the druid's. They rode down Reconciliation like some grand boulevard, and at the bottom Jeff continued on straight as an arrow toward the heartland.

Corin frowned at the distant mountains, considering, before turning to the druid. "Why are they already here?"

"Hmm?"

"I told you why I thought we needed to come here. I pled my case. But you were one step ahead of me. Why? Had you already reached the same conclusion?"

Jeff showed Corin a sardonic smile. "I only wish the Council thought the way you do. No. But you were right believing these two weren't safe anywhere within the Godlands."

"Why?" Corin asked again. "Is it true the gods' dominion doesn't reach this far?"

"Yes and no," Jeff said, choosing his words with care. "Obviously, they don't try to control this territory, same as Jepta and the Black Forest and the Isle of Mists."

"Why?"

"It's . . . fuzzy to them."

"Fuzzy?"

The druid shrugged. "I don't know. Oberon understood it. The elves tend to *feel* the world around them—not just through their senses, but through their instincts. They know how reality ought to be, and that gives them their ability to shape it."

Corin nodded, remembering. "Avery showed discomfort around Jessamine. He said she made him itch, that all justicars made him itch because of the way they twisted reality."

"Fascinating," Jeff said. "He is probably more sensitive than most, but that's the heart of it. But Oberon wanted to make this world a balance between Faerie and Yesterworld, so he built balances into it. He inscribed an enormous circle on the face of the world—"

"The Godlands," Corin said, imagining the boundaries Jeff had just described.

"That's how they gained their name," Jeff said. "Within the circle, the ancient elves have full access to their . . . whatever it is that makes them elves. I don't know. I was never a specialist in their kind."

"And outside the circle?"

"Outside the circle, they're half blind. Outside the circle belongs to the sons and daughters. It's a preserve for humanity. A sanctuary from the elves."

Corin laughed dismissively. "The Wildlands is a sanctuary? The Endless Desert? The Black Forest? These are dying grounds!"

Jeff sighed. "Ephitel has had a thousand years to make them so. He never shared in Oberon's vision. Who do you think brought the monsters out of Faerie to populate those lands?"

"That is the work of Ephitel?"

"Yep. He started it even before he displaced Oberon. After the war with the infidels, he proclaimed Spinola a vulnerability, positioned as it was. So he brought in the manticores to secure our borders."

"Gods' blood!"

"Uh-huh."

Corin considered this and shook his head. "But you still haven't told me *why* you brought them here."

"It was Auric's idea, really. He'd heard all the same legends you have, and he'd spent some time here, as you mentioned. When he heard us worrying over a place to keep them safe from Jessamine, he suggested here."

Corin shook his head. "Poor fellow. That was months ago."

"Oh, he wasn't boasting. They seem as safe as kittens."

"But living like that? With his princess? I'll admit she seemed satisfied to play some Raentzian farmwife, but roughing it out here in the wild? A princess?"

Not quite concealing his smile, Jeff looked sideways at Corin. "I think she's happy enough as long as she's with him."

"She won't be happy to see me, though," Corin said.

"No. No, she won't."

"Did you send word ahead for breakfast?"

Jeff nodded. Corin didn't ask him *how* he could have done so. Aemilia had once tried to explain the use of the arcane tablets they all carried, but she'd lost him halfway through.

"And . . . did you tell her *who* was coming?"

Jeff's grin broke free at that. "What, and risk her poisoning you before you get your shot at Ephitel? Never."

Corin breathed a little easier. He'd not expected poison— though she *was* a Vestossi—but the thought of missing breakfast seemed barely half a step below assassination.

His stomach rumbled, and Corin groaned. "How far is this hiding place?"

"The permanent camp is still three days' ride," Jeff said, raising his hand to forestall Corin's curses. "But breakfast is just beyond the next hill. There's a little gully, and a welcoming party waiting there."

Corin frowned, considering those distances. "How could they have come so quickly to meet us? Were you expecting me?"

"Not really. Actually, they're on their way back. We sometimes make trips up into Raentz for food and supplies. I sometimes stay behind to listen for rumors, see what pops up."

"Ah," Corin said. "And this time it was me."

"You're quite the rumor."

"You aren't wrong," Corin said, "and she'll be coming for me. There will be no more trips up into Raentz. Certainly not for those two."

"They've always traveled beneath a glamour."

"I can see through glamours," Corin said. "Can a justicar?"

Jeff scrubbed a hand through his hair, nervous. "I . . . I don't know."

"Then we'll assume she can."

"Of course."

"Are there others? That boy draws followers like a horse draws flies. We could send someone else in his place."

"I'm sure we could find someone," Jeff said, his expression suddenly unreadable.

Corin considered digging for an explanation, but his stomach growled again as he caught the scent of roasting pheasant on the air. He rose in his stirrups and narrowed his eyes to peer toward the ridge of the hill.

"Just beyond this hill?" he asked.

"Yep."

"Good," Corin said. "I'm starving." He kicked his horse into a gallop up the gentle hillside, and as he topped the ridge, he caught sight of the camp in the gully down below.

He understood Jeff's comment, then. Dozens of people scurried here and there throughout the camp. One or two had the look of druids about them, and Corin quickly picked out Auric and the princess, but the rest all looked like common folk: Raentzian by their dress, farmers by their complexions.

Jeff caught up with Corin while he stood staring down at all the people.

"What is this?" Corin asked. "Who are these others?"

"Refugees. I told you there were quite a few who wanted to leave a town Jessamine had visited twice."

"These did not all come from that sleepy village."

Jeff glanced his way, then nodded admiringly. "Perceptive. No. No, most of those moved to the ruins months ago. These are their distant friends or family or others who heard about a place of refuge and came looking."

"There are rumors about this place?" Corin asked, horrified. "And you let them come?"

"*He* lets them come," Jeff answered, and Corin understood with no more explanation. Auric wouldn't turn away a refugee. Not for anything. And he had a way of winning arguments.

Corin sighed. "This will be trouble."

"I've been saying that for weeks."

"How many are there?"

"Hundreds," Jeff said. "We've built a refuge in the Wildlands. Civilization has returned to Spinola."

"Fortune favor," Corin said; then his stomach rumbled again. "But breakfast first."

24

Corin spoke a word of caution to the druid as they descended on the camp. Then he dressed himself in the glamour of a young pirate he had met back in Rauchel. It was disguise enough to stop rumors among these refugees and to forestall Princess Sera's wrath, for a while at least.

He found a hearty breakfast, with buttered rolls and roasted pheasant and sweet red beets. All he'd had since leaving Aerome had been one loaf of bread and four sad apples, so he went back for a second helping and a third, and the woman tending to the food seemed all too happy to comply.

As he was finishing his third plate, she came to settle down beside him, groaning in a friendly way as she rested her feet after the morning's work. "Not too bad, huh?" she asked in Raentzian.

Corin knew enough of the language to carry on a conversation, if clumsily. Most pirates could do the same in any of the languages along the Medgerrad, but Raentzian and Ithalian were the most important.

This time Corin did his best and hoped the glamour would make up some of the difference. "Best food I've had in days. Seems like the only."

She nodded, sympathetic, and though she didn't mention it, she clearly noticed he was not a native speaker of her language. She ducked her head for a better look at his face. "You one of them Nimble Fingers?"

He started, but she laid a comforting hand on his shoulder. "Oh, no need to fret. My husband ran the tavern out of Loison. He was one of the first."

Something in her tone—a blend of grief and sympathy and deep, abiding hatred—made it entirely clear what she meant.

"The justicar," Corin whispered.

"Fires take her. Yes. You chose right in coming here. There is no shame in running from a foe you cannot conquer."

Corin blinked. "Avery said that."

"A husband talks," she said in answer. "I know some of your principles. There's more honor in them than some people think. Certainly more than this justicar has shown."

Corin frowned, considering. He'd taken the druid at his word that these refugees were all the friends and family of people from Taurb, but it stood to reason that if word had gotten out, there would be others. And certainly the wife of a man caught up in Jessamine's purge would have reason to want to flee.

But Corin couldn't let the Nimble Fingers get caught up in this. They were already paying too high a price, and if he meant to use his position in the Wildlands as bait to lure Jessamine, then associating the Nimble Fingers with the refugees could prove disastrous for them.

"Please," he said, worry gnawing at his spine, "don't tell anyone there is a member of the organization among the refugees. Will you protect my secret?"

She laughed and patted his back warmly. "Oh, it's no secret. You know how rumors spread among your brothers. Half the people in this camp are Nimble Fingers. I'm surprised that you don't recognize them." She nodded to herself in sudden understanding. "Oh. But you do come from a long way off."

"Aye," Corin said, falling back into his native Ithalian. And then he fall back onto the ground, staring up at the sky. "Fortune favor! What have I begun?"

Just as Jeff said, it took the refugees three days to reach the permanent camp, though Corin suspected he could have done it all in two, without the burden of such a large contingent. As it was, he felt the slow pace like a weight around his neck. He itched to spur his horse ahead, to leave them all behind and rush to his destination.

But that would not have served him at all. Even if he'd been able to pry useful directions from the druid, he didn't dare charge the farmboy's camp unexpected. If he came in disguise, they might well cut him down as a Godlander spy. And if he came in person, Sera might do far worse.

So he clung to his thin glamour and fought against his own impatience. He ate well for the first time since he'd left his cabin, and he found time for idle conversations. He sought out Jeff at every opportunity, if only for some company. Alas, the druid could not tell him much more than they'd already discussed. He had sent out requests for information on the missing dwarf, and he checked his tablet again every time Corin asked, but there was no news. Ben Strunk had disappeared.

Corin asked for details concerning Jessamine—some clue to her weakness that he might exploit—but the druids knew little more of justicars than did anyone else in Hurope. Their powers were mysterious—some strange convergence of Faerie and manling magics that only the druids and their gods could wholly understand.

That left them little to discuss, as all serious strategy would depend on Corin's conversation with Auric. More than once he considered searching for some chance to draw the farmboy aside for a quiet conversation, but there were a thousand problems with that plan. The first that occurred to Corin was a sincere doubt that Auric could tell a straight-faced lie. The boy wore pure-hearted honesty like a second skin.

But a more practical concern overwhelmed even that one. Auric was never alone. He always had a swarm of refugees around him, asking for advice, offering assistance, or just listening to his conversations with the others. Corin joined in on that, and he was startled to discover how much organization was truly going on.

Jeff had told him there were hundreds of refugees, but Corin hadn't really considered the full significance of that until now. *Hundreds* of civilians camping three days' journey into Spinola's lowlands? It was madness. Finding food and water for so many would be a challenge anywhere, but arranging shelter for them in such a hostile place as this? They could scarcely have found tents enough to house them, let alone the soldiers to protect them from raids by manticores or savages or both.

He grew more concerned about that with each passing day. How much would these refugees impede his plans? Jeff had said he'd wrestled with the same question, and Corin knew he'd run aground against the same difficulty too. Auric would not abandon them. He would not turn them away. He was a hero, not a statesman.

Corin heaved a weary sigh when he considered that. For all his generous heart, Auric lacked the ability to make the most difficult choices. No ship's captain lasted long with that naïveté, but a farmboy could preserve it, and so could an adventurer. If anything could wreck this venture, it would be Auric's tender heart.

More than once, Corin caught himself hoping for a manticore raid to resolve the problem. Then he remembered how many among the refugees were Nimble Fingers—how many of them were only here because of him—and the shame cut deep. Perhaps he needed more of Auric's heart.

For three days he wrestled with these things, constantly anxious for and dreading their arrival at the permanent camp. He rode always near the front of the contingent, eyes straining for the stain of a hundred tents sprawled along the bank of some muddy stream. Then late in the afternoon on the third day, no more than an hour after they had stopped for lunch, Corin crested a wide, tall hill, and looked down into a sprawling valley.

A river half a mile wide meandered down below, and nestled in a gentle bend of that river stood the ruins of an ancient city. Smoke rose in lazy tendrils from a hundred points within those ruins—cookfires and forgefires alike, from the things Corin had overheard. But this was nothing like he had expected. Everyone had called this place "the camp." Everyone had spoken of the hardships here. But there were soaring towers still intact. The ruins had a wall four paces high that ran unbroken around three sides, and a river deep enough to drown a horse protecting the fourth.

This was not a camp. This was a fortress.

"Gods' blood," Corin breathed, staring down at it.

Jeff was there beside him. Corin didn't know when he'd arrived, but now the druid clapped him on the back. "I told you. We've brought civilization to the Wildlands."

"It's true," Corin said, looking down into the future. "And next, we'll bring a war."

The first thing Corin did when he reached the city was find his lodgings. A friendly woman with tired eyes sent him to a vast, completely empty room within what might have been a cathedral to a pagan god. There was room to spare for anyone who wanted it, but almost nothing in the way of furnishings. She offered him a bedroll, a tin plate, and a battered pewter cup. Meals were available at the bells; and shares of beets and barley, at the storehouse.

He barely registered that information. As soon as she had finished talking, he bowed his head in thanks, then followed her directions to the room she'd promised. There he spread out his bedroll in the farthest corner and stretched out on his back, with the handle of a blade beneath each hand. The war would have to wait. He needed sleep.

He'd left his sickbed to ride day and night from Aerome to the Dividing Line, and he'd joined up with the refugees just at the start of a full day's march. Since then he'd had two nights' sleep, but they'd been nights beset with the anxiety of discovery and the constant nagging reminders that he was stretched up, unconscious, and exposed within the untamed wilderness of savage Spinola. And of course there'd been the rocks. He'd never found a comfortable position, no matter how he'd squirmed.

No, he'd found no rest beneath the stars. He'd been a city boy before he went to sea, and years of sleeping on a deck had done nothing to prepare him for a night stretched out on barren dirt.

He would have shuddered to think of it, but he never had the chance. No sooner had his head settled on the thin, hard pillow than his mind shut off. His breathing settled into a slow, steady pattern, and muscles he'd held tense for days gradually relaxed.

Within half a heartbeat, he fell into the quiet, restful sleep of men long dead.

Somewhere deep within that darkness, his dreams found him. He was working in the little cabin's kitchen with Aemilia, preparing a Sunday lunch for two. Then sometime later, he sat with her, discussing plans for thwarting Ephitel, trying to unravel the strange mysteries of Corin's powers.

And then the setting changed. A forgefire heat seemed to hang in the air, and the taste of ash soured his tongue, but in the next room over, he could hear Aemilia quietly at work. She was a scribe in old Gesoelig, and a prestigious customer had come to request a small favor.

Ephitel. Corin groaned, deep within the dream, and now Corin and Aemilia stood side by side at Oberon's throne. Outside, the city was burning. Innocent men and women died as Ephitel and his regiment marched upon the Oberon's stronghold.

Within the bower, the ancient, tired king of this world slumped in his throne, strain creasing his forehead and knotting hard the muscles of his shoulders. His hands clenched into fist, and perspiration beaded on his face. Somewhere behind them, Jeff's voice rose up in excitement. "It's working! A moment more. Good lord, it's working!"

The throne room rang out like a struck bell. The very world around them groaned, straining hard; and then, with a flash of light like a mighty thunderbolt, the world changed. A distant, impossible stone ceiling blotted out the sky, and the air around them echoed with the vastness of a stone cavern. Oberon's city had found its tomb.

And on the throne, the great king slumped. That final act of mercy had cost him more than strength. He would never again leave his living throne. But for the moment, his people were safe. He drew a weak, rattling breath, and Corin squeezed Aemilia's hand in his.

Then the king opened his bloodshot eyes and fixed them on Corin. Something like a smile tugged at his lips, showing teeth more fitting to a fox's grin than to any man's. "It is done," he wheezed, "but who is left to face the traitor?"

Corin started forward, but Aemilia didn't budge. He looked back at her, and she was beautiful, but the taste of ash still stained his tongue. *She looked beautiful upon her bier.* The thought rose up from somewhere else, some other awareness, and it awoke a flare of searing anger in his chest. He released his grip on her hand and turned away to throw himself before the king.

"I will face him!" he cried.

"It is no easy task. You will falter."

"Perhaps, but I will not fall! I will not forget! I will not rest until he has paid!"

Oberon looked Corin up and down with sad eyes. "Can I depend on you?"

"I swear it."

"I am spent," the old god said. "I can serve my people no more. But if I begged one final wish, it would be this: destroy the traitor Ephitel."

"Aye!" Corin shouted. "I swear upon the blood of gods, I will grant you vengeance."

The words rang out until they filled the vastness of the cavern. The throne room faded away, and with it the other inhabitants, but the echoes of his promise yet remained. They swelled around him, and everything else dissolved into perfect blackness. Still his oath resonated in the air. It hammered at him. It pounded him into nothing, and he became just another crying voice within the dead god's tomb.

·❦·

When he woke sometime later, it was sudden and complete. For all his deep fatigue, his instinct for survival ran still deeper. Footsteps, soft and careful, nonetheless rasped on the bare floor and echoed in the vastness of the room. Corin's position gave him time to recognize the sound, to wake and react.

In an instant he was on his feet, dagger in his right hand and knife in his left, ready to throw. Halfway across the room, Princess Sera stopped abruptly, though she did not let her flash of fear show in her expression. Instead, she raised her chin and looked down her nose at Corin.

"Master pirate," she said in icy greeting.

He looked down at himself, but he needn't have. The thin, distorting haze of the glamour still shrouded his eyes. Irritated, he met the lady's gaze.

"The druid?"

"He was worried when you didn't wake. He is in conference now with Auric. I didn't wait for them to find a resolution."

Corin frowned. "How long have I slept?"

"Two days now, and going on a third."

"Oh. Well. I rode hard to join you here."

"Clearly." She straightened her shoulders and aimed a pointed look at the knife still poised to throw. "Is that really necessary?"

He considered it. "I don't know. What do you intend here?"

She rolled her eyes. "I intend to talk with you. Frankly, I hope I can convince you to leave this place before the gentlemen are finished discussing you."

Corin sighed and put away his blades. "I'm sorry, Highness, but Fortune's brought me here. We all have our roles to play."

She shook her head. "For all I've disavowed their base morality, I was still raised a Vestossi, so I know better. Men choose the roles they'll play, Corin, whatever politics or powers they blame afterward. Gods preserve us, I know you've chosen yours."

"You couldn't be more wrong." Corin's voice rang cold in his ears, almost hostile, but he couldn't find the warmth to temper it. "Gods and governors have dictated my life since I was abandoned as a babe on the streets of Aepoli. I survive, Princess. That's as much control as I have ever had. I survive. Even now, even as I wage a war against the man who killed the woman I love, that's a destiny laid out for me by a god who died a thousand years before I first drew breath."

"You do not have to take that path," she said, her voice surprisingly gentle now. "I've told you that since the day we first met. I know more of your story than you will let yourself believe. I was born to be a Vestossi princess, Corin Hugh. Consider that dark destiny. And I do not blame my family or Ephitel or druids or my dear Auric or even you, Corin, for sending me to live in fear and poverty in the ruins of a pagan civilization. I do not blame the forces set against me, because they are the forces I *chose* to escape from. They are the forces I chose to battle. This is my destiny, Corin, but only because I chose a difficult happiness over a perfectly pleasant evil."

Corin sucked a deep breath and shook his head. "What would you have me do? There is no pleasantness for me. Not on either side of the coin. I war with Ephitel and die, or else I run and hide and still I die. I've tried both, Princess."

"Call me 'princess' one more time, and I will start to call you 'subject.' Do you understand?"

He smirked, but he bowed his head in acquiescence.

"In answer to your question . . . I don't know. I don't know what you should do. Perhaps you should chase freedom on the open seas. No gods can claim you there, and if ever there was a soul wild enough to escape the storms and shoals, it's yours."

He nodded. "I was an exceptional pirate."

"I have no doubts," she said. "Go back to that."

"I cannot. I cannot forget the things I know."

"Then it is personal," she said. "And though I find it foolish, that is the inherent nature of another's personal obsession. But I would beg you to keep the matter personal. Do not embroil all these people in your desperate war."

"My war is with the gods," Corin answered quietly. "Behind me and before me, there are gods. There is no one who will not be caught up in this." The echo of his oath—of that terrible dream—still rang in his memory. He nodded in acceptance of it. "I am not the instigator, Sera. I am not the agent. I am just the messenger. The creator of this world ripped me out of time to set me on this path. And whether he intended it or not, this is the simple truth: Ephitel dies, or else the world dies. I'm here to offer you the chance to choose a side."

She winced. "You cannot remain committed to such a misguided plan. After everything you've seen?"

He nodded, never releasing her gaze. "I am the harbinger of doom. You have only seen the hundredth part of the chaos I will bring."

She retreated half a step, then threw a glance over her shoulder as if searching for reinforcements. She wet her lips and reluctantly met his eyes again. "But . . . consider all these people."

"When I went to the ancient elves to ask their aid, they said the same. They refused to cast more manling lives upon the fire.

But I will tolerate this world no more. Oberon has shown me what he wants this world to be. And Ephitel has shown me what he intends." Corin closed his eyes, and a vision of Aemilia lying broken on the floor smashed free of his memory and nearly staggered him. He merely nodded.

"I have been running. I have been running from the truth and fighting for my life, but your husband offered me a place of refuge. I have had time to rest and to consider all the things I've seen."

She shook her head in quiet denial and whispered, "No."

He took a step toward her. "I tried so hard to forget everything they showed me. Both of them." He touched the pocket of his cloak that held the precious book of memories he'd stolen from Oberon's dream. He still had never found the courage to read it, though Aemilia had. It had made her fall in love with him.

He blinked back the tears that formed at that. He wouldn't let them fall. He straightened his back and marched on to meet the princess.

"Oberon vested in me the power to conquer Ephitel, and—whether he intended it or not—he gave me too the power to end this miserable dream."

"That is impossible."

"No," Corin said. "That is an alternative solution. Ephitel dies, or the world dies. Either way, the problem's solved."

He stood face to face with her now in the center of the enormous room, and somehow he seemed to fill the space. He felt like he could flex his shoulders and rip apart the stone ceiling a hundred feet above him, like he could stretch out his arms and push down the distant walls.

"You would never do that," Sera said, desperate to believe it.

"I am tired of their games. I am tired of their destinies. I am tired of their politics and ploys. They have hunted me across their precious nations and into the darkest godless corners of this world. They have stabbed at everyone I've ever cared about because I had the audacity to despise them."

"They are gods," she whispered.

"And I am their destruction. I will set you free of them, Princess. One way or another." A cruel smile touched his lips, though he could barely feel it. "Which will you choose?"

"I won't," she said. "I can't."

"Then let me speak with Auric." Regret stabbed hard at Corin's heart then, but again he barely felt it. The kindhearted farmboy would have to make one of the tough choices. It came with the territory.

"Ephitel or the world. What will he decide?"

25

After the massive grandeur of the room Corin had been given, he expected to find Auric in a proper throne room or something like an admiral's war council. But Sera's path took them down from the high hill at the heart of the ruined city, into what would once have been a warren of peasants' hovels. Fire and rot had long since cleared away the wooden structures there, leaving an empty field inside the city walls. But here and there stood old stone buildings—inns or old watch houses that had served the district—and Sera led him straight to one of those. It had been three stories once, but the timber roof was long since gone, and the upper floor had collapsed to fill the middle.

No grand palace, this, but it commanded a clear view of the city gate, and it offered room around it for the hordes of refugees so anxious to be near the farmboy.

There were craftsmen here, and cooks, and tidy organizers like the woman who had fed him that first night. There were guards as well. That took Corin by surprise, though it shouldn't have. Even without Corin, this encampment was a challenge to the gods' authority, and there were at least some among the residents who understood that.

A dozen burly soldiers dressed in arms and mail made a perimeter around the command structure. Their eyes tracked Corin closely as he followed Sera to the door, but no one moved to interfere with the princess. On the contrary: the pressing crowds and the hurrying messengers alike made way for her. She strode through the crowded yard as easily as strolling in her private garden, Corin ever at her heel.

Within the building's interior, Auric sat a court, his throne an upended wooden crate. He leaned his elbow on one knee and listened with apparent interest as a cobbler from Raentz demanded access to the camp's leather stores for his apprentices. "What good is armor if your soldiers are running barefoot into battle? Eh? Eh?"

The farmboy nodded thoughtfully, then told the clerk at his left hand to set aside a portion of the stores for leather. He also made a note to buy a lot more leather.

Corin raised his voice at that. "Send someone down to the stone quay due west of Marzelle. You'll find a flagpole there. Raise a banner in blue and white, and you'll have visitors within a day."

Auric and his attendants all turned to stare at Corin. The farmboy, at least, understood what Corin was suggesting. "Why should we trade with pirates?"

"Because southern Raentz is the worst place in Hurope to purchase leather in any quantity. The men who'll answer to that flag will bring the finest goods from Ithale and Orineth, and all at prices you'll find bearable."

The farmboy frowned at Corin for a moment, weighing the suggestion, and then his gaze drifted past Corin's shoulder to Princess Sera. Auric brightened. "Oh! Jeff had told me you were under a disguise. Come forward. Show your face and speak with me. I have heard no word from Tesyn, and I began to fear I would never learn what came of your adventure."

Corin stumbled at the scholar's name. Tesyn hadn't found his way home yet? That could prove troublesome indeed.

Corin swept a bow to mask his misstep. "I fear there's no time now to share the tale. I bring grim news indeed. I'd beg of you a private audience."

Auric blinked at that. He looked around the room, considering all the petitioners waiting for a chance to be speak with him, and he seemed startled to find them all there.

Sera stepped past Corin's shoulder. "Perhaps it would be best. These other matters can wait."

Auric shrugged sheepishly and raised his voice. "I'm sorry, folks. It seems I am to have a private audience. Go find yourselves some refreshment, and come back here in an hour. We'll get you sorted soon enough."

Corin watched, mystified, while the gathered crowd withdrew politely. No one wasted time in grumbling or complaining. They did just as the farmboy asked of them.

It wasn't that he'd found the world's politest refugees. Corin knew that much. It was a special kind of magic that belonged to the kind young hero. It had already worked on Corin, when he'd shared precious pirate secrets just to help outfit this camp that wouldn't last long enough to benefit from his advice. It didn't matter. He'd been caught up in the dream that wove itself around the farmboy.

He shook his head, staring. "You're remarkable."

Auric raised his eyebrows, clearly baffled by the comment. "I don't know about that, but you are really most unsettling in that disguise. Could I prevail on you to drop it?"

Corin nodded and dissolved the glamour.

The farmboy grinned in answer. "There's the man I know! Can't you tell me *anything* about your adventure with Tesyn?"

Corin had no desire to dwell on that. "The last I saw him," Corin lied, "he was safe and sound. We found the ancient elves and spoke with them. The Isle of Mists is everything you've ever heard, and more."

Auric whistled in appreciation. "What a tale that must be. I can't wait to hear Tesyn tell it."

"We parted ways," Corin said, "but I'm sure he'll find you in due time." Corin would have been happier by far if he didn't believe that last. But alas, the scholar had a way of turning up in the most surprising places.

"He always does," Auric agreed. The farmboy leaned back on his crate, bracing his shoulders against the wall. "Now. What is this urgent news you mean to discuss with me?"

Corin blinked. He'd done it again! Caught up in the farmboy's charisma, he'd lost the immediacy, the compelling drive that had brought him here. Now he straightened his shoulders and clutched at the looming intensity he'd used so effectively against the princess.

"The time has come to end the tyrants' reign. We have discussed these things before, but the time for conversation is done! I mean to see the death of Ephitel, and I would have you fighting at my side."

Auric nodded. "Done." He did not even consider it.

Corin blinked again. "This will be no easy task—"

"To kill a god? I doubt it! But I've seen enough of you to know you'll have some plan. Tell me where you need me, and I'll be there."

"Auric," Sera interrupted, cautioning, "I am not sure you have considered all the ramifications of the man's request."

Auric shook his head. "It doesn't matter. He's convinced me there's no justice in the gods' demands. Ever since we spoke on the matter, I have seen it with my own eyes. This world is twisted and broken beneath their power, and it demands a fix."

Corin stepped closer to him. "You see it, then?"

"Across the whole of Raentz, I see it. Across all Hurope! Do you know what the druids were telling me? There was once a different god, king of all the gods we know, and he had a different plan for Hurope. He meant Spinola to be a friendly place, a refuge for any man or woman who wanted to live free of the gods' strange rules."

Corin raised an eyebrow. "He told you that, did he?"

"Oh, yes. When he brought Sera and me to this place, he was telling me about the nations that stood here before. And then when that justicar came to Taurb and started scaring the people there, we invited them to stay with us and told them the same story. Soon enough, it spread."

The princess pressed forward, pinning Corin with her glare, but she tempered her tone for her farmboy's sake. "It spread because it is a compelling dream. We do not need a war to escape the gods' tyranny. All we require is a refuge, and I begin to think we've found it here."

Corin closed his eyes, considering. It was an alluring tale: a secret land of promised freedom, a nation built outside the gods' domain.

"How many have you gathered to this dream?" Corin asked.

"The next party to arrive will make one thousand." The farmboy sprang to his feet and clapped Corin on the shoulder. "But don't give me all the credit. Everything I said to them came from our conversation by the woodpile. And it was your friends within the Nimble Fingers who carried the message out into the world. They needed a refuge more than anyone, but they weren't greedy. They spread the word, and they've been working to smuggle men and women over borders and across the whole of Raentz unseen, just so they can join us here."

"You've done all this in three months?" Corin asked, awed.

"*We* have. All of us together. Sera's training for the throne made it so much easier. You'd be amazed how she can fashion order out of chaos. And the advice of the druids covered most of the rest. I just help out where I can."

Corin shook his head. "You are remarkable. And you will help me win this war."

Sera shook her head. "We do not need a war to make a place of freedom."

Auric glanced her way and nodded. "Can you imagine such a thing? And you would be the author of it, really. For all the darkness you've endured, you've helped us make a bright and shining light in this place. We'll change the world, Corin. Even if we never kill a god."

Corin didn't answer right away. His head was spinning with the things Auric had said. He could feel the allure of Auric's eager vision. He could already imagine a new Spinola, a manling kingdom carved out of the Wildlands, where justice reigned and elves might fear to tread.

It was impossible, but when bright-eyed Auric spoke, it seemed inevitable. That was all Corin truly needed. As long as the farmboy gathered refugees, as long as he could keep them here united, this camp would be a thorn in Ephitel's side. It was a constant challenge to the ancient gods, and one most personal to Ephitel himself, who had declared this land anathema.

For this, Ephitel would leave his throne on Attos. For this, he'd come to wreak his vengeance. He might send the justicar out first, but she would find no easy victories here, no compliant authorities. She'd find half a thousand Nimble Fingers displaced by her persecution, and at their head a hero who had defeated far worse monsters than a turncoat druid.

A smile touched Corin's lips as he considered it. Jessamine would break her teeth against the camp, and Ephitel would come in person to destroy it. He'd be focused on the farmboy, on the swelling army of Godlander rebels, and he'd never see the strike coming on his flank.

It was all a grand illusion, a puff of mist beneath the summer sun, but Corin had worked wonders with illusion more than once. If he could but build this one to the shape he needed, if he could hold it long enough, he'd have his victory.

He bowed his head toward Auric and answered him. "I am yours. Let us make it so. By my estimation, there are three things we need: resources, men, and time."

Auric nodded. "More men are coming every day, but every one we gain demands yet more resources."

"And I have given you the answer to that. Use the pirates. With the secrets I can give you, you can win their aid. They'll bring food and raw materials."

"I have craftsmen enough to build a city."

"And you will use them. We must make this place secure."

Auric nodded. "We're already hard at work on that. The manticores—"

"Are not the worst you have to fear," Corin interrupted. "You've taken great pains to bring these refugees here in safety, but the gods will not give them up so easily. They'll send justicars against you. They'll send spies to infiltrate your ranks. You must make this place a bastion they cannot compromise."

Auric considered that a moment, then he ducked his head. "Between us, we can manage that. What else?"

"Time," Corin said. "That's the key. If the enemy falls upon us while we're small and weak, he'll crush us. Even here. But if we can hold out for a month or two; if we can double our numbers; if Fortune lets us stay the summer here, I think we'll stand."

He didn't truly need so long as that, he hoped, but he certainly needed time. He had yet to find the sword. But surely this stronghold could stand long enough for that.

The princess seemed to read his thoughts. She arched an eyebrow. "And if the strike comes sooner? If they send an army to destroy us?"

Auric clapped her on the shoulder. "If we cannot fight for victory, we'll fight for glory." She glared up at him in answer, and he only laughed. "Everyone dies, my love. But for the things we're doing here, we'll live in legends at the very least."

Sera left off her argument with Auric and turned her attention to Corin. "Is that what you are hoping for?" she asked, her voice as cool as winter. "To die in glory?"

He opened his mouth to answer her, but she took a slow step closer and fixed him with her gaze. "Is that the destiny Aemilia would wish for you? For all these people here? How many have to die before you will be satisfied?"

Corin had to work moisture into his mouth before he could answer her. "Just one," he rasped. "It's only ever been the one."

26

Before the princess could find some new argument, a messenger appeared at the outer door. He spoke a moment with the farmboy, and then the two approached to speak with Sera. Corin caught the edges of their conversation. It was nothing of any great fascination for him—something about the weather—so Corin nodded in polite acceptance when the farmboy made his apologies. They left him in the war room, alone with his thoughts.

It troubled him how easily the young man had swayed him. Even now, he found himself imagining the glorious kingdom they could build upon these ruins. He shook his head, trying to dispel the image. His destiny lay elsewhere. The farmboy was useful in his way, but he could be dangerous. He didn't even really try. It was astonishing.

Sera's questions troubled him more. That cruel dream had given him the strength to defy the princess for a moment, but she had found his hidden fear. What would Aemilia think of this? How much sacrifice could she condone, even in pursuit of Oberon's design? He ground his teeth until his jaw ached, but he could find no answers.

They were the sort of thoughts that needed drowning deep in distilled spirits. No matter how desperate they were, a gathering this size would have to boast some form of tavern. Corin wrapped himself within his cloak and his careful glamour, and then he headed for the door.

As Corin passed outside, a spindly old Raentzman looked up with eyes full of hope. His expression soured when he saw that Corin was alone. He leaned aside, trying to catch a glimpse back into the empty building.

"You'll have to come back later," Corin said in passing. "The boy's been called away."

The old man furrowed his brow. "Again? Storm and sorrow, what will it take to catch him?"

Caught up as Corin had been in thoughts of Auric's special magic, the mild complaint stopped him in his tracks.

Corin frowned. He'd thought the old man looked familiar at first glance—like any Raentzman from the country, really—but now that he looked closer, he recognized the man.

"Jacob Gossler?" Corin asked. "From Taurb? Did you once run a country tavern?"

"I did," the old man said, his attention still mostly on the empty building. "Would you know if he means to return soon?"

"I couldn't say. But I can sympathize with your frustration. If you'll show me where to find one, I'd be glad to offer you a drink."

Jacob turned at that, finally submitting Corin to a close inspection. "I might know a place or two. New here, are you?"

"Aye," Corin said, following as the other man set a brisk pace back up into the city. "And you've been here awhile?"

"Near enough a month now, and not a day has passed I didn't try to catch the blasted hero for a chat. Twice a day, most days, and lately I've gone by there three, four times. Fortune's forgot me, friend. Storm and sorrow!"

Corin shared a rueful grin, but his mind was racing. This old man was a puzzle. A hundred others had happily abandoned their petitions at a brisk dismissal, but Jacob didn't hesitate to vent his frustration.

In a strange way, that comforted Corin. As exciting as Corin's life had become, it helped to see ordinary men behaving in ordinary ways. This Jacob was a country man, too old and gnarled to bend before the breeze of Auric's charisma. Yet he was here.

Corin frowned. "What brings you to the camp, Master Jacob?"

"This and that," the old man said. "And you?"

"Vengeance," Corin answered. He'd decided long ago that this man could be trusted, and it warmed Corin's heart to speak the truth. "Hatred. I want to see Ephitel punished for what he's done."

"Ah. The justicar. She's responsible for most of those who've come here."

"Not just her," Corin said. "Ephitel himself. How many senseless wars has he stirred up among our nations? How many deaths for his vainglory? This justicar is just the newest of his atrocities."

Jacob nodded, thoughtful. "I've heard some talk like that, though most of it has been more . . . circumspect." He walked awhile in silence, considering Corin from the corner of his eye. "You make it all sound personal."

"I've seen his face," Corin said. He closed his eyes and let the glamour melt away.

The tavern keeper gave a startled grunt, but that was his only reaction. A moment later, he nodded in recognition. "Now there's the face of a man who could bring a grudge against a god."

Corin looked away. "I never meant your village to get caught up in it."

"Anything worth doing has its consequences," Jacob said beside him. He walked a moment in silence, considering, then frowned sideways at the pirate. "I've heard an awful lot of rumors swirling around your name, but no one ever said you were a wizard."

"Not a wizard," Corin said. "I am a lot of things, but I am not a wizard. I couldn't be; I lack the discipline."

Jacob chortled at that. "Still, it's like living in a children's tale to watch a man change faces. Do you know any other tricks?"

"I know how to kill a god," Corin said quietly. "How would you like to see that firsthand?"

The old man didn't answer right away. He weighed the question, sucking on a tooth and staring at something far away.

In the end, he shrugged. "I can't say I'd rush to be at the front, but I'll tell you this: There's times even a good animal needs to be put down. Show me a justicar who treats innocent townsfolk like that girl treated Taurb, and I'll show you a god gone rabid."

Corin clapped him on the shoulder. "You're a good man."

"Not at all. But I take the world I'm given and do the best I can with it."

Corin carried those words awhile, turning them over. As hard as he'd tried to force the issue from his mind, Sera's questions still scratched at the back of his mind. But now the tavern keeper's words gave Corin a perspective to consider what he'd shied away from before. Eyes fixed on the ground, shoulders tense, he spoke his fears. "Auric thinks we can fix things without killing anyone."

"Young fellows get strange notions sometimes. Especially when they're in love."

Corin snorted. "Sera doesn't think we can fix things at all. She thinks we should come to terms with that."

"Huh. That doesn't really seem your nature, though."

"Not at all. But she also thinks—" Corin choked on the words he meant to say. He had to clear his throat, and still his voice came hoarse. "She doesn't think Aemilia would want me to do this."

The tavern keeper let a respectful silence take a breath, then he asked, "That's your girl?"

"She was," Corin said. "And Ephitel's victim."

"Well, there's an easy way to guess what she would want."

"Aye?"

"Ask yourself what she loved most. Was it your caution and careful sense, or your passion and your fury?"

Corin chuckled. "You have a way of cutting through the complicated problems."

"I've spent a lifetime polishing a bar. It's in my nature."

"You know what she really loved?" Corin said, staring off into the distance once again. "More than anything else, she loved Hurope."

"All of it?"

"All of it. Everything it represented. Everything it could have been."

"I get the feeling you're not including Ephitel in that."

Corin shook his head. "He was never supposed to be a god."

"Then that brings us right back where we started. There's times when even a good animal needs to be put down."

"Aye," Corin said. "I don't know if you'd remember, but when we first met back in Taurb, I asked of you a favor."

"Hah! How could I forget? That crazy old dwarf."

"You met him then?"

"Sure. He came through town two days behind you. Maybe three."

Corin drew a ragged breath. "And? You gave him my message?"

"I tried, but he would scarcely listen. The rumors reached him first."

"What rumors?"

"About you! You left Taurb with that justicar hot on your heels, and when the dwarf showed up asking after a stranger dressed in black, you can bet he found plenty of men willing to share the tale."

"Gods' blood," Corin whispered.

"You said it. Everyone thought you must be dead by the road somewhere, but the dwarf had to go and see for himself. I caught him halfway out the door, and he only stopped that long because I said I had a message from you. Told him everything you said to."

Corin sighed. "But I don't suppose he listened. That explains why Jane said there were rumors he'd been all over Raentz. Probably searching for some sign of me."

"He'd have gone by Rauchel, then. It wasn't half a week after you left before those rumors started slinking in. Every tavern in Raentz must have heard that Captain Corin had arrived a hero in Rauchel. And left that very night for the Isle of Mists."

Corin rubbed his eyes. "Oh, sweet Fortune, he wouldn't have tried to follow me there. Would he?" The thought of the city dwarf wandering through those choking fogs lay hard on Corin's heart.

The tavern keeper seemed to sense it. He lowered his voice and looked away. "I'm sorry, son. He seemed dead-set on finding you."

"He's an artist," Corin said. "He's a drinker and a gambler. He's not a hero. I never should have sent him from Aerome."

"Perhaps he's found his way back by now," the tavern keeper said, though he didn't sound as though he believed it. "Perhaps he never left Rauchel. I don't know where he'd have found a captain fool enough to sail him there."

"Then you don't know what a captain's willing to trade for a dwarven sextant," Corin said. He sank down on his knees, shoulders bowed beneath the weight of his poor choices. "I did this. I set him on this journey. I asked him to carry it for me, just for safekeeping, and now it's lost with his poor, stupid corpse somewhere on the Isle of Mists—"

"The parcel?" Jacob asked, frowning. "You're so concerned about that parcel he was carrying? Not for your friend?"

"We all die someday, tavern keeper," Corin said. "All of us but Ephitel, without that parcel."

The tavern keeper rolled his eyes. "I'd hate to call you friend, Captain Hugh, but I can soothe your heart at least. The dwarf did tarry long enough to hear your message, after all."

"Aye? And?"

"And he could no more guess at where to find a druid than I could. He was so anxious to get after you, no matter how I insisted, so he handed his parcel off to me. And I've been trying to deliver it ever since."

Corin stared up into the old man's eyes. "*You* have the sword?"

"It's not a sword. It's more a scrollcase."

"But Ben delivered it to you?"

"He said you'd clearly trusted me enough to ask the favor. Truth be told, he was far more worried about your safety than some artifact."

He said the words with accusation, but Corin felt no sting. His heart soared with hope. He had the sword.

Jacob was still grumbling. "A right nuisance it has been too. That's what brought me here. They said the farmer hero had a refuge with the druids, but you just try and find a druid who'll give you the time of day. Try to find a minute with the hero! He's always caught up in something. If I'd known *you* were here, I could have been done with it."

Corin was barely listening. His euphoria took on a sickly cast. He had the sword. It was here, with him. How long had Sera said he slept? Three days? Four? Long enough for Jessamine to sense the two in close proximity, no doubt. Long enough for her to report to Ephitel. Long enough for them to plan a strike.

He staggered to his feet and gripped the old man by his shoulders. "We have to find the farmboy. We have to warn him."

Jacob frowned. "Because I have some scrolls?"

Corin shook his head, furious. "We're out of time. It's happening too soon."

"What is? What's happening?"

"War," Corin said, remembering the force of soldiers Jessamine had brought to Raentz before. Ephitel could not be entirely blind to what was happening here, and Jessamine had abandoned all restraint since her visit into Faerie. She would bring overwhelming forces, if she thought she could capture him here. "How far would Ephitel go to keep his place on Attos?"

"He'd burn the world," Jacob said, unhesitant.

"Aye," Corin said. "But I suspect he'll start with us."

27

W here is the sword?" Corin asked.

"The *scrollcase* is in my room," Jacob said. "I'll be glad to turn it over—"

"Keep it," Corin said, his mind racing. Fortune favor, he would need it soon enough, but until then he hoped a little separation might be enough to keep Jessamine from walking straight to him. "Fetch it. Keep it close. I'll have Auric assign someone to watch you."

The old man raised his eyebrows. "I'm not a helpless babe."

"Against Jessamine, you would be."

Jacob shrugged, conceding the point. "But how do you mean to find Auric? I've been trying for weeks—"

"I was just in council with him," Corin said, sifting through his memory. A messenger had come to summon Auric to investigate some minor matter at the city walls. Something about the weather. It hadn't been half an hour. With any luck, he was still there.

"I'll find him," Corin said. "You go and fetch the sword. Then meet us at the war room."

Jacob opened his mouth to argue more, but Corin didn't wait. He turned and dashed back down the hill, rushing to the gates beneath the city walls. From half a mile off, he could see them gathered there. The messenger whipped his head around at Corin's fast approach, but the princess and the farmboy never turned from their consideration of the landscape outside the city.

"Grave news," Corin panted, stumbling to a halt at Auric's side. "We must . . . prepare . . ."

Before he could say more, the farmboy grabbed his shoulder and thrust him forward, showing him the wide, low valley spread before the city's gates. "Corin! I'm glad you're here. You've seen even stranger places than I have. Can you explain this?"

Corin didn't look. He twisted against the farmboy's grip, trying desperately to catch his eyes. "You don't understand! The Godlanders . . . they know . . ."

Auric shook his head. "No. That's what Sera thinks, but I can't imagine how a fog could be some sort of ploy. It's certainly strange, though; I've never seen its like."

Corin went still. He stopped fighting Auric and turned his attention to the east.

Fog lay across the valley, despite the afternoon's warmth. It was no normal mist, but a thick, roiling bank of fog two paces high and stretching out across the valley and up into the plains beyond. Even from a distance, it chilled him to the bone.

"I have seen its like," Corin said. "On the Isle of Mists. And Jessamine was there too."

Auric laughed. "You cannot mean she is responsible for the terrors that hang over that place?"

Corin shook his head. "I mean she might well have gotten the idea from there. What better way to move an army undetected?"

"An army?" Sera asked, alarmed. "What news is this?"

The messenger darted between them, stabbing a finger out toward the fog. "A rider! Who approaches?"

All four leaned forward, straining their eyes for a clearer view as a man on horseback resolved out of the fog. He'd been on an uneven path, aimed somewhere south of the city's ruins, but as soon as he broke clear, he dragged on the reins and bore his horse hard toward the city.

Corin recognized the rider half a heartbeat before Auric heaved a relieved sigh. "Hartwin! Noble Hartwin. Corin, you had me half-expecting a justicar!"

Corin felt no such relief, especially when he caught sight of the young soldier's grim expression. He was haggard, and his horse was blowing from a hard ride, but Hartwin did not relent. When he spotted Auric waiting, he bent lower and drove his spurs into the beast's sides.

"What news is this?" Sera whispered.

"They're coming for us," Corin said.

Auric squeezed his shoulder, reassuring. "It's only Hartwin." But he did not sound convinced.

The young knight sprang from his saddle at full gallop and sprinted the last distance. Auric pushed past Corin and ran to catch his friend in an embrace. It was likely all that kept the younger man from collapsing.

"What news?" Auric asked, pushing him out to arm's length but still holding him. "You were to wait at Taurb for more refugees."

"She's back," Hartwin said. "The justicar. She's kept it secret, but I have eyes and ears. She's back, and she means to end us."

Sera stepped forward. "How could she? On what grounds? We break no laws to gather here."

Hartwin shook his head, eyes rolling like a panicked horse's. "She does not bring police."

"Soldiers?" Corin asked.

Hartwin shook his head again. "Sharpshooters. Gladiators. And wizards."

Corin nodded. "That explains the fog."

"They're already marching," Hartwin said. "I passed by them at Reconciliation. Where else could they be going?"

"Gods preserve us," Auric whispered.

"How far?" Sera asked. "How long do we have?"

"A day at most. She has perhaps a hundred men to coordinate, but these are not foot soldiers. They travel light and strike fast."

"A hundred gladiators," Auric said, awestruck. "How could she bring so many?"

"Not all were gladiators," Hartwin said. "But they do stand out, and I saw at least a score of them. The rest were mostly crossbowmen."

"And wizards," Corin said, feeling numb.

"Those I did not see myself," Hartwin said apologetically. "But rumors spoke of them. And there is the fog, of course."

"That would take a mighty effort," Auric said, waving to the horizon. "Ridgemon could not do a hundredth part of that. Even if she brought several masters, it will take all their concentration to maintain it."

"And if she brought more than several?" Corin asked. It was a preposterous notion, but no less so than a score of gladiators. Those were the fiercest soldiers that Hurope had to offer; survivors of the ruthless Games, they were born and bred for battle. Rarely had any field seen more than one or two gladiators, but they were always decisive factors.

The young knight trembled. "I do not think we can win."

"They will not make war on us," Auric said, striving to encourage his friend. "We have done no wrong. How many innocent women and children are gathered in those walls? No justicar could unleash that kind of death upon them."

Corin met the princess's eyes and saw in them the same certainty he felt. Jessamine was lost to reason. She had become a plague, and if she had brought such a force as this into the Wildlands, she would scour these ruins down to bedrock.

There was another certainty in Sera's expression: This was Corin's fault. He'd doomed them all by coming here. The timing was too great a coincidence for it to have been anything else. She spoke no word of accusation; she merely held his gaze, but it was enough to convey how much she hated him.

Then she took the young knight's hand and pulled him away from Auric. "Come," she said. "We'll need to spread the word among the refugees, prepare them for her arrival. We can find you food and drink while we are at it."

He nodded, mute, and caught his horse's reins before shuffling after her into the town. She threw one glance back over her shoulder, and she spent her glare entirely on Corin. He'd made an enemy there.

But a far worse one was coming. He turned to Auric. "How many can you field? I've heard you have a thousand in your camp."

"Yes, but they are farmers and housewives. Fighting men? I might find a hundred men to throw against hers."

"You mean more former free lances?" Corin asked. "Men like you and Hartwin?"

"Some. And then some regulars who fought in border wars—"

Corin shook his head. "A decade gone?"

"Or more. We were not recruiting for an army here."

"I wouldn't wager on a hundred farmers who still own rusty swords against a single gladiator, and she has at least a score of them. But there are the druids." He heaved a small sigh as he remembered the druids he'd seen before. "How many are here?"

Auric shook his head. "A dozen, but they will not participate in armed conflict. They told me so from the first."

Corin cursed. "Then we cannot stand. Not here. Not now. We must run."

"Run? But you were so thirsty for a war."

Corin shook his head. "Not now. I told you I needed time—"

"But there is none," Auric said. "We make our plans and watch them crumble, and then we fight the field we're given."

Corin shook his head. "That's foolishness."

Auric met his eyes. There was no hope in his expression, no clever spark. He didn't even summon up the gentle lie he'd offered Hartwin. "You asked for a war against the gods. This is what it looks like, Corin. It's hopeless. It was always hopeless. But I will lead my men to battle regardless."

Corin shook his head. "I told you, I have a plan! I just need time. We can salvage this, but not if our only fighting men die in a senseless charge here."

"A senseless charge? This is the battle you've been begging me to fight. This is the proof of everything you've claimed. We did nothing to defy them, but still they raised against us a force such as Hurope has not seen since the pagan wars. If we had made camp any closer to the Dividing Line, we'd already be massacred."

"And you will rush to war against that very force. You're giving them the massacre they want."

Auric met Corin's eyes. "What do you propose?"

"We should withdraw. They don't know our disposition here. Even when they close on us, they'll do it with care, but we have time to slip away. I have hope that I can fool them with a glamour. If I make them think the camp is fortified, they'll come on slow."

"And where are we to run to?"

"Further inland," Corin said. "Anywhere away from them. You have friends among the savages. If we can evade them for a week or two, they will withdraw and leave us time to make a better plan."

Auric considered that a moment. "That seems a fragile hope for men defying gods."

"Better than going to their slaughter."

"Why?" Auric asked, his gaze penetrating. "Why such restraint now, when you've been begging for this conflict all this time?"

Corin chewed his lip a moment, considering his answer, before settling for the truth. "It's not gladiators and wizards I want dead. It never was. Win or lose, this is not the fight I'm looking for."

"Not the Godlanders? Then who—"

"It's the gods I want. I need you and your men to bring me Ephitel. What good have we accomplished if you kill a dozen soldiers?"

Auric's jaw dropped. "You mean that?"

"Every word of it."

"You're not a soldier, are you?"

Corin frowned. "I have been many things—"

"But not a soldier."

"No," Corin admitted. "I've never been a soldier."

"It shows," Auric said. "You're still talking about the war you planned for, blind to the battle raging around us."

"I'm not blind! I'm suggesting a better strategy."

"For your war," Auric said. "You're staring into the distance and dreaming how to use today's victory, oblivious to the certainty of defeat."

The certainty of defeat? From Auric, who could do the impossible? The sentiment shook Corin to his core. He couldn't let this man give up.

So he invested his voice with all the scorn he could manage. "Surrender, Auric? Before the fight has even been engaged? That is no noble sentiment."

"And I do not mean to surrender. I mean to fight."

"But you have said—"

"I've said we cannot win. You said it too. Your best plan is to slink away and buy some time."

"But if you don't hope to win, why fight at all?"

"To save the others."

Corin frowned. "What others?"

"The refugees. The women and the children. Your Nimble Fingers. All those who came here for your dream, not for my war." Corin sighed. "There are good souls among them, but none of those will decide this war. Would you really throw away our fighting men for the sake of our civilians?"

"Every time. Every single time."

Corin gaped. "But why?"

"That's what fighting men are for, Corin. We sacrifice ourselves to the horrors of war so that the rest of you won't have to. We pay a price in blood—our own and the stain of others'—to preserve the lives of men whose hands are clean."

Corin shook his head. "That does not explain your objection to my plan. If we delay the enemy forces and slip away—"

"Deeper into the Wildlands! One man in seven would be lucky to survive."

"You've survived there."

"And I'm a soldier. Every man I brought with me here was battle trained before he ever crossed the Dividing Line, and even so we've had our losses. Your Nimble Fingers might live like kings on the darker streets of their great cities, but they would freeze in terror at a wyvern raid. They would turn and fight beside a manticore against my men. I will not take civilians on a desperate flight into the Wildlands."

"But if they stay here—"

"If they stay here and fight, they'll die. If we wait for the Godlanders to come into the camp, they'll slaughter everyone here. But if the fighting men go out to face them, if we send a sally and they cut us down, the Godlanders will show mercy to our noncombatants."

Corin gaped. "That's your entire plan? You'll go off to die and let the Godlanders make prisoners and slaves of those you leave behind?"

"If it means they survive, I will. But it will not be as grim as that. They will most likely escort the survivors back to Raentz; perhaps some officer will question them, and then they will be free to go."

A brusque laugh escaped from Corin. "Ephitel is not known for his mercy."

"But Ephitel will not decide this matter. Soldiers will."

"And Godlander soldiers show such honor?"

"In this matter, they will. Out of selfishness, if nothing else."

"Oh?"

Auric nodded. "You see? If you were a soldier, you would already know this. Every camp has its followers—often wives among them, sometimes children, always friends. A soldier might slaughter his foes to the man, but they will show mercy to the camp followers, if only because next time, it might be their own."

Corin shook his head. "You've given up. You've given up completely."

Auric gave a laugh, though there was no joy in it. "I never thought we'd win a war against the gods. Did you?"

"Aye! And I still think we can. If you didn't believe, why in Fortune's fickle name would you have brought all these people here? Why welcome me against all Sera's admonitions?"

Auric cocked his head, confused. "Because it needed doing."

"But if you thought you'd die—"

"I know I'll die. All men die. If I can strike a blow before I fall, if I can go out fighting for what's right, I'll count it all a victory."

"But you could do so much more! You have a talent such as I have never seen before. Men follow you, Auric. They believe in you! Don't waste that for some noble gesture. Escape this massacre, and we can change the world. We can fix it for the better—not just buy a miserable escape for this little crowd of refugees, but for all mankind. For ages yet to come."

Auric rested a hand on Corin's shoulder. "With or without Ephitel, there will still be wars. There will still be tyranny. There will always be some injustice to battle, Corin. It's not a soldier's duty to change the world, but to do everything he can today."

"But you are more than a soldier, Auric!"

"No. You want me to be more, but that doesn't mean I am. I know how to be an honorable soldier . . . I cannot fathom how to be the creature you want me to be."

"I can see it in you, even if you can't. Trust in me."

For a long time Auric was silent, but then he shook his head. "If you weren't asking me to sacrifice civilians, perhaps I could.

But this is who I am. This is what I do. You're not a soldier, Corin. Hide among the other refugees, and I will buy your life with mine. It cannot be that hard for you to find another general to support your cause."

"You're more than a general! You're born to be a king."

Auric laughed incredulously. "A king? Me? I'm as common as they come, Corin. If you could make a king of me, you can make a king of anyone."

"You're a hero. For all your modesty, you don't deny that."

"I've seen too much evidence."

"Then embrace it! Forget this mad plan to die in glorious battle, and start devising some scheme to survive."

"If I can do it with only soldiers, I will. But if it brings the civilians into play, I'll die instead."

Corin nodded. "I understand. Give me half an hour, and I'll come up with something."

"To defy the gods? To overcome an army such as this?"

Corin smirked. "It's better odds than I could have hoped for. But wait for me. I need some time to think."

"I never meant to ride before tomorrow's dawn. I have yet to explain the truth to Sera, and she will want to offer her good-byes."

"Twelve hours, then." Corin shook his head. "Go to her, but tell her there's still hope. I will buy you years of happiness together, out from underneath the thumbs of Ephitel and of Sera's wretched family. That's what we're fighting for."

"And you think we can win?"

"I will not stop until it's done."

Again, Auric considered him for a long while. Then he shrugged one shoulder and put on a genuine grin. "I can't wait to see what you imagine, Corin Hugh. No matter what, it will be fun to try."

"We'll crush them," Corin said. "We'll force their god to show himself, and then I'll strike him down. And that will change the world."

"As I said, I'll try. Now you go to your planning, and I'll go to my wife."

"She won't want you to die, Auric."

"No. But she loves me for my honor. She won't want me to buy my life with another's blood either. You have my conditions, Corin. Devise a plan within them, or take advantage of my offer. Aught else would be a great betrayal."

"Have faith. I'll use you as you want me to."

Auric shared a smile before he left. "I suppose that counts as honor for a pirate."

Corin watched the farmboy climb the hill toward the battered stone building he used for a war room. When Auric disappeared within, Corin turned back to the fog and heaved a weary sigh. "I don't want honor, Auric. I want vengeance. Fortune favor me with both, or tomorrow we will bleed."

28

Corin wasted half an hour searching for some plan that might satisfy the farmboy, but he found nothing. When sunset cast her long red rays into the dancing fog, Corin shook his head and set off walking instead.

He headed up into the city and caught the shoulder of the first refugee he spotted. "Where are the druids? I must speak with them."

The stranger gave him a shrug in answer, and Corin found the same from two more refugees before a man in chainmail answered in a broken Ithalian. Up the hill and right at the crumbled tower. Half a mile down.

Corin had to ask a dozen times more and double back more than once, but sometime after sunset he poked his head in at the open door of some ancient storeroom and found Jeff himself stuffing dirty clothes into a linen bag.

The room was large enough to house at least a dozen men in comfort, and by the scuffs in the thick dust that coated the floor, Corin would guess it had seen recent use by at least half so many. But only one bedroll remained, and even as Corin watched, Jeff knelt and began packing that as well.

Corin slipped into the room and eased the door shut behind him. Then he turned to the druid. "Leaving? I guess you've heard, then."

Jeff raised his head at the sound of Corin's voice, but he didn't turn.

Corin went on. "I have seen the power of those silly trinkets your people use for weapons. You could make a difference."

Jeff shook his head. "We have our orders."

"Do you know how Auric means to save the innocents here? Do you understand exactly what it is your Council has decided to sacrifice?"

"We couldn't win this war for you," Jeff said, his voice strained. "You can't possibly believe a few tranquilizers would make such a difference."

"They have gladiators," Corin said. "They have wizards. We need anything we can get."

Jeff nodded, still unwilling to face Corin. "Yep. You're right. And you can't get any druids."

"Not even you?"

"Not even me." He climbed to his feet and slung the heavy linen bag over his shoulder. Then he turned to face Corin with his chin held high. "I have my orders."

"This is Jessamine," Corin said, accusing. "She's one of your own. How can you possibly pretend the druids have no responsibility here?"

Jeff ground his teeth and glared at Corin, but he gave no other answer.

Corin nodded. "Aye. You know. She has come here to reclaim the sword and destroy the only credible threat Ephitel has ever faced. In the process she'll carve a path through Auric and Princess Sera and countless other noble souls. And your Council believes their best choice is to stand aside and watch?"

"We cannot win this!" Jeff said. "You're right. Of course she's our responsibility. But so is everything else! All of Hurope depends on the druids, and if we threw ourselves away in some reckless battle—"

"You might just fix Hurope," Corin shouted. "It's broken, Jeff. It has been broken for centuries, and for all your efforts, you've never made it any better. It's time to fight! Fix it or end it."

The druid clenched his hands in fists and bounced on his toes, wrestling with Corin's plea, but in the end he shook his head. "I have my orders. You can't imagine how difficult it will be to repair what you've done here."

Corin answered with a sneer. "Oh, you have my deepest sympathy. I hope it doesn't trouble you too much." He spun on his heel and ripped the door open.

Behind him, Jeff called, "Corin, wait!"

Corin hesitated. "Aye?"

"I found one of the answers you were looking for. The dwarf Strunk. He's in a prison outside Pri, on the road toward Rauchel."

Corin's shoulders tensed. He'd heard how Jessamine treated her prisoners. "The justicar found him?"

"Nope," Jeff said. "Way I understand it, he propositioned the wife of a maréchal. He's missed all the excitement. If you want, I can probably make arrangements to get him sprung."

Corin didn't even answer. Breaking Ben out of a country prison wouldn't take him half a day. Fortune favor, old Ben would probably talk his own way free any moment this. That was all the druids had to offer?

Corin had no more patience for them. He slammed the door behind him as he left. Then he found a kitchen and consumed a bowl of stew, without tasting a single spoonful. He visited the tavern keeper, Jacob, and he very nearly buckled the ancient sword on his belt. But Ephitel would not be here, not on this field, and the sword was still too precious a thing to risk.

So instead, he gave special instructions to the tavern keeper and left him to his rest. He found a modest rapier instead, a simple and familiar weapon to complement the dagger and the knife he always carried. He armed himself by starlight, and then he went back to the city gates, to the same place Auric had left him, and he spent the hours left him trying in vain to find some way to win.

❦

The morrow dawned gray and chill, and sunrise showed the heavy fog now pressed right up against the city's walls. From his place beneath the city wall, Corin could hardly make out the orange glow of campfires among the enemy forces. He could feel them, though, like a blight upon the dream. If he closed his eyes, he could almost sense the circling snare of his enemies outside the camp.

How many wizards did they have? That was what Corin had to know. How many, and where were they? And could they see through Corin's glamours the way he saw through others'?

He wore no glamour now, but he would need one before this day was done, and if the wizards had any talent there, it could prove his undoing. The druids could have told him yea or nay. Aemilia could have. Why had he never asked her?

He tamped down the bitter flare of anger and regret. Aemilia was gone. She was reason enough to do what needed doing now, but dwelling on it wouldn't bring her back.

He clenched his fists and strained his eyes against the fog, searching for some last-minute flaws in his designs. He could not see any yet, but they would come once swords were crossed. They would come.

He heaved a sigh and turned away. "They'll be coming soon," he said. "If you're going to go, then go."

Auric sat astride his warhorse with two dozen men arrayed behind him. He looked down on Corin with a sympathetic gravity. "You have found no scheme to save us?"

There was no self-pity in the question, no remorse for the sacrifice he meant to make. There was only sympathy for the pain and frustration he knew he was causing Corin.

Corin hadn't found a scheme that would satisfy the farmboy, but he did have a plan. It wasn't one he dared reveal, though. So he painted his face with mock chagrin and shook his head.

"Gods preserve us, then," Auric said. "You have your part to play, and I have mine. I'll see you in another world."

The farmboy had never looked more a hero than he did this day. He nodded his good-bye to Corin, then raised up in his stirrups to better signal his commanders. He wore plate armor like a second skin, steel polished so it shone like silver. He shouted, "For honor!" as he raised his broadsword overhead. "For glory!" The blade caught the bronze light of a fog-shrouded sunrise, then flashed copper as he stabbed it forward to signal the charge. "For freedom!"

His golden hair ruffled in the wind as he spurred his horse toward the fray. The fool wouldn't wear a helmet. He *meant* to be a target on the field.

Corin couldn't deny the effect, though. A hundred fighting men swarmed after him, pounding hard across the ground, whether they were mounted or on foot, and every man among them seemed just as eager as the farmboy for a fight they couldn't hope to survive.

It was foolishness. But for all his craftiness, Corin had found no way to stop it. He *did* have a plan, but it was a risky one. And it would earn him enemies almost as terrible as those he already fought.

He planned to steal the farmboy from the fight. That was the best he could do. He'd wait until the fight was well engaged, until Auric had shown himself on the field and committed all his fighting men as he intended. Then Corin would conceal himself in a glamour, steal to Auric's side, and drag him off through dream while the others fell in battle.

He suspected it would serve the farmboy's goals. He'd have the rout he wanted, and Corin would have the farmboy alive and safe. He'd have preferred a victory, of course. He'd even have preferred to risk the Wildlands with all the people they'd already gathered. But Auric had denied him that, and the farmboy was too precious a resource to let slip away.

That still left a rocky course for Corin. If he stole Auric from the fight before it was truly engaged, before he was *seen* in the heat of battle, his own ploy wouldn't work. Auric's soldiers wouldn't charge to their slaughter without the farmboy in the lead, and without that, the civilians would be doomed.

That meant Corin had to wait. He had to time his strike. He had to keep much closer than he ever would have wished, watching for the perfect opportunity to snatch his prize away. And all the while, he and Auric both would be treading the fine line between life and death.

He bounced on the balls of his feet, trembling with nervous energy while he stared east toward the looming fight. Somewhere out there in the fog, trumpets sounded. The Godlanders were roused to battle.

Corin cursed. This was no place for him. He was no soldier. But he had need of one. He cursed again, touched the handles of his blades for comfort, then started forward, following the charging soldiers.

He hadn't gone three paces when a strong hand clamped around his shoulder. He spun in place, trying to tear away, but he couldn't fight that grip. His free hand found his dagger and had it half raised before he recognized the man who'd caught him.

"Kellen?"

Corin whipped his head left and right, searching for some explanation for the elf's sudden appearance, but he found none. The land was rocky and uneven here, crawling with the low fog, but still it was a testament to Kellen's prowess that he had crept so close entirely unnoticed.

Despite that prowess, the old elf looked older still since his encounter with the justicar. Dark lines creased his brow, and new scars marked his throat and collarbone. Yet he lived. And he was here. Corin stared in awe.

"Kellen," Corin said again, bewildered. "How are you here?"

"A mutual friend persuaded me to come and speak with you."

"Avery?" Corin asked. That was almost as astonishing.

"I believe he suffered some persuading too," Kellen said.

Corin nodded. That would be the work of the dear lady Jane. Even the elves of old Gesoelig could prove fools for a pretty face. Fortune favor, that would never change.

"Have you changed your mind, then?" Corin asked. "If you've come to join us in our fight against Ephitel, you've only barely made it. Our last, best hope is even now charging in to die."

"I've seen the same before," Kellen said, sad and weary. "No. It is but chance I found you on the brink of battle. I did hear rumors on the way, and I came all the faster, but in truth . . . I only hurried in the hope of catching you before you slipped away."

Corin's heart sank at that. "You came to speak, then?" He poured all the contempt he could find into that. "You came to reprimand me more? Good men will die today, but you did not come here to fight?"

Kellen raised his chin. "I came here because Avery asked me to." After a moment's hesitation, he dropped his chin again. He looked deep in Corin's eyes. "And then you surprised me. I watched you send your champion off into the fray. I understand his plans today, and there is much honor in them."

"Good men, dead," Corin spat. "And bad men, the only victors."

Kellen nodded. "As I said before. That is the way this battle always goes."

"Then why interrupt me?" Corin asked.

Kellen still held Corin's shoulder, and now his stare grew even sharper. There was something searching in it, like an investigator at the question, even as he offered answers. "Because you surprised me. I thought I knew you, Corin Hugh. Down through the ages I've known many men like you. And when I saw your champion ride off to die, I expected you to slink away, to find some way to escape your destiny that you might carry on your war."

Corin held his breath. He didn't blink, didn't twitch under the elf's intense scrutiny. He *had* intended to slink away, but if Kellen wanted to believe otherwise, Corin would be happy to encourage it. He looked Kellen square in the eye and spoke with deep sincerity. "I already told you once: I mean to fight this war with my own hands. I am not a king, and I am not a general. I don't know how to send other men to die, but I know how to dive into the fray."

Kellen held his gaze a moment longer, still considering. Then he bowed his head in admiration. "You are a better man than I had guessed."

Corin nodded, and then he turned toward the distant charge. Already, Auric's men were nearly lost within the fog, but the shining farmboy on his massive charger radiated like a beacon. Corin stabbed a finger after him. "There goes an even better man than I, and he leads a hundred souls dedicated to defying Ephitel. Will you stand here and watch them fall?"

Kellen showed his teeth. "Not willingly."

"Then let us go to battle!" Corin cried. "Kellen Strong will ride for Oberon once more!"

A cheer went up in answer to that. "Kellen Strong and Oberon!" Corin started as half a dozen more elves dashed out of the fog, every one of them as much a surprise as Kellen himself had been. They flowed forward across the uneven ground like a school of eels, settling in perfect formation behind Kellen. Then half a dozen long, sharp-edged rapiers stabbed toward the sky, and half a dozen fervent voices cried out again, "Kellen Strong and Oberon!"

Kellen ducked his head and ran a hand through his hair. In that moment, all the cruel years disappeared, and he was the same modest, gentle soldier Corin had met in Oberon's strange dream.

"I found a few who will stand with me," Kellen said in explanation.

Corin raised his voice for all of them. "Ephitel has sent some fierce assassins to destroy this stain against his pride.

There's at least a hundred soldiers charging through that fog, and they are more than pikes and bows. They have gladiators."

One of the soldiers sneered in answer. "And we have elves! I'll kill a hundred gladiators."

Corin felt a flare of hope, bright and painful in his breast. He'd watched Kellen battle Jessamine. If these others were half as good as Kellen, this handful of elves might well turn the tide of battle.

Corin nodded, thoughtful. "They might have wizards too."

"Then we will die in glory! But for my part, I'll do my best to take one of those wretched wizards with me."

They could win. The very thought felt impossible, but Corin couldn't quite quash the searing thread of hope. If they killed Ephitel's assassins, would that be enough? Would he come in person then? Corin had planned to build a vast rebellion, to steal away Auric just to start anew and wait for months, for *years* perhaps, to draw Ephitel out to settle their defiance.

But this could be enough. Here and now, he could have his vengeance. He drew a shaky breath and pushed the hair back from his eyes. "For justice," he said. "For Aemilia. To war!"

He turned to lead the charge, his heart hammering and blood burning with the thrill of it, but once again Kellen stopped him with an unshakable grip on his shoulder.

"Stay here, manling," he said, even as he motioned his soldiers on toward the fray. They swept across the ground like summer wind and disappeared into the distance. Kellen held Corin's gaze. "You may not call yourself a general, but you have vision we will need. Leave the war to warriors. But I will never forget you were prepared to charge."

He clapped a fist to his chest in proud salute, then turned and sprinted off after his men. Down in the valley, lost within the fog, iron rang on iron as the initial charge crashed into solid lines. Horses and men screamed and died as free men struck a blow against the armies of the gods.

It was begun.

29

On a sudden instinct, Corin raised his voice. "And you, Avery? Will you go rushing into battle for glory and honor?"

It had been a guess, a hunch, but the elf looked most impressed as he came around to stand before Corin. "Most men never hear me coming."

Corin spread his hands. "I am not most men."

"This is true," Avery nodded. "And in answer to your question: No. Like you, I have more valuable talents than the spilling of blood."

"But you do mean to aid me?"

"Jane would have my head if I did not. She bid me keep you safe."

"Oh?"

"Yes. Apparently there is a matter of some debt you owe her, which she thinks you could not repay as a corpse."

Corin nearly laughed at that. "That is all it took to rouse the elves of old Gesoelig to my cause? The earnest request of a pretty woman?"

Avery smirked, but it lasted just a moment. Then he shook his head, serious again, and said, "We have been reduced to ghosts, Corin Hugh. Can you imagine that? Haunting the edges of this world that was made for our glory."

"Aye," Corin said. "I know the feeling well."

"You stirred us up, for good or ill. After facing Jessamine, after seeing the dark powers Ephitel would vest in a helpless manling, dear Kellen found a need to act."

Corin nodded. Avery must have wrestled with much the same consideration as he watched the justicar persecute the Nimble Fingers, though he wouldn't bring himself to say it. But how far would that anger carry them?

"She must be stopped," Corin said, testing.

Avery snorted and tossed his head. "She's the tenth part of the problem. *He* must be stopped."

Corin showed his teeth. "I have the means."

"Then why do we tarry here? Let us lend our aid to the battle."

Corin touched the hilt of his rapier, but he found little courage there. He had no desire at all to rush into the fray. He glanced sidelong at the elf, and asked quietly, "Do you have a suggestion as to how?"

"The same way I've done every time dear Kellen has thrown himself into this mad endeavor. I'll find some fitting vantage point and try to spot the devious blow he won't see coming."

Corin breathed a heavy sigh of relief. "I know just the place." His own plans had depended on a clear view of the developing skirmish, and he'd put a great deal of effort into choosing where he meant to hide. "Come. I'll show you."

The fight itself was raging in a huge bowl-shaped valley, bordered on its west by the river that wrapped around Auric's ruined city, and on the right by steep crags that rose toward the distant plains of Raentz. The best overlooks belonged entirely to the enemy, but Corin had found a rise along the southern edge of the valley—a little twisting ridge that led eventually up and around to the eastern crags. But halfway there a narrow spit of stone looked out across the battlefield. The path was treacherous, littered with loose rocks, but the heroes of the Nimble Fingers walked the line with ease.

They'd barely left the valley floor before Avery struck up a conversation. "I must know: Did you honestly intend to join the soldiers in their charge?"

Corin swallowed a curse. For a moment, he was able to pretend intense concentration as he went on hands and knees up the steepest part of the slope, but beyond that he found easier footing again, and Avery still waited for an answer.

"These are desperate times," Corin said evasively; then he tried for a distraction. "Where is Jane, then? Did you leave her unprotected?"

Avery arched an eyebrow. "She is one of the deadliest creatures in Hurope, and I take pride that I was able to instill some portion of that. But yes, I left her in Ithale. I had to come through Faerie to arrive here in due time, and that journey tends to fracture manling minds."

Corin licked his lips. "I think I would like to know more about that place."

"No you wouldn't." Avery went ten paces in silence, and then he cleared his throat. "But we have gone astray. Did you intend to join the soldiers in their charge?"

It wasn't much, but now he'd had a moment to consider the question, Corin had an answer ready. He'd impressed the warrior with his bravery. With any luck, he could impress the trickster with his guile.

It was an uncertain gamble, but Corin had always considered Fortune a friend. "No," he said. "I didn't. I had other plans, but Kellen's arrival changed everything."

Avery considered that a moment, and then he nodded. "Kellen's always been obsessed with valor. You managed his nature well."

"And with you?"

The elf smiled disdainfully. "I cannot be managed. I am Avery of Jesalich."

"Aye, well," Corin said, "I'm only grateful to have such esteemed allies by my side. Now, we've arrived. Take a look and tell me what you see."

There wasn't much to see. It might have been the best vantage point below the eastern crags, but little penetrated the roiling fog. The world was gray beyond arm's length, but the noise of battle rose up all around them—grunts and groans and dying screams, and often enough the wet slap and muffled thud of a man dying to some unseen blow. It hung around them, eerily close and almost unreal without any vision to support the sounds.

Corin stretched on his belly on the stone, easing up to the very edge of the overlook. He strained his eyes, staring into the fog, but though the battle sounded near enough that he might reach out his hand and touch a soldier, he could make out nothing. Corin offered thanks to Fortune that the elves had come to join him. His own plan would not have worked at all. He could hardly judge the tide of battle through this fog. He only hoped the elves' strange nature gave them some advantage there.

As if in answer to the thought, Avery crept up beside him. He balanced on his heels, shading his eyes with one hand and pointing out into the blind fog with his other. He shivered. "What's happening there?"

"I can't see any—" Corin started, but he cut short as a spear of amber sunlight stabbed down from the heavens and tore a gaping hole through the pressing fog. It showed a scene of slaughter, men from both sides dead and trampled on the unforgiving earth. No one remained standing there.

The light was nothing natural. The sunbeam seemed almost a pillar of fire, thick and straight as a ship's mast. It burned away the fog for several paces in all directions, leaving a perfect circle perhaps fifty feet across. As Corin watched, the light began to shift, drifting west across the valley floor until it found a pair of soldiers locked in combat.

Another figure darted from the fog—too tall, too lithe, too fleet of foot to be a manling—and leaped into the air to kill the Godlander with a rapier thrust above his collarbone. The elf rolled when he touched the ground and sprang away into the fog again, leaving behind one of Auric's soldiers, stunned to have survived.

It all happened in an instant, and Corin was only half surprised when the drifting sunbeam shifted its direction to follow the disappearing elf. It twitched that way, almost instinctively, but then resumed its earlier path, patiently plotting west across the battlefield.

Searching.

"Is that your doing?" Corin asked, though he had little hope of it.

"Not in the least." Avery met Corin's eyes. "I'm itching. She is here."

Jessamine. Corin breathed a curse, and Avery nodded his agreement.

Down below, the questing sunbeam found a knot of fighting men. Corin knew them as gladiators because of their attire; they wore not a bit of armor, but rich silks in red and violet. These were the Godlanders' fiercest warriors, and here a dozen of them had come together against a scant handful of Auric's refugees. They had the refugees surrounded and now, moving in perfect unison, they closed in for the slaughter.

The sunlight paused on the scene for half a heartbeat—just long enough for Jessamine to see that her forces were winning there—and then it started south. She was quartering, meticulously searching the field for her prey.

Before the light had left the unfortunate cluster of refugees, a blur of movement burst into the ring of light. Not an elf, this time, but a manling on a handsome charger. Corin saw the golden hair and groaned.

Auric showed himself. It had been his plan, after all, but the foolishness of it cut at Corin all over again as he watched the farmboy dash into plain sight and fling himself upon Jessamine's most able warriors.

And win.

He had the advantage of surprise and a clear view of the scene as he rushed to the attack. He felled a gladiator with one huge arc of that heavy broadsword, and then kicked the second in the teeth with a steel-plated boot while he was still at full gallop.

The others had time to react, though, and that still left ten gladiators against a single man. Two of them peeled off to deal with this new threat while the rest kept their attention on the knot of refugees.

"Go," Corin whispered, begging. "Get back into the fog. You can sally again if you have to, but don't stand and fight where everyone can see you!"

Avery snorted. "Just like Kellen. Are all soldiers fools?"

"Only the heroes," Corin said. "Look."

"I see."

Instead of dashing off into the fog, Auric reined his charger short and stood up in his stirrups. As he'd done within the city walls, he raised his broadsword overhead so that it caught the fiery light of Jessamine's strange sunbeam and glowed like molten steel.

"For honor!" His voice boomed out across the valley floor. Even at this distance, Corin saw the sneer that twisted the face of one of the gladiators closing in on Auric.

A crossbow bolt flashed out of the fog and ricocheted off Auric's pauldron. He only stood up straighter and shouted, "For glory!"

And then a hundred voices cried out in answer, "For freedom!" Even the men at bay within the circle of gladiators shouted their defiance. They charged, foolish refugees against the Godlands' most elite soldiers.

But others came to join them. The Godlanders must have spread their lines to cover the whole valley floor, because that one crossbow bolt was the only sign so far of their forces converging on the light. Auric's forces, though, came boiling out into the clearing, still shouting Auric's battle cry, and makeshift weapons in sufficient numbers quickly overwhelmed the exquisite blades of the gladiators.

A dozen of them fell. Any nation in Hurope would have considered that a crushing loss, regardless of the outcome of the fight. But Jessamine had more to spare. Corin ground his teeth and prayed for Auric to see reason, to slip away in the confusion, but instead the farmboy forced his way to the center of the clearing. He sat tall and proud beneath the golden sunlight.

"For honor!" he cried again. Then he pointed his sword east, toward the crags, commanding a charge. And the fools around him obeyed.

"What manner of thing is this?" Avery asked, dumbfounded.

"I have yet to decipher it," Corin said. "But if I could find some way to keep him alive, I could make that man some kind of king."

"If that is your intention, I suggest you kill the justicar who's making me itch."

"I'd have to find her!" Corin snapped, irritated.

"She's there." The elf pointed to a spot atop one of the eastern crags. It was high enough to sit above the fog, and as likely a place as any, but it offered scrubs and boulders large enough to conceal a dozen men.

Corin could see no sign of the justicar. He squinted. "Are you certain?"

Avery scratched behind his ear and scowled. "As a gravestone. She is there."

Corin started to his feet, checking his weapons out of habit. He'd gone two steps before he noticed Avery had not yet moved. "Well?" Corin hissed. "Won't you help me?"

The elf looked wretched, but he didn't stir. "I . . . cannot."

Corin rolled his eyes and groaned. "This again? You've seen too much of war? Kellen's down there fighting. Surely you—"

Avery shook his head. "It isn't that. I . . ." He looked away. "I made a promise. To Jane."

"Oh." Corin's shoulders slumped. Despite himself, he thought of Aemilia. He clenched a fist around the hilt of his dagger, ready to destroy the justicar, but he felt a pang of sympathy for the elf too. "Keep your promise. I need you watching over Auric, anyway."

Avery nodded his head in gratitude for the lie. Then he turned away. Below, Jessamine's sunbeam still shone bright on Auric for everyone within the battlefield to see. Crossbow bolts came heavier now, a steady rain that met the refugees' upraised shields or clattered off breastplates when they didn't punch right through. Auric's answer was to keep his contingent moving, charging blindly against the fog, killing crossbowmen where they found them and overwhelming infantry by sheer fury.

There was no more sign of the gladiators. Corin hoped the elves were down there thinning their numbers, but he had little time to worry on it. He had a battle of his own ahead. How was he supposed to fight a justicar?

His instincts were the ones he'd learned in the Nimble Fingers: to investigate the situation, determine every vector of assault, and analyze the various risks before choosing an optimum approach. But while he made his plans, Auric and all his noble fools were down there on the battlefield dying beneath a beam of holy light.

That thought nagged at him. It pressed him faster and faster as he navigated the narrow, rocky ridge that twisted up toward the higher crags. Twice he encountered little gullies where the ridgeline fell away, and anxious as he was, he leaped the gap instead of climbing down and then back up the other side. The first time he nearly lost his footing when loose stones slipped out beneath his feet just before he jumped. The second time he misjudged the gap and barely caught himself on the other side. He hung there for a moment, feet dangling over a steep rockslide that would have deposited him neatly in the middle of the battle.

"Just like the rooftops in Aepoli," he told himself, easing his way up onto the crag. "Easy as a summer stroll. To meet a justicar who wants me dead."

That thought was enough to still his tongue. He went on ahead at a more careful pace, trying to remember the precise spot Avery had pointed to. The crags were uneven, but by his best estimate, she should be close to . . . there.

He stepped around a boulder taller than his head, and there she was before him. She stood staring out over the valley, all her concentration fixed on that huge beam of sunlight. It looked even more monstrous from this vantage.

Corin eased back against the boulder and cast a rapid glance around, but he saw no bodyguards. She'd committed her whole force to the assault. And why not? She'd survived everything Corin had been able to throw against her. She'd survived Kellen and a trip into Faerie. She'd survived Jane's firebomb. She was a justicar. What could she have to fear?

While Corin watched, she went down on one knee, straining out over the cliff's edge for a better view of the battle down below. Where was Auric? Was he still alive? And for how long?

Corin's hand closed around the hilt of his rapier. He had an urge to draw and charge her, but the distance was too great. The ground between them lay cluttered with loose rocks and hard soil; she would hear him coming, and Gods' blood, she was fast!

She was distracted, though. She stretched out a hand to steady herself and leaned yet farther over the edge. Corin licked his lips, watching her precarious position. He released the sword hilt, and quiet as a mouse, he bent his knees and scooped up a stone a little larger than his fist. He glanced around one more time for any sign of guards, and this time he spotted the figure lurking in the shadows.

Not a guard, though now that Corin looked in that direction, he saw the plated boots of soldiers stretched out on the ground there. No, this new figure wore a cloak and cowl, but beneath them he wore the strange outland dress of the druids. And even as Corin watched, the figure eased forward, his outstretched arm aiming the tiny glass-and-silver dartgun that Corin had learned to fear.

"Jeff." Corin breathed his name, and in the same moment, the druid pulled the trigger. A dart no larger than Corin's thumbnail flashed across outcrop and buried itself in the soft flesh just below Jessamine's right ear. Corin held his breath, expecting her to topple forward and down into the fray.

Instead, she rose up like a darter on an ocean's swells. She spun around in fury, drawing forth her heavy blade one-handed while she shook her head against the biting sting of the dart's poison. It should have dropped her. Corin had seen one dart incapacitate an elite elven warrior in the space of half a heartbeat, but Jessamine shook out her golden hair, narrowed her eyes, and shrugged aside the poison.

Jeff cursed, every bit as surprised as Corin was. He scrambled at his belt for another dart, but Corin had seen how fast this creature could move. Jeff was doomed.

Corin closed his grip around the stone in his hand and shook his head. Not today. Not when one of the blasted druids had finally defied the strictures to do something noble. While the justicar was still settling herself for the charge, Corin swung his weight into a huge step forward and flung the heavy stone right at the back of her head.

It should've been enough to brain her, justicar or not. At worst, it should have been enough to knock her senseless, especially with the druid poison in her veins. But somehow she sensed it coming. She dropped her sword without even looking in his direction, reached out her arm, and caught the heavy stone against her open palm. It rang out with a crack like distant thunder.

In the selfsame motion, she spun in place and hurled the stone straight at Jeff's skull. As soon as it left her hand, she was stooping, reaching, and she came out of her spin with the sword held high again.

The stone caught Jeff on the crown and snapped his head back hard. He grunted as his limp body hit the rocky ground, and then he lay still.

She stared after him a moment, breathing hard. Then she turned slowly to meet Corin's gaze with all her burning hatred. Her nostrils flared, her sword slashed once left and right. And then she charged him.

Gods' blood, she was fast! But she was human too. As she dashed toward him, the loose stones Corin had feared before shifted treacherously beneath her feet, and she lost her footing. Perhaps the tranquilizer had had some effect after all. Regardless, Corin saw it happening and stepped forward to meet her, drawing his sword as he went. He had no time to bring it to bear, but he smashed the knuckleduster hard into the side of her head.

She sprawled. She rolled again and found her feet, when most men would have fallen still from a blow like that. She staggered some, swaying as she rose, but before Corin could close with her again, she had her sword raised between them.

She'd survived everything he threw against her, but not without taking some scars. She'd lost an eye while fighting Kellen. Jane had told him that, but it was still unsettling to stare into the empty socket from four paces distant.

Jane's trap had caught her too. It showed in the bright pink scars that webbed the back of her sword hand and disappeared beneath the bracers on her wrists. She snarled as she recognized Corin now. This was no longer the same lovely woman he had seen in the Piazza Dei. This was the monster that had hanged a thousand Nimble Fingers. This was a living fury, righteous vengeance in a used-up, battered shell.

"I was looking for you," she said. Even her voice rattled weakly, though her sword was steady as a rock. "I am supposed to kill the rebels' leader, but I came here hunting you."

Corin tried a lunge, testing her with a high slash. He hoped his blow had slowed her, even a bit, but she met his feint and answered with a riposte that nearly cost him his hand. He leaped back two paces and set his guard, but she didn't chase him. She held her ground, untouchable.

Below them, the battle raged on. Even with the elves to aid them, how long could a hundred retired infantry stand against as many of the Godlands' best? How long could Corin stand against this fiend? He considered all the ways he might attack her, all the tricks of swordplay that he knew, and no matter how he tried, he could not imagine any of them working.

He heaved a weary sigh and lowered his sword. "Very well," he said. "It's me you really want. And I am tired of running. I'll drop my sword if you'll assure my safety."

She scowled harder. "You'll what?"

He nodded, all sincerity. "Take me into your custody and withdraw your men."

"I have my orders here—"

"Aye, and you have your responsibilities too. As a justicar, you cannot truly enjoy the slaughter that is happening down there."

"My orders come directly from my god."

"But we have left the Godlands. We both know Ephitel cannot see clearly here. You now know more than your commander did when he gave the order, and it would be a grave evil indeed to allow this slaughter to continue."

She considered it. That was more than Corin had hoped for. She withdrew half a step and cast a glance over her shoulder. In the distance, the beam of sunlight shifted. Fortune favor! Even facing Corin's best effort, she was able to manage the fight below.

It cost her half a glance, not time enough for Corin to take any advantage, and then her attention was all on him again. Worry tightened the corners of her eyes—worry at the things Corin had said—but she shook her head. "Your heart is black as midnight, Corin Hugh. I *will* take you before Ephitel, but I will not fall for your clever lies."

Corin sighed. "They say a justicar can taste a lie. Is that just a rumor, or is it true?"

She raised her chin. "I will not share the secrets—"

Corin spoke over her. "Know this, then, and I will speak it plain so that you might taste the truth of it: I can step through dream. You cannot take me anywhere against my will. I can close my eyes and go wherever I desire in all Hurope."

"How?"

He shrugged. "Consider me the justicar of Oberon—an older god than yours."

She frowned, and for the first time her sword's point drifted to the side. "You truly believe that!" she said, astonished.

He nodded, holding her gaze. It was true, then! She could taste a lie. And he could use that. He moved a half step closer, unthreatening, and said in perfect confidence, "It was I who brought this fight to Ephitel, not Auric. I am the one you should be chasing, not that honest farmboy. And I say again, I'll drop my sword if you'll assure my safety."

"Why? Why would you do this?"

"I want to see this matter settled. I swear by sky and sea, by driving wind and gentle rain, I will gladly stand before

Ephitel in the name of justice if it saves the lives of those below."

There could be no truer words. He meant to be the judge in that trial, but the justicar—true believer that she was—heard his claim in the only way she could fathom. And Ephitel's fancy magic told her it was true.

Corin had to hide his smile.

She lowered her blade to her side, but he knew how fast she was. He didn't dare strike yet. She considered him for a long moment. Then she nodded once. "You have my word. Now drop your sword."

"Withdraw your men."

Her voice turned hard. "You have the word of a justicar. Drop your sword."

Corin shrugged and dropped the sword. Its cage rang against the loose stones of the outcrop. Her eyebrows rose in surprise, and still she backed a pace away before she looked toward the battle. As Corin watched, the beam of light that shone on Auric disappeared, and a heartbeat later it fell upon the crag instead. On Corin and the justicar. Corin blinked against the brightness of it. On the field below, Godlander trumpets cried retreat. She'd done her part.

Auric's men would not know of this arrangement. They would push the fight and cut down the invaders as they ran. Perhaps noble-hearted Auric would try to stop it, but Kellen would see some scheme in play and Avery would seize an opponent's weakness. The Godlanders would be cut down as they run.

He'd won. Corin swallowed hard. He'd won the day. He'd saved the farmboy and the Nimble Fingers and all the other innocents he'd gathered here. For the day, at least, he'd won.

A footstep on the hard stone tore him from his reverie. The justicar came toward him, sword still at her side and iron in her voice. "On your knees, unbeliever. Our deal is done."

"Indeed," Corin said. He went to one knee and used the motion to disguise the hand that slipped beneath his cloak. She stepped up to tower over him, the justice of the gods in human flesh.

"In the name of Ephitel," she began.

He let her get no farther. In one motion he drew his knife and rose. She flinched, recoiling like a snake, but she was too close to get away. The blade went into her side beneath the breastplate straps and between her ribs. Hot blood flowed over Corin's hand.

She stumbled back, trying vainly to raise her sword, knees already buckling. Disbelief and hate warred in her eyes. "But how?" she gasped. "I tasted your sincerity."

He nodded to her. "Aye. I spoke the truth, and I will swear again. Someday soon I'll stand before your wretched god. And I'll see justice done."

She fell. Her lips writhed, but no words came. Corin stooped for his sword and turned to end the poor creature's suffering, but it was already done. She lay still upon the unforgiving stone, sightless eyes staring up into the brilliant sunlight.

The meaning of that light occurred to Corin half a heartbeat before a steel-tipped crossbow bolt pinged into the stone behind him. The Godlanders were converging on him now, and at least some had seen his attack on their commander.

Corin took one frantic step toward the place where Jeff had fallen, wondering how he might escape with the druid's weight across his shoulders, but he got no farther. The druid was gone. Just a splash of blood marked the place where he had fallen.

Corin scanned the ridgeline, but he could see no sign of the man. Blast him! Where'd he gotten to? Who had taken him away? There was no time to discover it, as a rain of crossbow bolts tore the air all around him.

Corin cursed and spun away. He was no soldier, no general, but this day he'd somehow won a glorious battle. And now the time had come to do what he did best.

He ran.

30

A very met him at the top of the ridge. Corin made the leap this time, and the two sprinted down the narrow path as though it were across a meadow. The fog was failing now, dissolving rapidly beneath the springtime sun, and it showed Corin and the elf in stark relief against the ridgeline. For ten dreadful paces, crossbow bolts fell like hailstones all around them.

Somehow, they both survived the volley, but Corin didn't slow his pace. He pressed harder, counting seconds beneath his breath. How long to crank a crossbow back? To load and fire a second volley? He counted past what he expected, but still no shot came. He risked a glance down into the valley.

And there was Kellen. The ancient warrior stood alone, dripping with the blood of men he'd slain, and all around him lay the corpses of two score crossbowmen. He raised his blade in silent salute, then dashed away to join a scuffle in the shadow of the crags.

Corin paused to catch his breath, looking out over the battlefield. It was an ugly sight. The Godlanders had been put to rout, and it was mostly Kellen's elves who killed them as they fled. They struck without pity or remorse. They struck in vengeance for a wrong they'd had to suffer for more than a thousand years. They killed Ephitel's assassination squad to a man, and even from this distant vantage, Corin could see that Kellen hadn't lost a single soldier in the fray.

Auric had. That fact crashed home for Corin as he picked his way more slowly west across the ridgeline. Jessamine's forces littered the battlefield—gladiators in their violets and red, crossbowmen in the white and blue of the Vestossis' regiments, and here and there a wizard robed in royal black—but they were not alone. Auric's desperate defenders stood out almost as clearly in their mismatched browns and grays, farmers' clothes. They lay broken and bleeding, and far too many lay still upon the earth. The farmboy hadn't fallen. He rode among the dead with a coterie of his survivors, searching for the wounded who could be helped back into camp.

It was easier in a pirate raid. The corpses had a way of ending up overboard, and a little breeze was usually enough to put the past behind a man. Corin tried his best to keep his eyes on the narrow path, to ignore the horror down below, as he made his way back to the city.

Twisting as the path was, and weary as the fight had left him, Corin had barely left the ridgeline when Auric led his band of survivors through the city gates. The distant cheer of victory that rose up from the ruined city paid no mind to those fallen on the field. Not yet. There would be time enough for grief later. For now, the survivors cried out in celebration.

Corin couldn't bring himself to feel it. Instead, he felt numb. Wrung out and used up. He stumbled mechanically forward, halfway to the open archway and the sound of merriment beyond, before he stopped and turned aside. He picked a path around the outside of the ruined walls, searching until he found a spill of rubble low enough to scale. Avery came along beside him, never uttering a word.

As Corin stole into the city he'd helped save, Kellen scampered over the fallen wall to join them. He held his silence too. One by one, the other elves trailed in, but no one spoke. Corin picked a careful path down the dark back alleys that the refugees had not yet needed to explore. They passed the empty houses, the fallen timber, the shattered ruins. He swept out in a wide arc to avoid the celebrations in the city square. Then, by what might once have been a narrow kitchen door, he slipped into the back of the vast cathedral that had been given him for quarters.

At last, walled off from the distant sounds of joy, he heaved a weary breath and looked around. Avery and Kellen stood before him, watching. The others leaned against the walls or prowled the wide room, curious as cats and twice as deadly.

Corin licked his lips. Reason and emotion warred within him, so riotous, so deafening that he felt numb. One thought rose up as clear as daylight, though, and he bowed his head toward his friends. "Thank you. Thank you both for coming."

Avery nodded in answer. "You earned it, when all was said and done."

Kellen smiled a sad smile. "You have begun to learn the price."

Corin ran a hand through his hair. "I don't . . . I thought . . ." He heaved a sigh. "We won?"

Avery arched an eyebrow. "You say that like it's a question."

"So many died."

"That's how it's done," Kellen said. "You claimed you were prepared—"

"I didn't know," Corin said.

The old elf nodded. "And now that you do, would you have chosen differently?"

Corin chewed his lip. He considered long and hard, but in the end he shook his head. "No. He sent the killers, not me."

Avery cocked his head. "You did assassinate his prince."

"Princes," Corin said automatically.

"Just one," Avery said. "The other lives. And he does not like you much."

Corin thought on that. Giovanni's throat he'd slit clean, so it had to be Pietro who'd survived, with a blade in his shoulder and another through his gut. Corin swallowed hard. "Even so. It needed doing."

Kellen nodded. "There's your answer. Don't try to place blame, because it has a way of shifting like a snake. Either it's worth doing, or it isn't."

Corin thought of Aemilia, and of everything he had discussed with the tavern keeper just yesterday. He nodded, more certain now. "I mean to see this through at any cost. Hurope deserves to see a day free of Ephitel's dark shadow."

"Then this might be the dawn," Kellen said. "You are a most remarkable manling, Corin Hugh. And your Auric too."

Avery nodded. "He'll make an uncommon king."

"And you will stand with us?" Corin asked. "The elves of old Gesoelig will fight for man?"

Kellen looked to Avery, and those two shared a silent exchange. Then both turned away from Corin, searching out the eyes of their other companions. As one, the warriors all nodded.

"It will never again be so easy," Corin said. "You won the day because you were unexpected here. The fog her wizards raised worked to your advantage, and Ephitel sent no elves of his own into the fray. Next time . . ."

Avery lay a hand on his shoulder. "Next time, we'll find some other way to catch them unprepared."

Kellen nodded once, certain, and gestured to the men behind him. "I bring you these today. And I will promise more. We'll never field an army—there are too few of us left—but I will bring you every man still loyal to the name of our fallen king."

"For Oberon!" the others chanted, reverent.

"For Oberon," Corin echoed. "Let's see this through."

Something of Corin's tension drained at that. He sank back against the wall, exhausted, and listened while the others settled into a more casual conversation. They compared their exploits, bragging over their own feats and admiring each other's handiwork.

Kellen never boasted of himself, but just among the deeds his companions had witnessed, the old warrior had answered for eight gladiators and half as many wizards on his own. The efforts of the other elves combined scarcely matched that, but Kellen only gave a modest shrug and turned away.

They went on boasting and laughing, and someone suggested a sortie into the camp to find some wine and brandy. In the midst of all of this, some instinct tugged at the back of Corin's mind, and he raised his eyes toward the outer door.

A man stood there.

He was dressed all in white, cotton clothing of a plain cut, though he wore a belt of midnight black, and he had eyes to match. He entered the chamber like a ghost from one of Tesyn's stories, drifting soundlessly across the floor, unseen by all the others in the room. Deadly warriors one and all, they ignored him, until Corin began to fear this was some hallucination.

And then he saw the wisps of mist that hung about the man, clinging to his plain white robes and glistening against his skin. He wore a glamour, and he wore it well. The intruder passed within a pace of Kellen, and perhaps the old elf's shoulders tensed, perhaps his eyes narrowed, but he did not react. He shook his head and carried on his conversation.

Corin let it pass. He waited, motionless, until the stranger came within three paces. Then he moved like lightning. He shoved off from the wall and drew his rapier in one smooth motion, slashing out until its point dimpled the intruder's throat.

Everyone throughout the room fell still, staring, but they must have seen Corin threatening the empty air. Corin didn't care. He met the cold black eyes of the intruder.

They showed no fear. They showed no surprise at all. He waited, silent, while Corin considered him.

"You've come from Ephitel?" Corin asked.

The stranger nodded.

"An assassin? To finish what his army couldn't?"

The stranger shook his head.

"Then what?"

The stranger spread his hands, showing them empty to Corin, then very slowly reached into the folds of his robe and withdrew a piece of folded parchment. He extended his hand and let it fall. As it touched the floor, half a dozen voices gasped.

Behind the stranger, Avery arched an eyebrow. While everyone else had been staring at the bit of paper, the old thief had positioned himself just beyond the tip of Corin's sword. He had a knife in his hand, held low and perfectly positioned to perforate the intruder's kidney.

He looked a question at Corin, and Corin almost smiled. Avery could no more see the stranger than the other elves, but he'd been faster than any other to interpret Corin's actions, and the old elf had moved with confidence to act on his guess. But Corin shook his head no and returned his gaze to the assassin.

"Tell your master I can see through all his clever tricks," Corin said. "Tell him if he sends anymore like you, they won't return alive."

The stranger nodded, still completely unconcerned.

Corin sheathed his sword and watched the stranger leave. Once again, the fellow slipped within a pace of Kellen, but Corin noticed that he left Avery a wide berth. Perhaps he had sensed what he could not see.

Here was something new. Corin had heard rumors of the gods' assassins, but he'd scarcely credited them. What use could they have for such delicate tools when they had access to justicars and gladiators and wizards?

Yet today those all had failed, and if not for Oberon's strange power, this one might well have carried out a different set of orders. Corin shuddered at the thought. Invisible assassins to add to his growing list of enemies. Delightful.

But there at his feet was the bit of parchment, and Corin could *feel* the anxious desire of all those elves to learn what the page contained. Corin knelt and unfolded it, leaving room for all the others to read with him.

The message was in the ancient language of the elves. It wasn't long.

"Under the circumstances of today's engagement, I must beg a meeting with you. I will not set foot on pagan ground, and I suspect you would refuse to meet me in my own dominion, so I recommend a neutral site. Join me in three days' time, at sunrise, where last we spoke. Ephitel."

Around the room, astonished gasps and busy chatter rose as the other elves comprehended the significance of that request, but Corin only nodded. His mind was reeling, but in a sense, he'd anticipated this moment since the day he'd gone after the

Vestossi princes. He'd anticipated it when he suggested Auric build up this stronghold in defiance of the gods. He'd anticipated it when the old elves joined him on the field of battle.

"You cannot mean to go," Kellen said, earnest. "It's obviously a trap."

"Obviously," Corin said.

Avery considered him a moment, and then he too nodded. "It is indeed. It is a trap our friend here has been laying out for Ephitel. How long?"

"Since he killed the woman I loved. No, longer. Ever since he killed your king. This has been my destiny."

"And do you have a solid plan to overcome him?"

"Be faster," Corin said. "Want it more. Get him before he gets me."

Kellen nodded. "Brave. Noble."

Avery showed his teeth. "Sincere and foolish."

"I do have an idea," Corin said, "but I need an answer first. Can Ephitel see through a glamour?"

The elves exchanged looks, considering, then Kellen shook his head. "Not easily. Not the way you seem to. But if he knows a strike is coming, he can dodge it anyway."

Corin nodded. "Then I'll have to make it quick. And from a direction that he won't see it coming." He ran a hand through his hair, adjusted his cloak, and then tipped his head in a bow to all the elves. "Thank you once again for everything you've done. Go find your wine and welcome among the people that you saved. It is well earned."

Kellen caught Corin's shoulder. "You cannot mean to go alone."

"If Ephitel sees elves with me, he will know it for a trap. He'll show contempt for a manling, and that gives me my only edge. I *have* to go alone."

Kellen still looked doubtful, but Avery clapped him on the shoulder. "He's right," the old thief said. "Let him go. Either he solves all our problems, or he ends this new rebellion at the start. Either way, he'll save us trouble, eh?"

Kellen didn't laugh, though it drew a smile from Corin. The warrior finally shook his head and released Corin. "Go in valor," he said softly. "For Oberon."

Half a dozen voices raised in exhortation. "For Oberon!" The ancient cathedral rang with the words. "For Oberon! For Oberon!"

Corin dipped his head. "For Aemilia," he whispered. Then he slipped away to find his humble tavern keeper.

31

It ended back where it had begun. The abandoned cottage in the border woods of western Raentz was three days' ride from the farmboy's stronghold, but it felt a world away. A lifetime. Corin made the trip with time to spare, and as the sun rose on Ephitel's appointed meeting, Corin waited already in the cottage's tiny kitchen.

He couldn't bring himself to look into the inner room. It would be empty but for dust, yet still it bore too strong a memory for Corin. He couldn't bear it. Better far to hold his place and wait for his guest.

He thought he knew what to expect here. After all, he'd faced Ephitel more than once before. The creature loved to prance and preen, to wallow in his threats and bask in his imagined victories.

Corin had landed a cruel blow by conquering his force in the Wildlands. He'd spread the word that manlings might find refuge in Spinola once again—two thousand years after Ephitel himself had named the place anathema. One way or another, he'd gathered up the force that killed some of Ephitel's most prized warriors. All of that would burn at Ephitel's pride.

But worst of all, he'd killed the justicar. *That* had been the blow that earned him this meeting. Corin was sure of it. It hadn't even been his plan, but three days' journey to this place had given him time to understand the significance of that action.

Corin had the sword *Godslayer*. It was the only weapon in the world that could kill Ephitel, and Ephitel *knew* it was in Corin's hands. He could never leave such a thing out in the world. Poor, mad Jessamine had offered Ephitel some hope before. She could sense the sword when the circumstances were right, and that had offered him the promise of securing it. But the moment that she fell, Corin had become too great a threat. So Ephitel set this trap to draw Corin in and seize the sword himself.

That was why Corin didn't wear the sword. After Kellen's caution, he didn't dare carry it on him, even under a glamour. Instead, he wore only his dagger at his side, and a knife in its sheath on his wrist. They were his favorite weapons, but here and now, they left him feeling naked. He chewed his lip and prayed Fortune that Ephitel showed soon.

He did not have to wait long. The sun lay low on the horizon when the outer door creaked open to admit Ephitel. A dozen gladiators were crowded in the garden behind him, as well as two men in the plain white robes and clinging mist of the gods' assassins, but Ephitel could see the room was empty.

He glanced to Corin's side and noted the sword's absence. He looked disappointed. He was an elf, after all, and Corin a mere manling. He doubtlessly believed that he could best any manling in a fight, even a manling armed with the one sword that could scar him. He'd have been all too happy to cut Corin down and secure the sword at once.

But without it, he had to carry on his ruse. He had called for this meeting, after all. He turned back, still in the doorway, and spoke a quiet word to his attendants. Then he came into the room and closed the door behind him.

"It is well you came to meet me," he said.

"We have unsettled business, you and I."

Ephitel shook his head. "You've made a valiant effort. I should have killed you last time we were here together. I thought the druids were the greater threat."

"Not to you," Corin answered, bitter. "To your ambition, perhaps, but not to your person. They want to see a stable world, and they will tolerate you if that is what it takes."

Ephitel arched an eyebrow. "You won't? You hate your god so much?"

"You are not my god," Corin said. "I have met Oberon while he still sat his throne. I have glimpsed the world this world was meant to be. I will never bow to your tyranny."

Ephitel considered Corin a moment, then shook his head. "I would so love to know your story. Perhaps when the rest of this is settled, I'll take the time to wring it from you."

"Is that why you called me here? To offer threats?"

"You seem glad enough to seize the opportunity."

"But I did not summon you. Why have we come here, elf? You can't possibly believe you'll end this thing by taking me."

"I can end this thing in an afternoon. A thousand filthy refugees cannot stand against the united armies of the gods."

Corin sneered. "They stood against your first strike."

"Impressive as that was—I'll even say astonishing—that one heroic stand was nothing but a gesture. Your rabble survived a strike force one-tenth their size, but I could send ten thousand men against them. A hundred thousand, if that's what it takes. We'll unite the world against this wretched band."

Corin showed his teeth. "If you believed it would be so easy, you would not be here now."

"You presume to know my heart?"

"I know what my eyes show me, Ephitel. Three days ago, you lost this war."

"There is no war! There is one pathetic enclave huddling in the godless wilderness. If they have blasphemed our names, we will strike them down. It's a distraction, not a war."

"I can't decide if you honestly believe that. It doesn't matter. You are wrong. You have seen the first engagement of a war that will change this world, that will rip it from your hands and restore it to the rightful inheritors of Oberon's ancient dream. You're finished, Ephitel."

The elf was incredulous. "You killed a handful of my men—"

"Not I. It wasn't I who killed your elite slaves, but a farmboy who dared to dream of a world governed by justice and honor. His followers are not gathered there out of need, but out of hope. The whole world waits in quiet desperation for something better, and Auric has now shown it to them. Even if you crush him, the world will remember what happened here. Your easy tyranny is at an end."

Ephitel considered this in silence for a moment. Then he shook his head, disbelieving. "Does he truly believe that? Do all his silly followers think his legacy can be so powerful? Does he honestly believe he can defeat me with a romantic gesture? That's why he does this?"

"No," Corin said. "You give him too much credit. He doesn't see the subtle truths that will play out over generations. Auric defies you for a much simpler reason. He does it because it's right. Because you are a cruel, petty master, and the whole world groans beneath your wickedness. Auric stands—at any cost—because someone has to stand against you. And his followers stand behind him because they believe in him."

"Noble heroes live short lives," Ephitel said dismissively, but Corin answered over him.

"Perhaps, but legends live forever. Auric drew first blood. He has shown that you are vulnerable. And while you're gathering your armies to destroy him, he'll be gathering followers as well. Not just pathetic refugees, but elves long lost in hiding and druids who have waited all these years to fulfill their promise to their fallen master."

Ephitel's nostrils flared as he huffed in frustration, but he didn't answer back. Corin nodded, masking the shock that bloomed behind his breastbone. He was right. He'd known it, he'd believed it, but he hadn't dreamed that Ephitel would see the truth.

But if the elf could see it through the bloody haze of his own arrogance, it must be true. It must be. Corin's desperate scheme was going to work. The sad alliance Auric had pulled together was going to change the world. Those who had died before the city walls would not have died in vain.

Finally, frustrated, Ephitel asked, "And you? Why have you done all of this? For Oberon? He was never perfect. He enslaved the dwarves. He welcomed insurrection and challengers for the sport they gave him. In the end, he was weak."

"He was," Corin said. "I saw him in those days. And he knew his own shortcomings, but he did his best." Corin drew a heavy breath, thinking hard, and despite his best intentions, his eyes cut toward the inner room. He nodded to himself, and answered loudly, "I did not do it for Oberon, but for Aemilia."

On those last two words, the inner door slipped open. It made no noise, and Ephitel never glanced back toward the figure now revealed. Jacob stood two paces behind the wretched god, and he carried *Godslayer* naked in his hand. Both man and sword shimmered with the misty haze of Corin's glamour, but still Corin's heart hammered in fear that the elf might glance around, might somehow sense this doom.

If the old tavern keeper felt that fear, he didn't show it. He walked with an easy step, firm but unhurried, a man about a necessary task. From time to time, he'd said, even a good animal went bad. Any farmer worth his salt knew how to put down a rabid beast. He took no joy in his task, but he understood his role.

He was no hero, but he'd said all the things Corin needed to hear, at just the moments when he needed to hear them. So Corin would stand here and face the tyrant's sneer, and Jacob Gossler would become a legend. They'd call him Jacob Godslayer through all the ages. He'd be the man who killed a wicked god. He'd end up next to Auric and Kellen and Aemilia and all the rest in the undying fame of true heroes, simply because he'd been willing to do the job that needed doing.

Still oblivious, Ephitel spoke into the silence. "However small your reasons, however wrong your motives, I do believe you've started something grim. I've met in council with the gods, and it was they who bid me meet you here. They offer truce. Despite all your people's sins, the offenders will be given pardon."

Corin frowned. "They don't want pardon; they want freedom."

"Very well. That answer was anticipated. None of mine will sacrifice his lands to rebels and traitors, but we've agreed to leave your people unmolested in the Wildlands. Resurrect old Spinola and call it your own. We will trouble you no more."

Corin staggered back a step, astonished. *This* he had not expected. The gods of Hurope were petitioning for peace?

Behind Ephitel, Jacob seemed to sense Corin's surprise. He stayed his hand, though nervous sweat now shone on his forehead. He waited, licking his lips, and cast a questioning look to Corin.

But Corin didn't have an answer. His mind was reeling as he considered possibilities. One thought kept intruding over everything else.

He'd won.

It would take time for these events to run their course—perhaps more than one lifetime—but the destiny was set. Mankind would finally shake off the bonds of Ephitel's cruel gods. Any foothold—even a ruined city in the godsforsaken Wildlands—would be enough to start a slow cascade. Humanity would thrive beneath that kind of liberty. Between its long-forgotten resources and its position on the trading routes, Spinola would rival Raentz or Ithale or even Rikkeborh once it was reclaimed.

And then the gods would fall. With or without a war, they'd fall. Mankind would abandon their cruel tyranny for the allure of their own nation. They'd forsake the gods, and Ephitel and all his cronies would be no more than memories and scary stories told to children.

He'd done what Aemilia had asked of him. For her sake, and in her memory, Corin had restored the world she'd loved so much. He'd won for her.

But it was not enough. Even as the thrill of that victory rang in his head, a fiery, overwhelming thread of hate still burned within him. It twisted tight around his heart, and for all his cautious reason, he couldn't shake it off. The monster that had murdered Aemilia stood here before him, unpunished.

Corin opened his mouth to answer, but Ephitel hurried to speak over him.

"There is one requirement," Ephitel said. "Your manling throng can have Spinola and a bond of peace for all time. But we require a token of your good faith as well. It's only reasonable."

Corin felt the answer in his bones, but he asked the question anyway. "What do you require?"

"*Godslayer*. Naturally. Your kingdom will live forever. And so will I."

He showed Corin a victorious smile at that.

"Is this the requirement of your brother gods?" Corin asked. "Or is it only yours?"

Ephitel frowned. "Why does that matter? Will it change your answer any?"

"Curiosity," Corin said. "How close do they stand behind you?"

"It was a unanimous request," Ephitel said coldly. "None of them would like to see a god cut down by a man. It sets an alarming precedent, you know."

Corin raised an eyebrow. "You're quite forthcoming."

Ephitel showed his teeth again. "You need to know the truth to make a wise decision. I know a little of your heart, Corin Hugh. You killed one of mine, so I killed one of yours. Tit for tat. But then you made it personal. Would you now throw countless lives—the fates of nations—on the cruel pyre of war just to cut me down in vengeance?"

"I'd consider it," Corin said.

Ephitel shrugged. "I'd be disappointed if you didn't. But know this, and know it for truth: You claimed you'd set a thing in motion when your commoner embarrassed me in that pathetic battle. You're wrong. That setback can be restored with time enough. But if you were to strike at me, if you were to bleed a *god* where all the world could see . . . every god on Attos would come hunting for you. Not just for you, but for anyone who knows your name. If you cut down one of us, you'll bring such a doom upon your manling crowd as you could not imagine."

Corin cocked his head. "Perhaps, but there'd be a bright side too. You'd be dead. You can see how I'm conflicted."

He *was* conflicted. Even with his nostrils full of the stink of this rotten creature, even standing here five paces from the place where the fiend had killed Aemilia, Corin wavered. Was he strong enough to choose the greater good? Could he sacrifice his own pride, his own consuming vengeance for the sake of a peaceful victory? Could he leave an immortal Ephitel unchallenged for all time?

Ephitel was not caught in such deep consideration. All he'd heard was Corin's casual slur, and now his lip pulled back in an animal snarl. He slammed his fist against the wall so hard the plaster cracked. "I should have killed you long ago, manling! I should have made you watch when I killed your pretty girl. I should have made her scream."

Corin closed his eyes and fought to draw a calming breath. "You should have kept that to yourself," he said softly.

"You wretched worm!" Ephitel bellowed. "I've offered you everything you want and better than you could have hoped for. Accept my terms."

"Can you give me back Aemilia?"

"Don't be a fool."

"Then give me Ithale. Renounce your authority, and you can live your life however you please."

"I am not here to negotiate."

"Nor am I," Corin said coldly. He'd hesitated for a moment. He'd wavered. It was an attractive offer, after all. And the consequences grave.

But he'd already told Sera his own terms. Ephitel died, or the world did.

The tyrant god stomped forward and caught Corin's shirt-front in a massive fist. He lifted him up and smashed his back against the cabin's ceiling. "Age of Reason, manling, you've had all you'll get from me. Give me the cursed sword!"

Corin tore his gaze from Ephitel's, and looked down to Jacob. He nodded once, and the tavern keeper did as he had promised. He killed a rabid god with one clean stroke.

And so began the Godlanders War.

About the Author

Julie Velez/2010

Aaron Pogue is a husband and a father of two who lives in Oklahoma City, Oklahoma. He started writing at the age of ten, and has written novels, short stories, scripts, and videogame storylines. His first novels were high fantasy set in the rich world of the FirstKing, including the bestselling fantasy novel *Taming Fire*, but he has explored mainstream thrillers, urban fantasy, and several kinds of science fiction, including a long-running sci-fi cop drama series focused on the Ghost Targets task force.

Aaron has been a Technical Writer with the Federal Aviation Administration and a writing professor at the university level. He holds a Master of Professional Writing degree from the University of Oklahoma. He also serves as the user experience consultant for Draft2Digital.com, a digital publishing service.

Aaron maintains a personal website for his friends and fans at AaronPogue.com, and he runs a writing advice blog at UnstressedSyllables.com.